STAR TREK VOYAGER®

SHADOW OF HEAVEN

BOOK THREE OF THREE

CHRISTIE GOLDEN

POCKET BOOKS

New York   London   Toronto   Sydney   Singapore

An *Original* Publication of POCKET BOOKS

POCKET BOOKS, a division of Simon & Schuster, Inc.
1230 Avenue of the Americas, New York, NY 10020

A VIACOM COMPANY

STAR TREK is a Registered Trademark of Paramount Pictures.

This book is published by Pocket Books, a division of Simon & Schuster, Inc., under exclusive license from Paramount Pictures.

ISBN: 0-671-03584-3

First Pocket Books printing December 2000

10 9 8 7 6 5 4 3 2 1

POCKET and colophon are registered trademarks of Simon & Schuster, Inc.

Printed in the U.S.A.

*This book is dedicated
to the memory of Gene Roddenberry,
without whom this particular universe,
that of* Star Trek,
would never have existed.

What if earth
Be but the shadow of heaven, and things therein
Each to other like, more than on earth is thought?
—John Milton, *Paradise Lost*

SHADOW OF HEAVEN

INTERLUDE

THE ENTITY WAS PLEASED WITH ITSELF. AFTER SO LONG drifting aimlessly throughout space and time, it had a purpose. A good purpose, a healing one, one that made it feel satisfied and content. It had not known it lacked, or perhaps had forgotten, these feelings until the Presence had contacted it, explained what was at stake, and begged for its assistance.

Dark matter, something simple and innocent of wrongdoing in its natural state, had been twisted. Mutated. Turned to aid evil. Both the Presence and the Entity were searching for it now, gathering it up, rendering it harmless, and helping restore the things it had damaged, sentient or no, to their true and rightful state.

The Entity had helped the Sikarians, the Beneans, the Kazon, and others. It had known these names, these people, these planets, but how? How had it known such

1

things? It tasted curiosity. Another new sensation for something as powerful and yet as formless as the Entity.

On and on it floated, finding pockets of dark matter hidden in a nebula, gently plucking it from a wayward asteroid.

And then it found the Vidiians.

CHAPTER
1

I'VE NEVER CONSIDERED MYSELF THE LITERARY TYPE. WELL, I've now learned the hard way that when you're stuck so far from home that you don't even know where home is, in a civilization that's nothing like everything you left behind, you can go nuts without something that connects you to the life you used to know. So I started this.

The Culilann are a little bit nervous about this writing thing I'm doing. It sort of feels like I'm violating the Prime Directive with the ABCs. But the Culilann certainly know about advanced technology, they just choose not to embrace it. The Alilann—well, suffice to say that if I were with the Alilann right now I'd be writing this on something resembling a padd, not on dried and stretched tree bark. I somehow think the captain would be proud of this.

Ensign Tom Paris paused and stretched his fingers, grimacing as they cracked. He was surprised at how badly his hand was cramping, but he wanted to get all this down. He used his hands all the time on *Voyager,* but he was learning that operating the responsive controls at his station and grasping a sharpened stick smudged with soot from the fire exercised very different finger muscles.

He continued: *My fingers hurt, but here goes, trying to make a long story short. A few—*

He paused again. How long *had* it been? This place, with its slow pace and repetitive days, blurred time for him. And of course, being injured for so long, he'd really been out of it for a while. He thought back to when the strange wormholes had been "following" *Voyager,* opening and closing like the mouths of some kind of space monsters. No one had suspected that it was the Romulan scientist Telek R'Mor, a man who lived in the Alpha Quadrant dozens of light-years and twenty true years ago, trying to find them at the command of the Romulan Tal Shiar.

What a weird tale Telek had told them, of powerful aliens called Shepherds, and of dark matter being mutated and causing terrible harm. They'd mistakenly beamed Telek aboard against his will, thinking he was in danger. What followed was one of the strangest adventures of Tom's life, and he knew he'd had his share of them. They had known something was dreadfully wrong when Neelix—quite possibly the nicest person aboard the entire ship—had tried to murder Telek R'Mor. It was the mutated dark matter, of course, affecting Neelix's mind. As it had affected Tom's own, as well.

He frowned, and scratched down his thoughts. *My personal experience with the dark matter was frighten-*

ing. It made me completely paranoid. I had hallucinations, lost my enthusiasm for things—it turned me into someone I wasn't. Someone I really didn't like. And it damaged people physically, too.

He thought about the two Romulan scouts who had managed to get aboard the ship, the awful things the dark matter had done to them. He decided he didn't want to write that part down.

It might have been Telek who got us into this mess, but he was also the one to get us out of it. He was able to track down one of the so-called good Shepherds, Tialin. She removed all the dark matter from our bodies and put it into a small, glowing sphere. She told us that she could give us the technology to do this ourselves, and asked Captain Janeway if she would agree to take Voyager *and gather up the rest of this dangerous dark matter. The captain consented. I don't think any of us believed she'd refuse.*

Again he paused, and shook out his right hand, cursing. It was not cooperating. He would have to wait until later to describe being dragged by Chakotay into this strange place, injured and weak. The aliens here had not greeted them with overwhelming warmth. They had even put him and Chakotay into a pit for a few days. The "Ordeal," they called it, a sort of test to see if he and Chakotay were acceptable to their gods, the Crafters. He didn't remember a lot after that until he got better.

Most troubling was the events of the last few days. Chakotay had mysteriously disappeared and the spiritual leader of the Culilann, a gentle young man named Matroci, had died. The Sumar-ka, the villagers, attributed the death to asphyxiation. But Tom had seen the corpse before it was ritually burned; had seen the unmistakable mark left on Matroci's abdomen by some kind of energy weapon.

Paris knew he was not under direct suspicion of Matroci's death. They didn't even realize their Culil had been murdered. But the tragedy occurring on the same night as Chakotay's unannounced disappearance had made the Sumar-ka uneasy around him. The result was that Paris, who had just started to think maybe he had made friends here, was again feeling isolated and itchy to leave.

But first, he had to find out who had killed Matroci. He had not voiced his suspicions, but he was going to emulate Chief Inspector Tuvok and see if he couldn't do a little detective work on his own. He would start his investigation tomorrow. His first suspect: Trima. She was the one who directly benefited from Matroci's death. She got promoted, from a mere Sa-Culil to the Culil herself. And she was so icy and unapproachable, she had to be up to *something*. He tried to pretend that he wasn't pleased at the thought of spending more time with her, for cold as she was, she was gorgeous. It wasn't cheating on B'Elanna just to want to look at and talk to someone he found attractive.

Was it?

He leaned over on the pallet stuffed with fragrant ferns and blew out the lamp. He did not look over at the empty bed where Chakotay had slept.

Trima wondered if the Stranger Paris had killed Matroci.

He and the one called Chakotay had come from a strange and far-off place, been accepted by the Sumar-ka, and then the same night as Matroci's death Chakotay had vanished. She had made certain that Paris's alibi had been investigated. He had led them to the tree and shown them deep, fresh gouges in the trunk that could have come only from the claws of an *iislak,* and a large one at that. Smaller footprints confirmed his story of a mother and cub in the area. Still not completely satisfied, she had shinnied up the tree herself. Sure enough, there were fresh breaks in the trunk, still oozing sap, in places where someone Tom's size could have been supported.

She felt his eyes on her as she climbed and was fairly certain that he was looking at her legs. This Tom was one for the females, it would seem, though he had never behaved improperly. Trima thought she had heard Yurula, who found both Strangers quite handsome, say something about Tom having a partner back in his old life. But Trima knew that ties loosened their hold on one after enough time had passed. One day, Tom would truly realize that he was to spend his life here in Sumarka, and set about looking for a mate among the Culilann. She imagined he would have his pick of willing females.

So his story had been verified—he had indeed been treed by an angry predator until the morning. But what if he had been treed while trying to flee with Chakotay, after they had murdered Matroci? Why was he still here while his friend had gone?

It seemed a sound theory, but for one thing: the reaction Paris had had to the dead body. She had been watching him keenly when he approached the pyre to pay his last respects. She had seen Paris notice the burn mark, seen him express shock and horror, seen those emotions quickly covered as he realized that no one else would recognize the mark for what it was. Would a murderer so give himself away as to react to the sight of his killing, especially if no one else even realized that murder had been committed? It did not make sense. So now she was confused, and not a little frightened.

Because of her position, first as Sa-Culil and now Culil proper, Trima could not express much interest in Tom's origins. One did not question where Strangers had come from. It only mattered that they were here. But Trima needed to know for reasons that no one else in Sumar-ka was aware of.

She went about her duties of morning prayer, placing a few leaves of the Sacred Plant in the small bowl of embers and taking care to fully open the windows. She was not interested in dying the way Matroci had died.

Her thoughts were not on the prayers she had uttered since childhood, but on the fair-haired Stranger.

She went through the day watching him when she could. Most of her time was spent talking to a bereaved people, assuring them that the Crafters had a plan for Matroci and that those left behind did not need to trouble themselves in fear for his fate. She was beginning to hate the lies. She did not even know if there were Crafters, and she certainly did not know of any plan. And yet the words of comfort came to her lips, and her people embraced her, called her Culil, called her good.

For years, she had told herself that her falseness was serving a higher good, but now she was not sure. Now, she might be a target herself, and things were very, very different.

There was a knock on the door and she started. She forced herself to be calm and rose languidly, the robes of a Culil swirling about her gracefully. She opened the door.

"Tom," she said, surprised. "You have never sought

solace from the Culil before. Why are you not helping Soliss and the others in repairing Ramma's hut?"

"Too many cooks spoil the broth," he said.

Her delicate blue brows drew together in a frown. "I do not understand your reference."

He grinned. "It means that sometimes you can have too many people doing one task, and you get in the way. They finally told me to leave after I knocked Kevryk off the roof. Accidentally, of course."

Despite herself, Trima smiled. "So that was what the shouting was all about."

"Soliss is busy preparing herbal drinks and Yurula is off gathering berries, I think. So, I thought I'd drop by and see if I could serve some useful purpose here."

"There is nothing I need you to do." She was about to close the door in his face when she realized this was a perfect opportunity to interrogate him. No one would know what they talked about, unless Tom told, and there was no real reason for him to. Everyone was busy, and those who weren't would assume that Paris had come for spiritual guidance.

"Oh," he said. "Well, if there is—"

"You could stay here and talk to me for a while. While I prepare the altar for the next prayer session." Her voice was still hard, and she could tell the offer sounded far from genuine.

He hesitated. "If I'm not intruding."

"No. Please come in."

He stepped inside, a little gingerly, she thought, and looked around. His eyebrows rose in appreciation. Trima was now living in Matroci's hut. It was the largest building for an individual or family in the village, and was furnished with the finest the Culilann had to offer their spiritual leader. Pillows and rugs covered

9

the hard-packed earth. A small table and chairs sat to the side, exquisitely carved and inlaid with precious stones gathered from the jungle. Trima, feeling unaccountably nervous, walked to the table and poured Tom a drink of water from a delicate earthenware jug.

"Some water," said Trima, handing him the cup. She waved a slender hand, indicating a bowl piled high with colorful fruit. "Please, partake if you are hungry."

"Thank you," said Paris. "This is beautiful. Nice place you got here."

"It is not mine. It belongs to the Culil of Sumar-ka."

He regarded her with steady blue eyes. "But you are the Culil of Sumar-ka. And unless I misunderstood what Soliss told me, you will be Culil for the rest of your life."

"Yes," she said, "but these are for the position of the Culil, not for me personally."

He shrugged broad shoulders. "Same difference."

The contradictory words baffled her. "What? Perhaps I do not understand your language as well as I thought."

He grinned, flashing white teeth. "Earth phrase, forget about it. What I'm getting at is, since you are the Culil, you get to enjoy these nice things, whether or not they're meant for Trima. It's a nice perk."

She nodded, regretting her impulse to ask him to stay. She was learning nothing, and he was making her feel uncomfortable.

"Do you think that is wrong?"

"Not my place to argue against the tradition of the Culilann. If they want to make their Culil comfortable, good for them."

"You are a Culilann now," she reminded him.

"Oh, no," he said. "I'm an honorary member of the village, but I'll have to get back to my ship one of these days, soon as I can figure out how."

Good, he had given her an opening. "Tell me about your ship," said Trima.

The blue eyes narrowed. "Why do you want to know about it? No one has ever expressed any curiosity about it before. Soliss said that it didn't matter where I came from, only that I was here now."

Trima thought fast. "That is true," she said. "But now that Chakotay is gone, I thought you might be feeling a little lonely and pining for your home, since you have no one to talk about it with. And as Culil, it is my duty to offer comfort."

He relaxed. "Well, you're right. I do miss it. I guess I have two homes—my real home, Earth, where I was born, and *Voyager.* It's become kind of a home for me as well. And the people there are just like family. Better than family, in some cases."

Trima poured herself some water and indicated that Tom should sit. He sank down among the cushions. She sat across from him, demurely arranging her robes. She listened while he spoke. She had the feeling that he had not come here to do that, but now that he had an audience, he was unable to stop the words from spilling out.

He spoke of a "star ship," a vessel that could cross light-years. Of a home farther away, he said, than she could possibly imagine, though he was wrong about that. Of visiting so many alien races that her head spun. Of instruments that replicated food, others that shot like an arrow from a bow.

"So," she said at one point in a stern voice, "you are like the Alilann. You value only technology."

"That's not quite true," he said, and then proceeded to utterly confuse her by telling her of a friend who loved to make music, of a place called Sandrine's where one danced, of a captain who was a scientist but who loved to paint, of a funny alien named Neelix who reveled in preparing fresh-grown food.

Trima stared, completely taken aback. For her, it was a new sensation. Little startled her, but this—

"How do you do it?" she demanded. "How can you integrate both castes like that?"

"Because we don't have a caste system," he said. "If your planet is a member of the United Federation of Planets, you can partake as little or as much of technology as you like. For example, Chakotay's family was pretty traditional. They grew a lot of their own food and didn't really avail themselves of all the technology they could have. I grew up in a family that was very involved with Starfleet, so my experience was almost the opposite. But even I appreciate a home-cooked meal or skill with the arts."

Trima realized she was gaping at him. She closed her mouth and tried to summon outrage, but for a long few seconds she couldn't do it. To imagine a life where one chose one's destiny. One could embrace either extreme or a middle ground, living in an Alilann-like city with art on the metal walls, eating fresh foods but sleeping protected from the elements—it was a revelation.

He looked at her curiously, and finally she remembered who she was supposed to be. She frowned terribly and stood up quickly.

"You speak blasphemy, Tom Paris," she cried. She didn't have to feign the trembling that shook her body, but she hoped he attributed it to outrage. "But since you are still very much a Stranger, I will forgive you. Speak no more of this obscene blending of castes among the Sumar-ka." A thought struck her. "Since I am your spiritual advisor, you may speak of it to me. But to no one else, on pain of expulsion!"

He sobered at that. "I get it, Trima. Culil, I should say. Sorry to have offended you."

She turned her back to him, uncertain as to whether her shining eyes would give the lie to her words. "Go, now. We will speak further of this, in private."

She heard him walk to the door, heard it close behind him. Trima didn't move for a moment, then turned around. Yes, he was gone. She let out her breath in a rush and clapped a hand to her mouth. What he had said shook her to her very marrow. Could it really be so? Did his people truly live like this? She needed to hear more about it, and soon.

But in the meantime, she had duties to attend to. Trima went to a carved wooden chest, opened it, and removed the false bottom. There, looking spectacularly out of place, were five items. Two were communications devices they had found on the Strangers, which looked more like jewelry than technology. Two others were weapons, also recovered from Tom and Chakotay. These looked like the weapons they were. The fifth item was a small handheld communication device unlike the ones the two Federation representatives had carried. It sparkled in the shafts of sun that filtered through the shutters, and one corner of it pulsed bright green.

She removed it and checked for a message. There was one, short and to the point. Yet another Culil in another village had died under mysterious circumstances. This made the sixth one in almost as many moon cycles.

And now, she was Culil. She sat the device on her lap, and began to manually enter a message—quick, efficient, full of detail, and to the point. As all her missives to the Alilann were.

Our Culil was found dead several days ago, a clear mark of a directed energy weapon on his chest. Fortu-

13

nately, or unfortunately, whoever committed the atrocity was clever enough to cover his tracks. The Culil's domicile was filled with the smoke from the Sacred Plant, which was directly responsible for his death; the energy weapon was obviously set to only stun. No one in the village has noticed, though I think this alien Paris might suspect something.

Either that, or he or his companion Chakotay is the killer. Chakotay disappeared the night of Matroci's murder, which makes me very suspicious. They could be the ones killing the Culils, wandering from village to village, place to place. They had the weapons, though I think it odd that Chakotay and Tom would have been able to find where I had hidden them, used them, and then returned them.

You must let me know if Chakotay was Recovered or if he fled on his own. And if the former, then why did you not take Tom Paris? I am in danger now. Please advise.

Trima paused, then recklessly continued, voicing her emotions. *They are only Culilann, but they are not beasts to be slaughtered so. Matroci was a voice of calm reason in this village, and his death is a setback for everything save an increase in hostilities. Was this authorized? I repeat, was this authorized? If not, and if Chakotay was indeed Recovered, then, Implementer, you have a rogue on your hands, and no one is safe.*

Trima sighed, then tapped in her signature: "The Silent One."

CHAPTER
2

IT WAS A COMFORTABLE CELL. CAPTAIN KATHRYN JANEWAY
had to give the Kwaisi that. But a cell it was, nonetheless, and she was in it, and she had to get out.

She paced back and forth like a caged animal, the
repetitive movement helping her mind to focus. She
couldn't believe she had been so easily captured, and
even with a security-guard escort! She hadn't expected
the Kwaisi to react in such a fashion, or else she'd have
been more alert. After all she and her ship had done to
help them, too.

With an uncharacteristic bitterness, Janeway recalled
her first encounter with the Kwaisi. Sensors had picked
up eight heavily armed vessels, riddled with mutated
dark matter. It was a wonder they weren't falling apart
right before her eyes. The leader of this fleet was one
Captain Ulaahn, a deluded, suicidal being who was

convinced that somehow his ships had managed to decimate an entire star system a few light-years away.

It was the dark matter that had infested his brain talking, of course. He had destroyed one of his own vessels before Janeway had managed to transport him to *Voyager*, remove the dark matter from his body, and talk sense to him.

She leaned against the metal wall and chuckled without humor. She'd abducted him against his will. "Tit for tat," she said aloud, though no one could hear.

It was after she had helped him that she realized the Kwaisi weren't the most pleasant of the alien races they'd encountered in the quadrant. It wasn't that they were aggressive, they were just extremely arrogant and litigious. And it was the latter characteristic that had landed her in this Kwaisi jail, awaiting trial. It seemed that while the Kwaisi were grateful for *Voyager*'s help in purging their planet of the dangerous dark matter, they also held her responsible for the stuff being there in the first place. Her pleas that they release her, so that her ship could save more people the way they had saved the Kwaisi, had fallen on deaf ears. They were bound and determined to drag her to trial, although Eriih, head of the Kwaisi council, had confided that he was certain she would be exonerated. Janeway supposed that was something.

They had let her speak with her ship. After explaining the situation, Tuvok had replied, "We will, of course, manage to free you, Captain."

They were welcome words, and the steadfastness with which Tuvok uttered them filled her with pride. "There's too much at stake for *Voyager* to be delayed," she had told him. "My orders are for you to take the ship on to the next patch of dark matter. They won't hurt me here." She felt certain it was the truth, but as she uttered the words, she realized she had doomed herself to at least a year in this place.

There was a long pause. "At the present moment, with you in the hands of the Kwaisi, I am the acting captain of *Voyager*," said Tuvok. "I hear the logic in your words, Captain, but surely having you back in command of this vessel can only aid our quest. I repeat, I will explore every avenue to ensure your freedom. It is only after that exploration that I will allow *Voyager* to depart."

Stubborn Vulcan. Janeway knew better than to argue once Tuvok had made up his mind. It wasn't direct disobedience, just enough for him to manage to get his way despite her orders to the contrary.

Anger at her impotence rose inside her and she banged a fist on the metal wall. It did nothing, of course, except hurt her hand, and as she rubbed it she wondered what Tuvok was doing to try to get her out of this damn place.

"Please," said Telek R'Mor. "You must let me speak to the Kwaisi Council."

"Dr. R'Mor," said Tuvok, "I have already explained that you were the original target of the Kwaisi Council. They wished to try you for your so-called crimes, and took Captain Janeway in your place as she is, for the time being, your commanding officer. There is no doubt in my mind that if you transport down to the planet, the Kwaisi Council will be delighted to have both of you to be placed on trial."

Telek closed his eyes briefly, seeking calm. For the first time in his life, he envied the Vulcan. None of this seemed to be bothering Tuvok.

"Commander Tuvok," he said with exaggerated patience, "the information I have just received from Tialin will convince the Kwaisi to release the captain. Our mission is far more dire than any of us realized."

"If you would tell me what you learned from the Shepherd, I will consider your request."

"I told you, it is for the captain's ears only!"

"As the captain is not present," said Tuvok, "then your information must needs remain unheard."

"*Veruul!*" cried Telek, and stormed off the bridge. He was shaking, with fear and anger combined. "Deck Two," he instructed, and the turbolift hummed into motion.

He tried to calm himself, clasping his hands in an effort to stop their trembling. Tuvok was right, as far as he knew. To him, it would indeed be folly to simply allow Telek to beam down and himself be captured by the trial-hungry Kwaisi. But Tuvok didn't know what Telek knew, and the Romulan feared he could not convince the Vulcan chief of security with mere words.

Alone in his quarters, Telek lay on the comfortable bed, his body tense and his mind racing. What to do, what to do? How to convince a stubborn, emotionless Vulcan that—

Yes. It was the only way.

"Telek R'Mor to Commander Tuvok."

"Go ahead, Doctor."

"I would appreciate it if you would meet me in my quarters immediately."

"You are hardly in a position to make requests, Doctor. Our captain has been kidnapped. My place is on the bridge, orchestrating a rescue attempt."

"Your place is to protect the security of this vessel and its mission. Please, Tuvok. Come to my quarters. After that, if you do not agree with my suggestions, I will make no more of them and stay out of the way."

A pause, perhaps the longest in Telek R'Mor's life. Then, "Very well. But this will be brief, Doctor."

I don't know how brief it will be, thought Telek, *but I will wager you will stay longer than you think.*

Young Ensign Kim was a reliable officer. Tuvok did not hesitate to leave the bridge under his temporary command. Kim knew enough not to do anything drastic without consulting him first. Still, the Vulcan felt the faintest tendrils of annoyance creep through him as he stood in the turbolift en route to Telek R'Mor's quarters.

Gently, he pressed down the unwanted emotion. Dr. R'Mor had obviously learned something of great import when the sphere had spoken to him with the Shepherd Tialin's voice. As the entire purpose for being here hinged on Tialin's request, Tuvok was inclined to pay attention to what she said. That Dr. R'Mor, as fine and logical a non-Vulcan scientist as Tuvok had ever met, was as agitated as he was by this unknown message was not dismissed by Tuvok. He was prepared to listen with full attention to what R'Mor had to tell him.

He exited the turbolift, strode down the corridor to R'Mor's quarters, then stood at the door, waiting to be invited. "Come," called Telek.

The door hissed open. "I assume you are prepared to tell me what Tialin told you?" asked Tuvok.

"No," said Telek, surprising Tuvok. "But I am prepared to show you."

It took a second for Tuvok to realize what R'Mor was proposing. He did not like it. The Vulcan mindmeld was not something to be used like a tricorder, as a mere diagnostic tool.

"I do understand the personal intrusion that a mind

19

meld represents to your people," said Telek gently. "I would not ask for such a thing lightly. But it is the only way I can truly convince you of what I know."

Tuvok cocked his head quizzically. "I do not doubt what you will tell me, Dr. R'Mor. You have not lied in the past, and there seems little reason for you to lie now."

"Thank you, Tuvok. I appreciate your trust. But you need to know this as I know it. Tialin didn't just talk to me. She spoke to my brain, implanting the information in a way that—" He fumbled for words. "It is a deep sense of knowing, Commander. That's all I can tell you. And you have to experience that as I did, as a knowing, not a telling."

Tuvok's dark brown eyes searched Telek's. Precious seconds were ticking away on the bridge.

"Very well," said Tuvok. "I agree."

They sat down on the edge of the bed. Telek smiled slightly.

"What is it about this situation that you find amusing?" asked Tuvok.

"There are dissidents on my planet who secretly follow the Vulcan path," he said. "This has gone on for generations. They hope for unification, someday. I was just thinking how pleased and excited some of those people would be to be involved in a mind-meld, as I am about to be."

Tuvok frowned a little. "If they react with pleasure and excitement to a mind-meld, then they are not truly following the Vulcan path, are they?"

"Spoken like a true son of the planet," said Telek.

There had been enough chatter. "Close your eyes and take a moment to calm your no doubt racing thoughts," said Tuvok. He did the same, though he was much more tranquil than the agitated Romulan. He was not looking forward to this. The mind-meld was an intimate act, one Tuvok had shared only in the most dire of cases with anyone who was not a Vulcan. He was not eager to plunge headlong into the chaotic mind of a being as passionate as Romulans were believed to be. Admittedly, Telek's years of studying science had taught him discipline, but even a disciplined non-Vulcan mind was a riot of emotions to a true Vulcan.

He opened his eyes. Telek sat silently, expectantly. Tuvok lifted his right hand and placed his fingers with exquisite gentleness on the Romulan's ridged brow, temple, chin.

"My mind to your mind," he said, intoning the ritual words. "Your thoughts to my thoughts."

And those thoughts came, rushing toward him in a stampede of colors and emotions and feelings. It was not the most volatile mind Tuvok had encountered; that dubious distinction belonged to the late sociopath Lon Suder. The feelings and thoughts of others with whom he had melded joined in the cacophonous chorus: Janeway's warm sincerity, Paris's cocksure arrogance tempered with insecurity, Kes's thoughts before she spiraled away from them into an existence they could only imagine. Voices, words: *You are my soul, my husband—My dearest friend, Tuvok—I only want to do something for the ship. . . .*

Carefully, Tuvok took the many voices, many thoughts, and separated them strand by strand. With great gentleness and respect, he laid them aside, focusing on the vibrant thread that was Telek R'Mor. Quick images flooded his brain, not what he sought but nonetheless vital to understanding that final goal. He saw an elegant Romulan woman holding an infant daughter. *I am a husband. I am a parent,* Tuvok thought, his mind automatically seeking all resemblances to ease the shock of sharing another's thoughts. He beheld the face of the chairman of the Tal Shiar, Jekri Kaleh; such a young, fair face to house such cruelty. He saw a blond man, humanoid, with a twist of contempt to his full mouth. Lhiau, the rogue Shepherd.

For a moment, Tuvok resisted the flow of Telek's thoughts and branded everything the Romulan knew about Ambassador Lhiau onto his own brain. Knowing one's enemy was wisdom. This was their foe, Tialin had said, and thus far nothing Tuvok had learned had made him inclined to doubt her.

On swept the relentless tide. Tuvok experienced grief and horror at the words uttered by Kaleh: *Your family is dead.* Telek knew more than most about the atrocities that the Tal Shiar sometimes perpetrated in the name of protecting the interests of the Empire, and now Tuvok was the shocked recipient of that knowledge. He saw himself through Telek's eyes, saw Janeway, Chakotay, Seven, Torres, Neelix, who had tried to kill Telek. The images rushed past, merging together in a kaleidoscope of color until it coalesced into a hovering, purple sphere.

It was the orb Tialin had given them, their means to understanding how to extract and contain dark matter. The orb glowed, and spoke without speaking.

Tuvok listened. Despite his lifelong control over his emotions, his heart sped up and sweat broke out on his dark skin. His eyes went wide, dilated, and he almost stopped breathing. He had never imagined such a horror, such a complete and sweeping disaster, as what was being imparted to him now.

It was no wonder Telek had not wanted to put this into words. To do so would be to drastically reduce the profound impact of this knowledge, though speaking this information would be horrific enough. Tuvok wanted to break the contact at once, to deny what had been imparted to him, had been burned onto his brain like a brand.

Instead, he regained control. He gently disengaged his mind from that of Telek's, returning to the Romulan the thoughts that were rightfully his and his alone. He thought a brief statement of gratitude at being allowed to share those thoughts; a Vulcan ritual.

Tuvok was trembling by the time his mind returned to him and he stared at Telek R'Mor.

"Now," said R'Mor shakily, "you know."

"Yes," said Tuvok. "We must beam down to the Kwaisi Council at once."

CHAPTER 3

THEY WERE MOVING HER FROM THE HOLDING CELL TO her permanent place of imprisonment, and they had blindfolded her to do it. Behind the blindfold, which was sealed to the individual contours of her face, Jekri Kaleh's eyes still foolishly struggled to focus. She smiled to herself, then forced her lips to uncurve. There was no telling what these guards would do if they thought she was laughing at them.

But the former head of the Romulan intelligence service the Tal Shiar was not laughing at them. She was laughing at fortune, which had raised her from the streets only to throw her back down even harder. And she was laughing at the familiarity of all of this, although up until now she had only witnessed these events from the other side.

There was terror here, of course. She'd be the worst

sort of *veruul,* knowing all the ghastly details as she did, to feel no fear. But she also knew exactly what was being done to her, and why, something that most prisoners did not have the luxury of knowing. The blindfold was to make her feel vulnerable, to force her to trust to the goodwill of the guards—who naturally had none—to save her from tripping or slamming into something. Her ankle was slightly twisted and there were bruises forming on her forehead and right elbow already.

Next, possibly, would come the psychological and physical experiments. Many a cure for disease had come from trial and error upon living patients. And new types of interrogation that did not involve elaborate equipment were always tested on those unlucky enough to come down on the wrong side of the law—or, Jekri mused bitterly, on the wrong side of Ambassador Lhiau.

She was glad she thought of Lhiau, because the hatred that flooded her at the thought of his loathed, handsome face gave her strength and courage. She was here wrongly accused, and she was certain that almost everyone involved, save perhaps the Empress, knew it.

Ah, righteous anger. How often have I seen it in others? Jekri did not delude herself that all the prisoners she had had arrested, interrogated, imprisoned, or executed were true criminals or traitors to the Empire. Some were just inconvenient, and she had watched with cool detachment as they raged and pled.

As, no doubt, those in control of her fate were watching her. It was a dreadful thing, to be inconvenient.

She had no idea where the guards were taking her. Intellectually, she was familiar with the elaborate prison system, but she had no personal experience with it. She had had no desire to sully her hands with that sort of unnecessary detail, but now she wished heartily she had taken an interest. She would have had access to every plan, known every weakness, every possible avenue of escape.

They went up a turbolift, walked some more, went down a turbolift. They marched her outside at one point. She could tell by the feel of the sun on her face, though the opaque blindfold did not let her even see a lightening of her darkness. This was another part of her mental torture. They were confusing her, trying to disorient her. It would have been much simpler to merely transport her from the holding cell to her permanent one. At some point, they would do that. She knew the routine well. But for the moment, it was important to them to start breaking her.

They would fail.

Finally, she was shoved forward. Her foot caught on a step and she tripped, falling heavily as her hands were bound and she could not catch herself. She was hauled to her feet, moved roughly into position, and then she heard the hum of the transporter.

Cold assaulted her when she rematerialized. A voice came from nowhere. "Your bonds have been removed. You may take off your blindfold and behold your new home."

Slowly, her heart thudding in her abdomen, Jekri did as she was told. Even this dim light hurt her sensitive eyes, and she blinked several times before her vision adjusted.

She gasped, then steeled herself to react no further, for she was certain she was being watched.

They had imprisoned her beneath the palace, in the ancient cells that had once held the worst sort of traitors hundreds of years ago. They were not often used anymore, and the significance of her being in this place was not lost on Jekri.

She would die here, alone and forgotten. And she would die soon.

Over the next few days, Jekri got to know her ancient cell very well indeed. It was small, only about three meters by two. The walls were meter-thick and made of stone. Moisture beaded on their surface. In the small space was a pile of rags that Jekri was supposed to use as bedding. She sat down experimentally on it and coughed at the stench. The old rags nearly dissolved beneath her weight, and dust rose in a choking cloud. There was also a hole in the floor for elimination, a grated hole in the ceiling for air, and a jug of stale-tasting water. With a little imagination, she could be a prisoner from eight, nine hundred years ago.

Of course, twenty-fourth-century Romulans did not rely on centuries-old security measures. There was a forcefield in place instead of a heavy metal or wooden door. Her food, such as it was, was transported in. She knew her activities were being monitored day and night, though there was no day or night here. But she suspected that she was not being watched at every moment. It would be a poor use of a guard's time. Heat sensors would record the presence of a living body. When she died, they would record that too, and someone would come to haul her corpse away so that some other prisoner could die in this place.

Her guard was a son of a *fvai*. She knew he was trouble when he swaggered up, leering, and shut down the forcefield. Before Jekri could seize the opportunity he had fired his weapon right at her.

Jekri went sprawling. Her body trembled in convulsions as she stared at her tormentor. Tingling pain raced through her and she felt saliva trickle from her lips as she spasmed helplessly. She could not stop it.

He threw back his head and laughed. With a quick touch of his fingers, the forcefield hummed back into place. He patted his weapon as he returned it to his belt.

"Lowest setting," he told her. "Come to check on the little prisoner."

The needling pain was ebbing, and Jekri clumsily wiped at the spittle on her face. She swung her legs underneath her and clambered to her feet, swaying. "What was that for?"

The guard grinned. "For fun," he said. "You're my prisoner now, Little Dagger. And we're going to have a great deal of fun for as long as you can take it."

Her body was under her command again, and Jekri stood at her full petite height. She caught his gaze and held it. She did not say a word.

It was the guard who finally looked away, muttering. As he stalked off, Jekri realized that she had probably made a mistake. As he had said, he had used the lowest setting. Next time, she would be treated to something stronger. Jekri knew people, and she did not doubt that this was just the beginning of the barbaric games the guard planned to play with her.

She sat down and picked at the food, and actually laughed out loud. It would be just as simple to program something nourishing and tasty as what was set before her, yet someone had gone to a lot of effort to specify partially rotting meat, dry, stale bread, and raw, old vegetables.

Idly, Jekri picked up a slice of some sort of root and threw it at the forcefield. Her eyes widened when the small tidbit was vaporized almost instantly. Of course, something larger, say the former head of the Tal Shiar, would not be so destroyed, but she would be incapacitated and perhaps injured. They had put the highest level forcefield on her door. Interesting. And good to know.

"That was ill done," came the disembodied voice.

"I like my vegetables cooked," Jekri snarled, searching for the source of the sound. She finally found it, hidden in a natural crevice of stone. She had just inserted a finger, thinking to retrieve the device and examine it, when a noise at the door made her turn.

Despite herself, she swallowed hard. Three doctors stood impassively outside her cell, and they had almost certainly not come to heal her.

One, a female, seemed to be in charge. With a graceful movement she tapped the controls and the forcefield was lowered. "Prisoner 8754, accompany us."

8754. At least the guard had named her. But she was in the "system" now, and that was no place for names, for identities, for individuals with emotions and families and talents and skills. She thought at first to fight, but she had only her hands, and there was no doubt in her mind that the doctors had hypos at the ready to render her docile.

She stepped forward, head held high. This was it. They would begin the torture session now, and everything she knew would be revealed. Then they would throw her back in this awful place and there would be no more transported food, only the stench from the elimination hole and her own body as it decayed.

I am a Romulan. I have lived like one, and now I die like one.

Bonds were snapped onto her hands at once. "Energize," the female doctor said.

They rematerialized in a room as far away from

Jekri's cell as could be imagined. Everything was bright and clean here, sharply so. Sterile. Metal gleamed, glass shone from instruments and containers with which Jekri was almost completely unfamiliar. It promised torture, but Jekri tasted relief. It was not the sort of mental torture session she had feared. That would have broken her. This, she could withstand.

Two of the doctors left. As Jekri watched them go, the remaining doctor, the female, said with a hint of amusement, "They have gone to watch the session, 8754. There are guards outside the door. Do not think of attempting to escape."

Jekri did not grace the woman with a reply. With as much interest as she might show toward a lab animal, the female doctor ordered Jekri to strip and step into a sonic shower. Jekri complied without argument. She had little interest in her body, save when she could use it physically for defense or sexually as a tool, and shed her filthy clothes without a qualm. The sonic shower felt good. They might be preparing her for agony, but they had given her a brief moment of feeling like a sentient being again.

"Lie on the table." Naked, Jekri clambered up. At once heavy metal cuffs slammed into place around her neck, wrists, and ankles. Now she did feel vulnerable, nude, exposed, and trapped.

And when the doctor began, despite her resolution, she screamed.

Jekri awoke in her cell, naked and cold. Her body ached all over, and when she tried to sit up, her stomach roiled. She crawled on her belly over to the elimination hole just in time to vomit up what little she had eaten of the poor food they had given her. She tasted bile, and her stomach heaved again, straining to empty itself of something that wasn't there.

Shivering, Jekri wiped her mouth with the back of her hand. She crawled over to the pile of dirty clothes and with an effort began to dress. Her head ached, and there was a burning pain in her wrist. She looked down at it. The flesh was an angry green. She touched it gently, hissed, and pulled her finger back, but not before she had ascertained there was something hard and round embedded beneath the skin.

Was this how she would die, then? Were they going to keep infecting her, inserting things into her body, and see how long it took her body to surrender? What she would not give for a clean execution!

She was sick, and weak, and wounded, and the rags did not seem so foul this time when she clambered over to them and collapsed. Jekri fell asleep at once, and dreamed of good food, Romulan ale, clean clothes, and the touch of Verrak's hands.

Jekri was jolted awake by agony and the guard's laughter. She flailed like a fish and was certain that for a moment her heart had stopped. He had indeed set his weapon for the next highest level. She wondered how many were on this particular one. He wouldn't kill her, not deliberately anyway. She heard the hum and crackle as the forcefield snapped back into place. Heavy footsteps told her the guard was leaving.

She made a decision. She could not live like this. Somehow, some way, she had to either escape or find a means with which to take her own life. With every minute that passed in this hole, the latter option looked like the most appealing.

The hum of the transporter made her turn her head. There it was, another plate of the awful-looking stuff that passed for food. Despite her earlier illness, Jekri found she was hungry. Her stomach growled as her eyes took in the sight of old cheese, moldy bread, and withered fruit. At least there was some variety, she mused with dark humor.

The fruit looked the least offensive. She picked up the puckered, lumpy shape of a *quaeri*, sniffed at it, and cautiously took a small bite.

Her teeth bit down on something hard. She dropped the fruit and her hands flew to her mouth. *Quaeri*s did not have hard pits; they had tiny, digestible seeds. What new torment was this?

She spat the offending object into her palm, and stared at it for a second, not recognizing it. Then all at once, hope spurted through her and she stared with round, wide eyes.

Embedded in the fruit, beyond visual detection, as if it had grown there, was a small, hexagonal piece of metal. She had almost swallowed it. She was not certain what it was for, but her mind raced with possibilities: a disruptor, a communication device, a piece of medical equipment that she could adjust to neutralize the forcefield.

Slowly, so as not to attract more notice than she already had if someone was monitoring her, she closed her fingers around the precious piece of metal and took another bite of the *quaeri*. Its luscious juice had long since evaporated, and it was tough and chewy, but she barely noticed the taste. It was nourishment, and she would need every ounce of her strength when the time for escape came. Someone from the outside was helping her. He or she had managed to materialize the piece of metal into her food by placing its signal on that of the standard meal transport. "Piggybacking," the Earthers called it.

Then another thought came, and the food turned to ash in her mouth. What if this were merely another type of torture? Nothing was beyond Romulans, as she well knew. Would they study her reactions, tease her with the illusion of freedom, merely to observe? Or was it Lhiau? Did he truly hate her so much that he would go to such elaborate lengths to get her hope up simply so he could crush it back down again?

She swallowed the bite, then took another. If that were so, then she would turn the tables on them. She would take their test and make it work for her. She imagined their faces, one day finding her cell empty, and realizing that they had unwittingly helped her to flee.

Or it could be true. Though Verrak had been as false as it was possible for one to be, she never had learned the identity of the mysterious friend who had sent messages to her in her quarters that night when she had been attacked by Sharibor. This person could be very high placed—high placed enough so that he or she could help Jekri without attracting attention.

With sudden determination, Jekri realized that the only way her enemies would win would be if she gave up. She finished the pathetic excuse for a meal and lay down on the rags, secreting the precious part of a tool deep in the dusty center.

She would escape, and she would mete out justice, both to those who had aided her and those who would see her dead. It was a thought as sweet as a ripe *quaeri* in season, and this fruit would be plucked soon enough.

INTERLUDE

THE VIDIIAN DOCTOR WENT BY THE NAME OF DANARA PEL. *The Entity knew her. Not of her, but knew her, the way it had known Maj Culluh. It did not understand how it came by this knowing, but merely accepted this fact.*

For over two thousand years, the Vidiians had battled a dreadful disease they called the Phage. Their desperate drive to stay alive as a race had prompted them to do terrible things. Often, they killed innocent aliens and harvested their organs. Skin grafts were necessary to replenish flesh as it died and sloughed off. They ought not to have survived, but they had, and their medical knowledge was almost unsurpassed in this quadrant.

As was the hate and fear they engendered.

The Entity had a deep connection to the Vidiians. What was it? It had lost something, had given it up.

Had it once been a flesh-being, and had its organs harvested? That was close, but it was not quite right. There was a nobility about the Entity's loss, a sense of yielding that transcended victimization. What was it, what was it?

The thought went away as it regarded Danara Pel. She still bore the scars of the illness that had ravaged her body, but was no longer a macabre patchwork of other beings' parts. She was cured of the Phage.

And imprisoned.

When the Phage had been cured, it had seemed like such a blessing at first. Kuros and his group of mercenary intellectuals had offered a cure in exchange for Vidiian medical knowledge. It had seemed so little to ask. But as with so many things, there was a dark side to the request. In earlier times, the Vidiians were known as educators, artists, explorers. Once the Phage had been cured, many raced to embrace these neglected passions, looking forward to the chance to contribute to, instead of prey upon, the other aliens in the quadrant. But others had gotten used to the casual brutality of a mind-set that rationalized murdering fellow sentient beings and using their organs.

Dark matter, floating through this system, had escalated the conflicts. Civil war had erupted. At a time when the species ought to be rejoicing in its deliverance, they were fighting one another. The Sodality had imploded and the Vidiians were easy prey for a variety of alien races desirous of revenge.

So it was that Danara Pel, compassionate doctor who had never wanted anything more than to help her people, was a slave. She was forced to use her knowledge to perform experimental surgeries and vivisections to appease cruel masters. At least the Vidiians had done what they had to survive. This alien species, the Charasin, merely wanted conquest.

They, too, were infested with dark matter, sensed the Entity. Their commander, one Pektar Sirumal, was quite mad because of it. And Danara Pel, a cancer spreading through her internal organs, knew it. The Entity felt terror coming off the woman in waves as she sliced and cut and speared and dissected. The victim moaned softly on the table. The white cloth on the table had turned bright purple with its blood.

The Entity knew pain. The pain of the victim, and the pain of the doctor.

And it knew anger at the dark matter, anger at those who valued torment over healing, subjugation over art. It did not drift upon Danara Pel, it charged her, hurtling through her system and ripping the dark matter from her cells. Danara gasped and staggered backward, a bloody instrument in her hand. Recognition passed over her face, and the Entity realized that Danara knew it the way it knew Danara. But it did not linger for confirmation.

Borne by the heat of its anger, it swept through the ship. It hurtled through the bodies of the slaves and masters alike, gathering the wrong things and neutralizing their darkness. It paused for a moment, hovering beside Pektar Sirumal, repulsed by the dark matter writhing in his body and systematically devouring his brain. If it removed the dark matter, there was not enough natural matter to keep him alive. To purge him would be to kill him.

The anger faded. The more familiar sensation of compassion took its place. It had to be done. The mutated dark matter had to be retrieved. The Entity would kill as kindly as it could.

Gently, like the softest of rain showers, the Entity descended on the leader of the Charasin. They were a hard people, and their ideology was not one of understanding, but they were not monsters. No species was, though individuals could become monstrous. The Entity coursed through Pektar's system, as tenderly as it could, and in his angry, infected brain, it planted thoughts of pleasure and calm.

Pektar stiffened, then relaxed into his command chair. He saw before him scenes from a long-ago childhood. Faces long dead smiled at him. Slowly, softly, the Entity plucked the dark matter from his brain. There was not enough natural matter to take over the higher functions, so the Entity told Pektar to sleep, sleep deeply and well. And as he closed his eyes for the last time, he thought he saw another face, one he did not know; that of a beautiful woman standing before him, wreathed in gold, with a smile of tenderness upon her lips and compassion in her blue, blue eyes.

CHAPTER
4

CHAKOTAY'S MOUTH HURT FROM SMILING SO MUCH. HE hadn't realized how much he missed the little luxuries he had come to take for granted living in the twenty-fourth century. The sonic shower beat sluicing down with algae-infested rainwater hands down, and if the dinner hadn't had the delicious flavor of fruits freshly harvested or meat roasted slowly over an open pit, at least it had been served on a table with eating implements and napkins. It didn't hurt that he was being treated as an honored guest and feted to the nines, either.

He stepped out of the shower, the second one he'd had that day, and began to dress in the tailored, fitted clothing he was coming to realize was standard among the Alilann. Ramma the weaver had made him and Tom beautiful robes that fit well and were exquisitely comfortable. More comfortable and more attractive, truth be told, than the clothes he shrugged into now. But these felt right to him in a way that the Culilann clothes, beautiful, functional, and handmade, had not. He made sure to fasten the small gold translation device to his chest. The Culilann might have a facility with alien languages that bordered on incredible, but the Alilann, just like the Federation, had to rely on artificial means of translating language.

He had to admit, he'd enjoyed his time with the villagers of Sumar-ka. But he was glad to be among an advanced species again, with comforts that were more familiar to him. And now, he finally had a chance of locating his ship, something that would have been impossible if he had lingered in Sumar-ka. His only regret was that he had not been permitted to say farewell to the people who had become his friends, and that the Recovery team had not been able to bring Tom along, though Ezbai reassured him that a second attempt would be made immediately.

Chakotay sat on the edge of the bed—an actual bed!—and tugged on boots that had been replicated to fit his feet exactly. Rising, Chakotay surveyed himself in the mirror. He ran a hand along his clean-shaven jaw; shaving had not been possible among the Culilann. That, even more than the clean clothes and the shower and the meal, made him feel like he had finally come out of the jungle for good.

There came a soft chiming sound. "Come," called Chakotay. When the door didn't open, he belatedly recalled that chimes meant verbal communication. "Chakotay here," he said.

"Commander Chakotay." It was Shamraa Ezbai Remilkansuur's voice. It was his Recovery team which had taken Chakotay from the village. "I apologize for interrupting you. I realize you are exhausted and were probably looking forward to retiring, but . . . ."

"If you need me, Ezbai, bedtime can wait," Chakotay said with a little smile. "And actually, I was just about to take a stroll, get a little better acquainted with your command center. What's going on?"

"We were going to do all this in the morning," Ezbai lamented. "Your medical examination, your debriefing, everything, but the Implementer insists."

"Ezbai, it's all right, I really don't mind," Chakotay repeated, mildly amused at Ezbai's profuse apologies.

"You are gracious, Chakotay, and it *is* important. I will escort you to the meeting room," said Ezbai. Chakotay knew that it wasn't because Ezbai didn't trust him. It was because the Alilann command center was so vast that Chakotay couldn't hope to find his way there alone.

In a few moments, another sound came, an unpleasant buzz. Chakotay stepped forward and the door opened. Ezbai looked awful. His pale blue skin was paler than ever and his eyes darted this way and that.

"What is it? What's wrong?" Chakotay asked.

Ezbai opened his mouth to reply, then obviously thought better of it and shook his head. "Come on," he said. "You'll see. Oh, Chakotay, it's just awful."

And that was all Chakotay was going to get out of the distraught Interceptor. Ezbai led him through a labyrinth of gray metal. Chakotay had not been impressed with the design or décor of the place from the minute he had transported into its dry coolness from the hot, humid jungle. There was nothing here that was not simply functional. Even his room, which Ezbai assured him was the finest of the available guest quarters and usually reserved for the highest-ranking diplomats, was devoid of personality. The bed had felt comfortable when he sat on it, but there had been no decorations, no art on the walls, nothing to really set it apart.

The corridors down which Ezbai led him were utilitarian, nothing more. At first he'd thought this was a military compound, in which case the lack of decoration would make more sense. But Ezbai had assured him that while the place was a command center, it was also a place where people lived and children were raised. An Alilann city, domed and completely shut off from the natural environment of the planet's surface. It did not feel or look like a place where children's laughter was a welcome sound.

Chakotay was glad of Ezbai's presence. He'd have gotten lost within a few moments on his own. Left, right, left, left, down, into a turbolift, left again—it was dizzying. Finally they reached a mammoth door, which hissed open for them.

There was a large, round, metal table in the center of the room. Approximately twenty people sat at the table, all clad in clothing identical to Chakotay's. There were glasses, pitchers, and several bowls filled with small gray-brown nuggets of some sort. The room was octagonal and the walls were covered with eight floor-to-ceiling viewscreens. Seven of these were activated, displaying various planets, star systems, or what Chakotay presumed to be key sites on this or other planets. The eighth was ominously dark.

A very fat man sat at what was clearly the head of the table. A half-empty bowl of the gray-brown nuggets was at his elbow, and his hands were clasped in front of him. He looked extremely upset. His skin was flushed a darker blue than that of the other Alilann surrounding him, and Chakotay had a mild fear for his health.

As they approached, the man rose with not a little effort. "Implementer," said Ezbai, "may I present Commander Chakotay of the *Starship Voyager.*"

"So," wheezed the Implementer, regarding Chakotay with piggy blue eyes, "this is the one you managed to get, eh? I apologize, Commander. I understand that you had to suffer through the Culilann's barbarous Ordeal. If Shamraa Ezbai had been doing his job correctly, you and your friend would never have fallen into their clutches in the first place."

Beside Chakotay, Ezbai flushed blue, but said nothing. He stood rigidly straight. Chakotay felt embarrassed on his behalf.

"I'm none the worse for my Ordeal, and it was Shamraa Ezbai who did Recover me, as you pointed out. Besides, I don't count my time among the Culilann as wasted. You have two fascinating cultures on this planet."

There were disapproving murmurs around the table. The Implementer's piggy eyes went cold, and Chakotay suddenly realized he had no desire to get on this man's bad side, comical though he might be at times.

"We don't consider what the Culilann do to be, ah, *cultural,*" said the Implementer. Nods of agreement went around the table this time, as if everyone else were sheep to this man's ram. There was an expression of faint disgust on all the faces. Chakotay recognized the same contempt and hostility that Yurula, the mate of the man who had healed them, had displayed when she was talking about the Alilann. He realized that he had blundered onto a very sensitive subject, and while he could feel his own righteous anger rising at the slurs against the people who had treated him so kindly, he forced himself to smile pleasantly.

"Commander Chakotay knows of my sister," blurted

Ezbai. "We were to debrief him in the morning, but since everyone is gathered here—"

"Shamraa," said the Implementer, sitting back down in a chair that seemed far too small to hold his great weight, "we will discuss that later. You brought Commander Chakotay here for another reason. Or have you forgotten?"

"N-no, Implementer." Ezbai's voice was a whisper. The big bully had him totally cowed. Chakotay decided he really, really didn't like the Implementer.

"Please sit, Commander." The Implementer waved a fat hand, then lowered the hand into the bowl. He popped a few nuggets into his mouth and chewed. "Have some articrunch," he suggested. "These things are so tasty. And I bet you're hungering after some real food after your time with the Culilann."

Chakotay sat down. Ezbai slid into the seat beside him. Chakotay looked at the dry, unappetizing nuggets that were called "articrunch." The very name quelled any hunger he might be experiencing. He thought back to the feast with which the Culilann had initiated him and Tom into their rank. Fruits picked at their ripest. Fish and birds and other meats roasted to perfection, basted with fruit juices and served with mashed roots and tubers. Sweet desserts, tangy savories, all manner of food infinitely more "real" than this bowl of brown crunchy things.

"No, thank you," he said with exaggerated politeness. "I'm still full from dinner."

"More for me, then," said the Implementer, and laughed uproariously at his own joke. Halfhearted titters went around the table. Chakotay was rapidly coming to the conclusion that, aside from Ezbai, he didn't really like any of the Alilann he had met.

His gaze fell to the table. There was a metallic rectangle embedded in the surface. As he regarded it, it hummed to life and glowed bright green.

"Please place your right hand on the tester, if you would, Commander. It won't harm you," the Implementer said.

"What is it?"

"It's a way of ascertaining whether what you are telling is the truth."

A smile twisted Chakotay's full lips. "So, I see the Alilann have their own version of the Ordeal." Nonetheless, he complied. He had no intention of lying to these people. The metal was warm on his hand as he placed it down. The woman sitting directly across from him activated something; he couldn't see what, but immediately his hand began to tingle. It was not an unpleasant sensation.

The Implementer sobered. "I don't know how much Shamraa Ezbai has told you. I wouldn't be surprised if he hasn't told you *anything*. We have a spy planted in almost every Culilann village. The one located in the village which imprisoned you—"

Chakotay couldn't help it. "They didn't imprison me, and the village's name is Sumar-ka." Even as he spoke in defense of the Culilann, Chakotay wondered who this spy could be. Soliss? He seemed sympathetic enough toward the Alilann at times. Winnif? She had appeared reconciled to the loss of her infant to the so-called Crafters, but what if it was because she knew that the infant would be rescued by the Alilann? Trima? Yurula? Ramma, the weaver? Or someone else?

The Implementer glowered at him, then continued. "Sumar-ka, then, if you will have it so. The spy in Sumar-ka is quite frankly a bit of a triumph for our side."

"I didn't know the Culilann and the Alilann were in conflict," said Chakotay.

"We're not, but there are most definitely two sides, Commander. Surely you cannot have failed to notice that. This person was planted deep, at a young age. We do not even know the spy's gender; that is highly classified information. This person sent us a message shortly after dawn." He nodded curtly, and one of the young men standing at attention beside the dark viewscreen tapped in a command.

In its own way, the communiqué was almost as primitive as the Culilann. There was no face, no voice, only white words scrolling across a gray screen. Chakotay saw an English translation alongside the strange letters of the Alilann language. They were fast translators, these people. Doubtless, this was to protect the spy's identity.

Our Culil was found dead several days ago, a clear mark of a directed energy weapon on his chest.

Chakotay inhaled swiftly. Matroci, murdered?

Fortunately, or unfortunately, whoever committed the atrocity was clever enough to cover his tracks. The Culil's domicile was filled with the smoke from the Sacred Plant, which was directly responsible for his death; the energy weapon was obviously set to only stun. No one in the village has noticed, though I think this alien Paris might suspect something.

Chakotay had his problems with the impetuous ensign, but he knew one thing for certain. If *Voyager*'s pilot and medical assistant had seen the mark of which the spy spoke, he'd know precisely what it meant.

Either that, or he or his companion Chakotay is the killer.

Chakotay's grief and horror at Matroci's murder became something more personal as every head in the room turned to regard him. He started to speak, but the Implementer waved him to silence. There was more to the message.

Chakotay disappeared the night of Matroci's murder, which makes me very suspicious. They could be the ones killing the Culils, wandering from village to village, place to place. They had the weapons, though I think it odd that Chakotay and Tom would have been able to find where I had hidden them, used them, and then returned them.

You must let me know if Chakotay was Recovered or if he fled on his own. And if the former, then why did you not take Tom Paris? I am in danger now. Please advise.

They are only Culilann, but they are not beasts to be slaughtered so. Matroci was a voice of calm reason in this village, and his death is a setback for everything save an increase in hostilities. Was this authorized? I repeat, was this authorized? If not, and if Chakotay was indeed Recovered, then, Implementer, you have a rogue on your hands, and no one is safe.

It was signed "The Silent One."

Chakotay stared as the words on the screen faded. Before he could speak, the woman across from him said, "His reactions were genuine. He knew nothing of the death."

"You killed Matroci?" the Starfleet commander demanded, ignoring the woman.

The Implementer looked unhappy. "It was not authorized. We may loathe the Culilann, but we are not murderers. The worst of it is, this is not the first time a Culil has been killed in one of the Culilann villages. Over the last six months, five Culils have died under mysterious circumstances."

"During Recoveries?" Chakotay asked.

"Once or twice, as with this Matroci. Other times, no. I brought you here to ask for your help, Commander. These murders are a bad thing for us. They could stir up resentment against us among the Culilann. Tell us everything you learned during your time with them."

Chakotay regarded the Implementer. "I don't know that the answers lie with the Culilann. It sounds like an Alilann, or a group of them, have been acting on their own and killing the Culils. We should start an investigation here."

"And we will, don't worry," said the Implementer. "But first I would like to start an investigation of *you.*" He leaned forward, his blue eyes penetrating. "You and your friend didn't arrive in the normal fashion, or else even Shamraa Ezbai would have been able to Intercept you properly. We saw no ships, heard no communications—you suddenly were just here, on our planet. How did you do this? And why?"

"It's a long story," Chakotay warned.

"We have nothing but time," the Implementer answered frostily.

So Chakotay started at the very beginning, trying to condense years of adventures into a few words. He explained how they had ended up in the Delta Quadrant, his alliance with Captain Janeway. He spoke of their first encounter with Telek R'Mor, and how bitter it was not to be able to transport home when it seemed as though the opportunity had finally arisen. He went into greater detail about the more recent events, telling them about the Shepherds, the Romulans, and the mutated dark matter which had such deadly, devastating results.

The more he spoke, the more rapt his audience became. At one point, the Implementer seemed to have completely forgotten about his beloved articrunch and leaned forward, barely blinking. Even the woman who was supposed to be monitoring him for deception seemed to forget her task and simply stared at him. *Father would be so proud of me,* Chakotay thought, amused. *I've become a storyteller.*

Finally he came to the part about finding Khala. "You see!" interjected Ezbai, unable to contain himself. "Khala is with Chakotay's people, and he and Tom are here. We've got to help him find his ship!"

For the first time, the Implementer seemed as excited as Ezbai. "Yes, we do. We need to learn more about this dark matter as well. Perhaps we too have encountered some, and aren't even aware of it." A thought seemed to occur to him. "It could be that this is what is motivating the killers. Dark matter renders one's judgment unreliable, yes?"

Chakotay thought of Neelix, attacking Telek with a kitchen knife. "Sometimes," he said. He did not say what he thought in his heart: that someone among the Alilann, or a group of them, had simply decided that they hated the Culilann enough to kill their spiritual leaders. He would like to be wrong, would like to blame it on the dark matter; but he was all too aware that sometimes evil existed quite well without any assistance.

The Implementer nodded, as if satisfied. "Well, problem solved. It's clear to me that this dark matter is the culprit."

Chakotay couldn't help it. "Dark matter can't wield directed energy weapons," he said. "We need to stop these killers before they strike again."

"Of course," said the Implementer, nodding as if the two of them were in perfect agreement rather than conflict. "We need to concentrate on being able to detect this dark matter. That will stop the killing."

"Will it?"

"Chakotay, you are not familiar with our people. Perhaps your species has problems that routinely result in murder and chaos. We do not. The Alilann and Culilann have existed side by side for centuries with only the occasional minor conflict. We're not killers by nature. It's plain to me that it is the dark matter that is affecting the killer, or killers. And you will help us detect it, Chakotay."

"I'm pleased to be of what assistance I can," said Chakotay, "but I'm no physicist or engineer. Your efforts would be better spent trying to find my ship. I'm certain our crew has made great strides in my absence, and they have the sphere of the Shepherds as well." He spoke no more of his fears. There was no point. It was obvious the Implementer was too confident in the peaceful nature of his people and had seized upon the dark matter as the scapegoat.

"And then we could bring Khala home," said Ezbai.

Chakotay's hand was getting tired. "Can I move my hand now?" he asked.

"Certainly, certainly!" enthused the Implementer. He seemed jolly now. No doubt he thought that the dark-matter explanation would solve everything. "Thank you for indulging us. We know you are telling the truth now. It won't be asked of you anymore. However, there are some things that puzzle me. You speak of things like the Delta Quadrant. I've never heard that term. And all of the aliens of which you speak are unfamiliar to us."

That troubled Chakotay slightly. These people did not strike him as insular. "It's a big quadrant, and perhaps you have another term for it," he said. "But surely you know of the Borg, or at least have heard other aliens speak of them."

The Implementer shook his bald head. "Not a word."

"Consider yourselves lucky, then."

"From what you have told us, I promise you, we do." He rose, and everyone else around the table, including Chakotay and Ezbai, emulated him. "We are pleased that you and your companion were not the killers. And it sounds as though you have solved the mystery about why these killings are taking place at all. Ezbai will see you back to your quarters, and come fetch you in the morning. We'll want you to undergo your medical exam first thing, so that you can join us in helping us find your ship."

Chakotay regarded him for a long moment. He was delighted that he and Tom were no longer under suspicion, but felt certain that things were not as simple as the Implementer made them out to be.

Things were not that simple at all.

CHAPTER
5

"COMMANDER TUVOK," SAID ERIIH, THE HEAD OF THE Kwaisi Council. "What a surprise." The flat tone in which he uttered the words indicated he was anything but surprised. By this time Tuvok knew the species well enough to be able to recognize annoyance on the angular, mottled face. Deep, sunken eyes glowered at him.

"You must be a species that enjoys wasting time," Eriih continued. "Didn't you say something about having to rush off and save other planets from the dark matter?"

"Indeed we do," said Tuvok, "and we require our captain for that task. She is our commanding officer. This crew has served her loyally for many years. Our ship is more efficient with her at its head, and we will require all the efficiency we can muster."

Eriih sighed heavily through his beak-like nose. He leaned forward, and spoke with what appeared to be genuine compassion. "Commander Tuvok, you must not think us ungrateful. Your ship and your technology saved our planet. But because you have saved us, our legal system is still intact as well, and you must respect our way of doing things."

"I do," said Tuvok. "But there is more at stake than you yet realize. I request a gathering of the council, the crews of your defensive vessels, and Captain Janeway. Telek R'Mor and I have information that you need to know. We are certain that once you have this information, you will release our captain and permit us to continue our quest unhindered."

"You are stubborn," said Eriih, with not a little respect. "And intriguing. This goes against protocol, but I would say that the situation warrants it." He spread his hands. "We are a reasonable people, after all."

Tuvok lifted an eyebrow. He thought otherwise, but refrained from saying so.

"We will contact you when we are ready."

"Ulaahn," said Janeway with surprise as the Kwaisi captain stood at the entrance to her cell. "I thought you were awaiting trial, like myself."

"I have been permitted to remain free until my trial date," Ulaahn explained while the security guard deactivated the forcefield. "I am Kwaisi. I will not attempt to elude justice."

A smile twisted Janeway's lips. "And I might?"

"You have indicated a tremendous desire to rejoin your crew," Ulaahn said. "You are not of our people, you do not have obedience ingrained in you."

And thank God for that, thought Janeway. Obedience was a good thing, up to a point. But every individual had to decide what that point was. And blind obedience, certainly, was never good. She knew how vital it was that her ship continue gathering up the dark matter. Ulaahn's assessment of her had been correct. She was not going to sit around, languishing in a Kwaisi jail, while innocent people died or went insane.

"Is there a reason for this visit?" she asked mildly.

"I have come to escort you to the council chambers. Your Commander Tuvok has managed to convince the council to reconvene regarding your trial. It seems he feels he has new information that will persuade them to change their minds and set you free." Ulaahn's voice dripped skepticism.

"Let's hope he can," said Janeway, but she felt as skeptical as Ulaahn appeared to be.

"Two to transport," said Ulaahn, and a moment later they stood in the center of the Kwaisi Council chambers.

The room looked slightly better than it had when Janeway had last seen it, several hours ago. Most of the debris had been removed and the dust cleaned up. The fine carpeting that covered the floor still had slash marks, and colorful murals still bore cracks and what looked to Janeway like the Kwaisi equivalent of graffiti on them. Deep gouges marred the table at which the council sat. The last time Janeway had been in this place, she had been an honored guest. Now, she was a captive of the Kwaisi government, awaiting trial. She was not invited to sit at the table.

Instead, Ulaahn indicated a chair to the right of the central table. When Janeway sat down, a forcefield sprang into place around her with a faint hum. The Kwaisi were clearly not about to take any chances with their prized prisoner.

A few moments later, Tuvok and Telek materialized. Janeway was surprised to see the Romulan, and worried. Telek had been the first target of the Kwaisi. They had decided that he was, directly or indirectly, responsible for the spread of the dark matter in the first place, and that therefore he should be tried for his crimes against the Kwaisi. Janeway had argued with them. For that protest the Kwaisi had taken her, as she was R'Mor's commanding officer, in his stead. She had no doubt but that they would love to get their hands on him as well. What was Tuvok thinking, beaming him down here?

Tuvok caught her gaze. He nodded, slightly, slowly. Janeway recognized that gesture. Tuvok knew something she didn't, and obviously thought it worth the gamble. She settled back in her forcefield-enclosed chair. She had to trust him, and she desperately hoped he was right. The ship could continue on its mission without her, but it could not hope to do so without R'Mor.

"Let me first thank the council for agreeing to hear us out," said Tuvok without preamble. "With your permission, I would like to open a channel to our vessel, so that the crew may witness this revelation as well."

Revelation? A big word. Tuvok did not bandy words about. He always chose the precise term necessary. Janeway was desperately curious as to what this was all about.

"Certainly," said Eriih generously. "We have nothing to hide."

"You may also wish to broadcast what is about to transpire as well," said Tuvok. "Your people should be aware of—"

"You may decide what your people get to hear, and I will decide what mine do," said Eriih, his sunken eyes flashing. "We will record this and decide later if it is worth notifying the populace. Per your request, the crews of all the defensive vessels formerly under the command of Captain Ulaahn are being permitted to witness the proceedings."

Tuvok inclined his head. "As you wish." He squared his shoulders and, to Janeway's astonishment, looked uncomfortable. He looked like someone who did not know where or how to begin. Finally he said, "Dr. R'Mor, you are the one to whom this knowledge was imparted. Do you wish to explain the situation to the assembly?"

Telek looked even more uncomfortable than Tuvok for a moment. Then, he took a deep breath, and stepped forward. He indicated a padd he held in his right hand.

"I am no public speaker, or politician," he began. "I cannot hope to sway you with charisma. I must convince you with facts, and my own sincerity. I have here some notes to which I will be referring." He paused. "Among my people, we have something called the Right of Statement. It is given to every prisoner before his sentence is carried out. Captain Janeway has, I understand, told you a little of our adventures to this point. As far as my people are concerned, I am a traitor, though in truth I am none. I have been preparing my Right of Statement in the event that I am able to return home, where I will be tried for treason."

A lump rose in Janeway's throat. She had no idea that Telek had been drafting his last words.

"I will not read it, for that is not appropriate. But I will consult it from time to time. Are there trained scientists here?"

Several heads nodded. "Good," said Telek. "You will be able to verify many of my statements. I will make certain assumptions of your knowledge; please feel free to ask for clarification if you require it."

He was silent for a moment, looking down at his feet, gathering his words. At length, he raised his head.

"My friends—for you are my friends; at this moment, all innocent peoples are—I speak to you today of dark matter—and dark matters.

"Over ninety percent of the matter in the universe is composed of dark matter. The rest is matter that we know and understand. We call it baryonic matter, and it is what composes stars, planets, this table, our very flesh. Even when we understand dark matter, its mystery lingers. Most of the time, we cannot see it, although we know that it is very nearly omnipresent. There are untold amounts of it in this room right now, perhaps hundreds of particles in a single strand of my hair. Dark matter is only visible when it interacts with subspace distortions, as in a dark-matter nebula. We have since learned," and here he glanced over at Janeway, "that the reason we cannot detect it normally is because it exists simultaneously in all universes. The reason it becomes detectable in a dark-matter nebula is because the interaction with subspace pulls it completely into this universe."

"Remarkable," said one of the council members. "That is a theory that we have been working on for years. How did you prove this?"

Telek looked uncomfortable. "We were told this. We have documentation of the event, should you wish to see it."

Janeway took a deep breath. If only they had solid data, rather than Tialin's word! Though she knew, as others could not, how true that word was.

"Captain Janeway has perhaps told you of a being calling himself Ambassador Lhiau, of a race called the Shepherds. They have spent eons manipulating dark matter. Lhiau came to our people and offered us a cloak which would render our ships and even individuals completely undetectable. We, I regret to say, leaped

56

upon the opportunity without investigating it completely. We have paid dearly for that mistake. Lhiau also used his ability to manipulate dark matter to assist in our creation of wormholes of practically limitless size."

He was warming to the audience, who, to give them credit, were listening attentively. Janeway found herself leaning forward, even though nothing Telek had said so far could be termed a revelation.

"For what purpose did this alien Lhiau decide to help your people?" asked one of the scientists. "What did he offer, and what did he want in return?"

"He offered us quadrant domination. With the dark-matter cloaks, we had an advantage over every known species in the Alpha Quadrant. It was a very seductive offer. In return, he asked us to help him defeat his enemies. To the best of my knowledge, he has yet to reveal who these enemies are, or what grudge he has against them. But we have found out."

Telek's dark eyes flickered over to Janeway. "We encountered another member of his species, a being called Tialin. She told us of the true nature of dark matter, and that Lhiau was deliberately trying to pull dark matter fully into this universe. She told us he was a rogue, and that the Shepherds were desperately trying to gather up this mutated dark matter before it could do more harm. She enlisted our aid and gave us the technology so that we could assist them. Council members, you have experienced the effects of this mutated matter; you know what it does."

They nodded solemnly. Across the room, Janeway saw Ulaahn look down. Many eyes went to him. He had been driven mad by the dark matter and had killed the entire crew of one of his own ships, convinced that they were all wretched, evil beings who needed to be destroyed. He would be tried for that.

Janeway was not fond of the Kwaisi in general, or of Ulaahn in particular. He was arrogant and rude, but now, at this moment, she felt a deep wave of compassion for him.

They had to listen. They had to see how awful this obscene, unnatural matter was. They had to let her go.

"What it did to planets and people it came into contact with was bad enough," said Telek. Janeway's head whipped around. What? There was more?

"But Lhiau's evil goes far deeper than doing damage to a few solar systems. Let me digress for a moment, and discuss another theory. That of the nature of the universe."

Janeway didn't like where this was going. How was the nature of the universe tied into all this?

"We know that, first of all, ours is not the only universe there is. There are many others, some of which we know about, others which remain only theory. What lies inside a wormhole is not of this universe, for example. The small bubble inside *Voyager*'s warp core, which is safely containing all the dark matter we have been able to retrieve, is a universe unto itself. There is a mirror universe, which contains all of us, but in which our natures are very different. There is a theory of a Shadow Matter universe, related to our own only through gravity. There are Shadow people, Shadow planets, just like those in our more familiar universe. I confess, that is my favorite of the theories. It's the imaginative romantic in me."

Chuckles rippled through the crowd at the thought of the apparently staid Telek being an imaginative romantic. He smiled a little. Janeway raised an eyebrow in appreciation. He knew how to handle a crowd better than he let on.

"To return to the topic of the nature of our own universe, as usual, theories abound, but no one knows for certain. We know that the universe is expanding, and has been since its creation. Some believe it is what is called an 'open universe,' and it will continue to expand forever. Matter will be spread out more and more sparsely, and the average temperature of the universe will fall steadily toward absolute zero. My people call this 'the Freeze.' "

Janeway nodded her understanding. "The Big Chill" was what humans called it.

"Others feel that there is enough matter present in the universe to halt this expansion. Everything will collapse back inward. The universe will become compressed, and become a 'closed' universe. We call this 'the Squeeze.' "

The Kwaisi scientists were nodding too, now. Janeway knew this was "The Big Crunch," another playful human term for something quite dire.

"Now," and Telek placed the padd on the table and raised his hands in a helpless gesture, "some accuse scientists of wasting time on things like this. After all, they say, the universe should continue as it is for an unimaginably long time before either scenario occurs."

Janeway had to smile to herself. Once, as an exercise, she'd had to write down just how long it would be until, by all estimates, the universe either Crunched or Chilled. She'd written down the numeral 1, followed by a hundred zeroes. It was quite a long time.

"You will observe that both of these theories hinge on the amount of matter present," said Telek. He had clasped his hands behind his back and was walking back and forth at the front of the gathering. Janeway realized what he was doing. He was turning this into a lecture at the Romulan Astrophysical Academy. He was in his element.

"Too much matter, and we have the Squeeze. Too little, we have the Freeze. Therefore, dark matter, which comprises ninety percent of the matter in this universe, has a significant role to play in either scenario."

So that's what this digression about the nature of the universe has to do with dark matter, Janeway realized. *But how does it tie in?*

"But there is a third option." His dark eyes caught and held the gaze of first one scientist, then another. "And when I say it, you will realize why I can call myself an imaginative romantic for even entertaining the idea. This is the concept that our universe is neither open nor closed, but flat. There is something called a critical density."

Janeway was familiar with the critical-density concept. She tried to remember—ah, yes, one hydrogen atom per cubic meter, or about one ounce for every fifty billion cubic kilometers. It was amazing what you remembered from your Academy days sometimes.

"A flat universe," Telek was saying, "is one in which that density is exact. If our universe is indeed flat, it would keep expanding, but slowly, never quite turning the corner. It would exist forever."

The scientists in the crowd were frowning now. Janeway wondered why Telek had even brought up this ludicrous theory. No one had ever truly entertained it for centuries. All it did was undermine his authority with his fellow scientists.

"Of course, such a thing could never naturally occur," said Telek, soothing the ruffled feathers of the scientists. "But what about—unnaturally?"

Janeway's heart skipped a beat. The hairs along her arms and the back of her neck rose up. All of a sudden, she suspected she knew where Telek was going with this little lecture. And she didn't like it at all.

The room was utterly silent. "Suppose," said Telek, "for the last few billion years, the matter in the universe has been toyed with? A little taken here, a little put there, to keep it precisely at this critical density? Everything in balance, everything working out just perfectly?"

He whirled and slammed his hands on the table. "*That* is what the Shepherds have been doing!"

And it made perfect sense. Even the name made sense now—*Shepherds*, good tenders of their flocks. No wonder Tialin hadn't wanted to tell them this at the outset. She feared they'd be too frightened to do anything, paralyzed with the sheer horror of it all, as Janeway was paralyzed now.

There was nothing less than the fate of every single universe in existence at stake.

Her mind flew to what must be happening in the Alpha Quadrant. Eager Romulans, piling on cloak after cloak, creating more mutated dark matter, pulling more matter into this universe than there ought to be. The stuff expanded at an exponential rate. How close were they to oblivion? Years, months, days, moments?

She realized that she was cold, was trembling. She'd faced challenges before, even looked Death square in the eye, but this—her limited, human mind was having trouble wrapping itself around the concept of the end of everything.

"That perfect balance," Telek was saying, "which allows all of us to be here in this room right now, is what Lhiau is trying to tip. Lhiau is tricking us into playing with the mutated dark matter, to create more matter in this universe and less matter in others. Our universe will suffer the Squeeze; others, the Freeze."

"But why?" The voice was plaintive, frightened. Clearly, at least one member of the council believed what Telek was saying. "Wouldn't Lhiau destroy himself as well?"

"Not at all," said Telek. His face shone as if lit with an inner light. Righteous anger sat upon his features. "You see, the Shepherds live in the rifts between the universes. It is as if they are playing a game. When this is done, the playing board will be cleared, ready for a new game. I cannot do anything to stop my fellow Romulans from contributing to their certain doom by using the dark-matter cloaks, but the ship *Voyager* may be able to help delay the destruction long enough for the good Shepherds to stop their renegade comrade. This, my friends, is why you must let Captain Janeway go. We need to embark as soon as possible to—"

"My compliments, Dr. R'Mor," interrupted Eriih, a sardonic smile twisting the slash in his face which served as a mouth. "Captain Janeway did not tell us you were so accomplished a storyteller."

Telek gaped. For a moment, Janeway's world swirled in a mist of red and gray, fury and shock warring for her consciousness. They did not believe Telek!

"Your tales will no doubt help your time awaiting trial to pass quickly." Eriih gestured, and at once two guards stepped up toward Telek.

"No!" Janeway wondered who had yelled so loudly, and then realized it was she herself. She moved without thinking, and cried wordlessly as the forcefield surrounding her chair sent a shock throughout her system. "Didn't you hear him?"

"What Dr. R'Mor says is true," said Tuvok. "I have mind-melded with him and read his thoughts. He cannot lie in such a contact."

"But he can lie verbally to us. And you can too," said Eriih.

"Vulcans do not lie," Tuvok replied calmly.

At that, Eriih threw back his head and laughed. "I will say this for you Federation representatives, you do have quite vivid imaginations. My time was not wasted today. I was well entertained, and you have given us Telek R'Mor as well."

"No."

The voice was as quiet, as assured, as Janeway's had been frantic. She looked around, to see who was daring to utter such a defiance.

Ulaahn stepped forward. He held a weapon pointed directly at Eriih. "You will release them both," he said in that same calm tone.

Eriih stared at his old friend. "You cannot mean that you believe this tale? Ulaahn, we are not children, to be bought off with a story!"

"You have not seen what I have seen," said Ulaahn. "I have been aboard their vessel. I have seen how they utilize this Shepherd technology. And," his voice cracked slightly, "I have been in the clutches of this dreadful dark matter. It has driven me to murder, Eriih. I have seen too much, I know too much, to believe that they would concoct so elaborate a lie just to free their captain."

He looked over at Janeway. "You," he said to the guard standing behind her. "Shut down the forcefield."

The guard did not move. "Do it!" cried Ulaahn. "I have killed two hundred and eighty-three people already. I will not hesitate to kill one more to do what I believe is right!"

Now the guard did move. He pressed a button on the wall and the hazy yellow-green forcefield disappeared. Janeway rose, surprised her legs would hold her.

Ulaahn threw something in her direction. Her hands came up automatically to catch her comm badge and phaser. As she affixed the badge above her left breast, she demanded, "Ensign Riley. He comes too."

"Do it!" Again the security guard touched the buttons on the wall, and Ensign Riley materialized in the room. He quickly moved to stand beside his captain, Tuvok, and Telek R'Mor.

"You will pay for this disruption of our legal system, Ulaahn," warned Eriih. He was furious, but there was nothing he could do.

"I certainly shall," answered Ulaahn, "with rejoicing in my heart that I have not been obliterated by a rogue Shepherd's pique. Every day I have the privilege of being alive to stare at my cell wall I shall count as a blessing. Go, Captain. You have a duty to perform." His eyes held hers. "See that you succeed."

"We will, Ulaahn," she told him, fiercely willing herself to believe the words as she spoke them. "I promise you."

CHAPTER
6

IN A DISTANT, LOGICAL PART OF HER MIND, THE PART THAT
was not obsessing about food and dwelling on the agony
coursing through her veins, Jekri Kaleh marveled at the
efficacy of the Romulan penal system. In just a few short
days, she wasn't certain exactly how many, they had
come close to breaking even the former chairman of the
Tal Shiar. How did lesser mortals manage to hang on to
their sanity?

The dispassionate physical exams and experiments.
Waking her at odd hours while she tried desperately to
sleep, to steal time to repair her injured body. The
thrice-damned guard, shutting off the forcefield, firing
his weapon at stronger and stronger levels, reactivating
the field, then walking off laughing. The pitiful food.

Her logical self latched on to that thought. In the
food had come her chance of salvation. Each meal

brought something new. She was no technical expert, but the equipment was not unduly complicated. Besides, she welcomed the mental stimulation of trying to assemble the tool her mysterious benefactor was sending her. By this point she realized it was a laser scalpel. She had hoped it was a small disruptor, one of the tiny ones the Family of the Blade sometimes carried, but she would gladly accept whatever weapon she could get. Thus far, she could detect no energy cell. Whoever it was obviously planned to save that for last. If there were any investigation of the process by which her food was sent to her, it would be more easily detected than simple metal.

If only her wrist would heal. But it gave no sign of doing so. The doctors had embedded something just beneath the flesh and it was becoming infected. From time to time, they would check on it, but made no move to stop the infection. It itched, and hurt, and the flesh was a sickly puffy green. It was hot to the touch.

Jekri steeled herself and began to probe her left wrist with her right fingers. The pain was excruciating, but she pressed her lips shut against the shriek that wanted to escape and continued. The object was hard, round, and artificial. A tracking device, in case she should escape?

The thought unnerved her totally. Escape was what was carrying her through the hours of torment. It was the light that kept her focused, kept her from going mad or committing suicide. She had to remove the thing embedded in the soft, infected flesh of her left wrist.

Of course, she might do nothing more than hasten her own demise. She was no doctor. She did not know which veins lay where, or what tendons could be damaged if she tried to remove the foreign object. And once she removed it, provided she was successful, they would notice it right away. What would they do then? Probably insert another one, perhaps in her back, where she could not reach it.

Perhaps it wasn't a tracking device. Perhaps it was a pellet of slow poison. Maybe it was—

She shook her head. "No," she whispered fiercely. Panic and flights of terror-riddled fantasy would avail her nothing. But the thing in her wrist could be trouble if it was not removed.

The only thing missing was the energy cell to operate the laser scalpel. Otherwise, she was ready to make her move. Every day had brought a piece of the scalpel. Surely today the final piece would arrive. Jekri made her decision. The thing in her wrist had to come out. Now.

Jekri looked around her cell. Everything was filthy, even the little bit of water they gave her once a day. She'd have to risk further infection.

She recalled a Vulcan meditation, one that Dammik had told her would help her control her reactions to pain. True, pain was a physical thing. It was the body's reaction to something amiss, a way to alert the brain to damage that could result in injury or death. But the brain determined whether the damage was great enough to warrant attention. The damage was the message; pain was just the messenger. Once one was alerted to the damage the pain signaled, Dammik had told her, one could decide what to do about it. The pain no longer served a useful function. One could ignore the pain to the point of banishing it altogether.

Jekri first made sure that the recording devices she had discovered were still broken. It had become almost a daily ritual. Jekri would break all recording devices and, while she was gone, someone would come in and repair them. But at least she had a few hours of true privacy.

Confident that she was not being watched, she sat down on the pile of rags, closed her eyes, and began to consciously calm her mind. She addressed the agony in her wrist, and acknowledged the message it delivered. Feeling a bit foolish at first, she intoned, "I have heard the pain. I know what it is telling me. I dismiss the pain, for it is no longer of use to me." She repeated the ritual phrases several times, then opened her eyes.

She stared levelly, dispassionately, at the inflamed area. She concentrated on turning down the volume of the message the pain screamed to her, until to her surprise it was merely a throbbing ache.

Now.

One of the pieces of metal which her outside assistant had transported was long and, if not sharp, then at least sharper than her stubby fingernails. She felt for the piece in the rags, extracted it, and poised it over her wrist.

There is no pain.

With a cold focus, she began to cut at the inflamed skin.

The pain exploded along her nerves, right down to her toes, and she gasped. No, she would not be defeated by her own weakness! There was no pain, not for Vulcans, and for this moment she was no Romulan, but a Vulcan, born and bred on the red, hot planet, where there was no pain, no pain—

She placed the sharp tool against the hardness of whatever had been inserted into her body and dug around. Jekri hissed between clenched teeth, and clung to her mantra of "there is no pain" like a lifeline. Blood and pus trickled down her pale skin, and she smelled the scent of rot.

The metal tool found the base of the implant, and

carefully levered it upward. Rotting flesh parted and a small circle popped up and out, to land in the rags.

There is no pain.

Except her inflamed nerve endings shrieked loudly to the contrary. There was a bloody hole in her wrist now. Gingerly, Jekri flexed her fingers. Everything moved properly, though for a moment the world went gray and she feared she was about to lose consciousness. Grimly, she bound the injured limb with filthy cloths, applying pressure to stop the bleeding. Green liquid seeped through the cloth, but eventually slowed and finally stopped. The white-hot agony subsided to a sharp, angry ache.

Sweat dotted Jekri's face. She turned her attention to the small implant that had been embedded in her wrist. It was covered with blood and other fluids. She poured water on it, wiped it off—and joy shot through her.

Her salvation had been in her body all along. One of the doctors was part of this outside plot. Jekri held in her hands the energy cell that would operate the weapon that had been transported to her in bits and pieces. The female doctor, who had done such dreadfully painful things to her, was also apparently an ally.

Quickly she gathered up the pieces and began to assemble them. Her body was still reeling from the incredible pain she had just subjected it to, and she was growing weaker by the day for lack of sufficient nutrition. Her fingers were clumsy and her brain was not as alert, as sharp, as it ought to be, but she managed. Within a half-hour she had before her a laser scalpel. It was not the ideal weapon, but at this point, Jekri was willing to use a rusty spoon as a weapon, if it would mean getting out.

She had three escape routes. The first was the way

she normally entered and exited the cell. She would somehow need to dismantle the forcefield, then find a way out of the area without being captured. If only she had had a chance to study the layout of these old prison cells, she'd have a better chance of escaping via that route.

Another was the elimination hole. She had considered and dismissed that for the simple reason that, small as she was, she could not fit down into the chute. A few more weeks, she mused to herself, and she might be able to do it. But she had no idea where the elimination hole led. Had this been a more contemporary prison, there might have been some sewage system into which her excrement was emptied. But these cells were hundreds of years old. Most likely they were simply holes, covered when filled.

The final option was the ventilation shaft. It was covered by a grate, but that would yield to the laser with ease. The shaft was wide enough for her narrow shoulders. Once, she knew she could have climbed the smooth surface with ease. Her body was strong and well disciplined. Now, she was weaker. She did not trust her body as once she used to, but there might be no option.

Jekri wanted badly to test the laser scalpel, but she knew that its operation would make a distinctive humming noise. To activate it would be to draw attention to it. She could not risk detection until she was ready to use it to escape.

Now that she had the means of escape within her hand, she felt strangely hesitant. Every step along this dark path had been familiar, though she had never experienced any of it firsthand before. She knew that what she was feeling was a predictable reaction. Some prisoners grew used to their prisons, and as a result eventually became as tractable as anyone could wish them. Jekri's dark brows drew together in disgust at the thought of herself falling into that category. She was a warrior, a warrior of shadow. She was the Little Dagger, and she would never surrender, not in mind, not in body, not in spirit. She clutched the small tool until her hand hurt. She had to leave soon, before she lost her will altogether.

She stood and looked up at the grate. Extending a hand, Jekri probed along its edges, as she had done many times before. Her fingers could find the edges, red with rust, and see the welds that had set it deeply into the stone ceiling. Up inside the shaft was darkness, but it was from here that air came. If she could follow that shaft far enough, she—

Footsteps. The guard. Jekri almost quailed. The sadism of the guard had been the most difficult thing she had had to endure here. She could steel herself for the doctors, choke down the poor food, but the guard came at unpredictable intervals and each time he fired, the setting was one notch higher.

She flung herself down on the rags, feigning sleep. The laser scalpel was in her hand, hidden beneath the rags. He liked this the best. He was a coward of the vilest sort. Looking into her eyes while he fired unnerved him. She heard his heavy breathing, a rumble of a chuckle. The familiar sound of the forcefield being turned off reached her pointed ears.

She sprang more quickly than she would have believed. His eyes widened as she leaped on him, her mouth open in a silent snarl of pure hatred. His weapon was drawn. As if in slow motion, she saw him lift, point, squeeze.

Jekri slammed into him, bringing her damaged left hand down as hard as she could on his wrist, causing the weapon to clatter onto the stone floor. He was a big man, and scars crisscrossed his face, but now that ugly face wore an expression of terror. He knew who she was, what she had done, what she was capable of, and what he had done to her.

She brought her small, clenched right fist crashing down on his windpipe. It crunched most satisfactorily. He gurgled, his eyes still rolling in his head. Deftly she flicked the laser scalpel and heard the soft hum. It was working.

Jekri could feel him tense. In an instant he was going to utilize his superior weight and pin her beneath his large body. She had the element of surprise, but he had strength. She did not hesitate. In one smooth arc she brought the laser scalpel down and plunged it into his body.

He cried out and writhed in pain. She sprang off him, a dancer now, awaiting a second chance. As he rolled over, attempting to rise, she found and took it. She darted forward and sliced him from throat to belly. He fell forward and green blood began to pool beneath the writhing form.

It was perhaps the most morally just murder Jekri Kaleh had ever committed. She stepped back, panting and trembling from the exertion. She was so weak! She hated herself like this. Once she caught her breath, she armed herself with the dead man's disruptor. She almost took the communication device as well, but at the last minute decided against it. Who would she be talking with? And perhaps they could trace her through it. Best not to risk it.

She quickly scanned her cell, her home for the last— who knew how long it had been. She had the only thing she needed. Hope gave her energy as she sprinted off to find an exit. She would need to hurry. She did not know the guard's route or how long it would be until some-one missed him.

The area was enormous. She guessed it was at least a square kilometer, perhaps more. And it would appear that she was the only prisoner here. She grimaced; it was a dubious honor. Moving as quickly as she could, she trotted past cell after cell. Nothing, no one, no exit. Cursing the precious time lost in this fruitless quest, she ducked into the nearest cell and looked upward. Yes, there was a ventilation shaft here as well. She lifted her face toward it and sniffed. Cold air, but fresh. And this grate was in worse shape than the one in her own cell.

Quickly Jekri thumbed the controls. A blue blade sprang to life. She wished she were taller; she could only just reach the grate if she extended her arm fully. Red chips of rust flaked down onto her upturned face. She wiped them out of her eyes and continued. One more side . . . .

She stepped back quickly, not knowing if the grate would fall immediately nor how heavy it was. But it didn't move. It would require some help. Hoping that she wouldn't be crushed by the weight—now, *that* would be an irony—Jekri again moved underneath the grate and tried to dislodge it.

It shifted, ever so slightly. Then, all at once and too quickly for Jekri to catch it, it gave way and fell with a loud clang onto the stone. She tried to slow its descent, but all she managed was to divert it from falling di-rectly on her head. It caught her shoulder and almost wrenched her right arm from its socket.

She swore softly and froze, listening with all the ten-sion of a forest creature. The guard she had killed would seem to be the only one assigned her. She moved quickly. Luck had been with her thus far. She would not tempt it more than she had to.

Carefully switching off the laser scalpel, she inserted it and the guard's disruptor into her clothing. She wished she had a proper belt, but she'd have to make do with what she had.

She sprang upward. There was absolutely nothing to hold on to and she fell back onto the floor. Pain shot through her ankle. She had twisted it slightly. She attempted to stand. It was not broken, at least. Grimly, Jekri tried again. Again, she failed.

She took a deep breath, closed her eyes, and centered herself. She focused on what she would need to do to succeed. Jekri went through each step in her mind's eye: the leap that would be high enough to propel her sufficiently deep into the shaft; quickly extending her feet to wedge herself in; each move of hand and foot as she climbed upward to freedom.

When she opened her eyes, her heart rate had slowed and she was calm. She gaze up, determined where she wanted to be, and jumped.

This time, she went several centimeters higher. At once she kicked out, her arms flying outward to secure a hold. This time, she stayed, though she felt her enemy, gravity, pulling her down. It was dark, but she did not need to see. Her questing hands and feet told her what she needed to know. Centimeter by centimeter, her body straining, she began to move upward.

The rough walls scratched her already lacerated skin, tore at her clothes. Once, she almost got stuck and panic closed in. She forced her roiling thoughts to be calm and continued. Sometimes Jekri found handholds, cracks in the wall that assisted her.

At one point she extended her hand and found nothing. She flailed for a second until she realized that this was another shaft, a horizontal one rather than a vertical one. It would be much easier to negotiate. If it petered out, she could always back up and return to her vertical climb.

Carefully, she clambered up, patting around for a hold and then hoisting her torso onto the horizontal surface. For a moment, she lay there, gasping, grateful for the reprieve. Carefully, she got to her hands and knees. The corridor was wide enough so that she could move this way, though her head scraped the upper part of the shaft.

This was much faster. She scuttled along purposefully for some time until her hand landed on something hard. She snatched it back. In the utter darkness, she had no clue as to what might be in this place. Gently, she reached out and her fingers closed on something long, thin, and hard. It was like a stick of wood, but what would wood be doing here? Frowning, she kept exploring with her fingers. More sticks, of different sizes. Now she felt something soft. Material. When her hand reached something round and hard, with two holes in it, she realized what it was. It was a skeleton.

Another prisoner had tried to escape via these shafts, long, long ago. She was surprised his bones did not crumble at her touch. What had killed him? Had he gotten stuck in the narrow crawlspace? Had he starved to death, or been injured or ill?

Jekri shook her head angrily. Such musing would not serve her. All she needed to be concerned about was that she not die like this unfortunate wretch had. Determinedly she moved the old bones and clothes to the side, clearing enough room to continue, and pressed on.

From time to time, she heard voices. At such moments she would sit as still as possible, trying to breathe softly, and strain to listen. She could not make out words, but by other sounds she could sometimes tell where she was. Once, she even heard the strong voice of her Empress. Lhiau's baritone in answer made Jekri so angry that for a moment she couldn't breathe.

Revenge. It would be sweet.

Other shafts opened from time to time and, guided by whim, she would take them. At one point she wondered if she would ever find her way out of the maze. She thought it quite likely that she would die here, utterly lost. But at least she would die free.

Her stomach growled, eager for the poor food it had been given. She ignored it, ignored the increasing trembling in her limbs, the pain of her ravaged left wrist.

Finally, she realized that the darkness was beginning to lighten. Up ahead was a patch of white—light shining down a shaft. Hope spurted through her and she crawled forward as quickly as she could. When she reached that patch of light, she stared at it, and a slow smile spread across her face. She would get out. She was the Little Dagger.

She edged forward, blinking against the brightness, and looked up. It was too far for her to distinguish where this led. She would have to climb it. She closed her eyes briefly, allowing herself a moment of utter weariness, then rallied and began to climb upward.

The light on her face was enough. It almost pulled her along. She must not be too eager, though, and risk exposing herself too soon.

A grate came into view, but as unlike the one through which Jekri had first shinnied as could be imagined. This was made of a contemporary alloy. The ventilation holes were frequent and tiny. She listened, straining to maintain her awkward position of back against one wall, feet against the other. No sound. Whatever this room was, there was at present no one in it.

Carefully, Jekri reached inside her garments and removed the laser scalpel. It would take longer, but would be much quieter than simply firing the disruptor. And right now, stealth was key. She had not come this far to fail.

She cut through the grate quickly. This one was lightweight and easily maneuverable. Quietly, she pushed it upward and slid it aside.

At that moment, hands seized her wrists and hauled her upward. She kicked violently, trying to break free.

"Here you are at last," came a familiar voice. Jekri turned and stared into the eyes of Verrak, her betrayer.

INTERLUDE

What a sad, war-torn place this planet was, the Entity thought as it approached. Brother against brother. Law versus power. An old, old story.

As more information came to the Entity, it became disturbed. Once again, it knew this place. Ilari. It was becoming used to this strange sensation of familiarity, of knowledge of places it did not know it knew. But this was different, more intimate knowledge.

It had lived here.

It had been an Ilarian.

Yes—no—yes and no, right and wrong. Emotions buffeted the Entity: anger, fear, selfishness, selflessness. Battles, fought on the inside, reflected on the outside of this poor planet's scarred surface.

It floated down toward a turreted fortress. This was where the autarch ruled.

It had been an autarch, and tried to be one again, and—

The Entity did not like these sensations, and concentrated on what it had come here to do: seek out and neutralize the wrong things, the things that could soon destroy every universe save the ones that the Shepherds had created for themselves.

It was two youths who had been in conflict; youths they were still, not men, not old or weary or wise enough to realize that they should love and honor one another, regardless of who wore the ancient talisman. And following them, those who followed one or the other. It ought to have ended soon after it had begun, and they had thought that ended when they had left—

They? Who were they? Again, the perplexing questions that distracted the Entity from its task.

The Ilarians were a rugged people. They were not too far away from savagery, though they strove to honor the ways of peace and art. That savagery, lurking beneath the surface at all times, had erupted when a man long dead had risen to try to reclaim what he had lost two centuries earlier. The autarch had been murdered, and his sons squabbled over the right to rule like dogs over a bone.

A name floated to the surface of the Entity's conscious thoughts: Tieran.

It had been Tieran.

It felt angry with itself, and floated into the fortress like an unseen mist. It did not matter if it had been Tieran, or had not. Both it knew to be true and factual, though seemingly contradictory. But it was here to do what it could to soothe the damage that Tieran's bid for power had wrought, though only time and wisdom would do that.

The dark matter was strongest here. The Entity ex-

tracted it from walls and hangings, from plants and statuary and flagstones and flesh. It removed it from the reigning autarch, Demmas, as he ate alone late at night. And it left a sweet breath of spring behind. Demmas paused and looked around, sensing he was not alone.

His several nostrils flared. "Who is there?" he called, tense and frightened. This was his life, now; the fear of the assassin, or worse, the friend who betrayed. Gently, the Entity comforted him, and he relaxed and returned to his meal. Demmas thought of the fighting going on, how his troops were punishing those found to be loyal to his brother, and wondered if perhaps it wasn't time to forgive. He called his First Castellan to him and began to talk in quiet tones.

In another part of the fortress, Ameron languished. The food was poor and riddled with the dark matter that was turning his imprisonment into a living nightmare. Gently, the Entity came to him, taking into itself the hatred and fear and sickness caused by something that ought not to be causing harm at all.

It lingered, waiting for something, it knew not what. But when the door to the younger brother's cell swung open, and the First Castellan appeared, then the Entity knew why it had stayed.

"Your brother wishes you to join him at dinner," said the Castellan, and Ameron's heart swelled with joy and gratitude.

CHAPTER

7

ENSIGN PARIS'S PERSONAL LOG, STARDATE ... HELL, I don't know.

The whole village has been busy the last couple of days. Apparently we're heading into the season of "trading," though I don't know how they can mark seasons in this climate. How did they do it on the Earth's equator again? The rainy season and the dry season? Probably that's how they do it here too. I'll have to ask.

So we have stopped doing things like repairing huts—

And here Tom Paris paused and looked vexedly up at his own ceiling, through which a steady trickle emerged to plop into several pots he'd hastily scrounged. Rainy season. Definitely.

He resumed his log entry: *—and instead are spending our time making crafts, drying food, and coming up with other things to barter when the traders come by.*

Frankly, fond as I am of the people here in Sumar-ka, I am looking forward to meeting some new people. This might be a good time for me to disengage myself and start trying to contact the Alilann.

Except that he still didn't know what had happened to Matroci. Unease stirred in him. It was one hell of a bad coincidence that Chakotay had vanished on the night Matroci died, but coincidence Tom knew it to be. Chakotay would never murder anyone. Kill in a fair fight, or for a worthy cause, yes. But Matroci's murder had been calculated, cruel, stealthy—as un-Chakotay-like a thing as Tom could imagine. But who else? Someone knew more than they were telling.

With a sigh, Paris put down his makeshift "log." Over in the corner, his task awaited him. He stared at it. It seemed to stare back. He rose and went over to it.

It sat on the hard-packed dirt floor, reproaching him silently.

Tom hadn't ever been good at anything creative, other than coming up with fibs to get himself out of trouble. He couldn't play an instrument like Harry did. He couldn't sing, like the Doc. He couldn't paint, like the captain. His decision to keep a log merely highlighted that writing wasn't his hidden talent, either.

He sometimes made up pretty funny limericks, but that didn't count.

Before him were six earthenware pots of various sizes and shapes, all made by the talented hands of Resul the potter. His job was to paint them. He'd done two so far and they looked dreadful. He had first tried a pattern on one. Bad idea. The lines were squiggly and even a simple checkerboard made his eyes hurt when he looked at it. The second one, free-form art, was even more atrocious. It was a muddy swirl of colors that looked like someone had been sick all over the pot.

He sat down cross-legged in front of the pots, picked up the smallest one, and held it in front of him.

"What am I doing?" he asked it. "You're a lovely little pot. And I'm going to ruin you. I'm sorry. You must just have had some bad pot karma."

What the hell, he thought. This time he'd just dip his fingers in the pot and cover it with polka dots. He opened the sealed jars, poured small amounts of color into shallow, flat-bottomed bowls, and dipped his five right fingers into the liquid. First the black. He pressed his fingers to the brown-red surface of the clay jar. Kinda fun. Now a little yellow—

"Crafters give you a good after-sun, Tom Paris."

Tom started, knocking over the entire pot of blue paint. He swore and almost made the mistake of scooping the blue mud back into the jar.

"I am sorry," said Trima. "I did not mean to startle you. We were supposed to meet at this sun-place, remember?"

He groaned. "You're right. I'm sorry. I got engrossed in finishing these."

She looked gravely at them for a long moment, then said, "Perhaps Resul would prefer it if you were not quite so engrossed."

He had to laugh at that. "Perhaps she would, at that. I'm just ruining them."

"Do not worry about it," Trima said. "There are other things you can help with. A runner has come and said the traders will be here by nightfall. We need to build a fire and prepare the feast. Perhaps you would be more use assisting there than being engrossed in painting pots."

He looked at her closely. Her voice was dead serious—but was that a hint of a twinkle in her eye? Did Trima actually have a sense of humor? He was probably imagining it. But he would have bet his pots would make anyone laugh. Well, except maybe for Resul.

"Happy to help," he said, getting to his feet. "Let me wash the evidence of my crime from my hands and I'll be there in a moment."

The minute the words left his mouth, he desperately wished them back. Trima did not react, but he sensed something—a chill in the air, where before there had been camaraderie and even humor. He forced a smile and went to rinse off his hands. She left without saying anything.

The water in the basin turned a blue-black color. There wasn't enough to completely rinse his hands, so he wiped them dry as best he could with a makeshift towel and headed outside.

Did Trima know what had really happened to Matroci? Certainly, directed-energy technology wasn't something that the Culilann encountered on a day-to-day basis, but they weren't ignorant of its existence, either. The Ice Princess had always struck Tom as being a little more savvy than some of the other inhabitants of Sumar-ka. She might know enough to realize that Matroci's death wasn't just caused by smoke inhalation.

By the time he reached the central, cleared area where he and Chakotay had been guests at a feast in their honor, many of the villagers were assembled. The fire was already going. Laughing, several women prepared a roast something-or-other—Tom still couldn't keep the names of the wildlife straight—by rubbing it with oils and herbs.

He called a welcome and was rewarded with smiles. Paris plunged in to help eagerly, and soon his skin was covered with soot and perspiration from working so near the fire.

"So," he said to Winnif, who was peeling fruits with which to stuff the Something-Or-Other prior to roasting, "it seems like everyone is anxious to meet with the traders."

"Of course we are!" laughed Winnif, a hint of "silly boy" in her voice. "It is the only time we get to meet Strangers, except when they arrive unexpectedly like you did. We will have new fabric with different colors, and pottery of different shapes, and new foods to enjoy. Sometimes, they even bring the young of certain animals, that we may breed them and either use their fur or their flesh."

"Will they undergo the Ordeal as well?"

"Only rarely. They usually come from the nearest village, and they will bring a token from the Culil which shows that they have been determined to be acceptable to the Crafters."

"Lucky them," said Tom, and smiled. Winnif didn't seem uncomfortable by his alluding to the Ordeal. It was just a part of their culture. They were not embarrassed. Only Soliss had expressed remorse and resentment over the tradition. Soliss, who was the only Culilann who had a counterpart in Alilann society. Could he have pressed a weapon to Matroci's chest and coldly left him to die? It did not gibe at all with what a healer stood for. But people had been known to do things that went against what was expected of them before now.

"What about the runner who came earlier?"

"He stood at the edge of the jungle and shouted his news. He didn't come into contact with anyone. He'll join the rest of his group when they arrive. By the way," she added, looking up at him, "I saw Resul on my way here. She wants to know if you are done painting her pots."

Far too slowly for the people of Sumar-ka, it would seem, the suns finally sank below the horizon. Blue skies turned to purple, then faded to gray after a few moments of a spectacular sunset in which scarlet, gold, orange, magenta, and lavender spread their glorious hues across the skies.

Paris helped light the torches. The Something-Or-Other turned slowly on the spit. Its scent made his mouth water. One thing was for certain. He'd never eaten this well in his life.

The villagers gathered, milling about aimlessly, waiting for the guests of honor. Finally, Paris thought he heard a faint booming noise. Distant thunder?

Yurula's eyes lit up and she turned to embrace her partner. "The drums! They are coming!"

Sure enough, the drumbeats increased in volume. The Sumar-ka began making music of their own, beating their drums to guide the traders in the right direction. Even Paris was caught up in the power of the rhythm and felt excitement and anticipation rising in him.

The sound grew closer, and now he could make out shapes in the distance, just beyond the ring of the firelight. The Sumar-ka drumming ceased, and after three strong beats, so did that of the traders.

One of them stepped forward, a man in his middle years. Tom saw many of the villagers smiling; they obviously knew this man. He said something that was completely unintelligible to the human, and Paris was disappointed. Of course. The Sumar-ka had taken the time to learn his language. These Strangers—and he had to laugh to himself when he realized he was thinking of them in those terms—had not yet had the chance. There was a lot he was going to be left out of tonight.

He felt rather than saw someone step next to him, and glanced down to see Yurula. "I will translate for you," she said, smiling at him.

The head Stranger began to speak. "The man is Weymar, and this opening is a traditional speech," said Yurula. "He says, 'We are the Traveling People. We go from village to village, spreading the joys of the Crafters throughout. We ask for permission from your Culil to approach, and receive the gift given us from the Culil of the village of Nagar-tem.' "

Trima spoke in her own tongue, and again Yurula translated. " 'I am Trima, Culil of the village of Sumarka.' " Tom couldn't understand the words, but he was watching everyone closely and didn't miss the reaction of the Traveling People to seeing Trima, not Matroci. Their faces grew terribly sad. " 'Approach, and show me your offering.' "

Weymar did so, extending a small carved statuette. Murmurs of approval went through the crowd. Tom couldn't see it clearly but it looked pretty ugly to him. Yurula chuckled at his expression.

"It's a very good gift," she explained. "It is a representation of a Way-Walker. They walk between the worlds, between our world and that of the Crafters. A depiction of a Way-Walker is said to ward off harm to the village it guards. We already have several, but the more, the better." She paused, and added softly, "Perhaps this one will be more effective in his duties. There has been harm enough done here."

Paris nodded his comprehension and sympathy.

Trima accepted the gift and held it high over her head for her people to see. She spoke clearly, in the fluid language that was the Culilann's native tongue.

" 'We accept the gift of the Culil of Nagar-tem,' " translated Yurula. " 'We accept that these Strangers are clean of illness, are pleasing to the Crafters, and bring no darkness with them. Welcome, then, to the village of Sumar-ka.' "

Trima embraced each of the traders in turn, after which they happily came forward to greet old friends. Their blue eyes kept wandering to Paris, and he knew he was an object of great interest. He worried about the language barrier, but laughter, food, and drink did not require words to be understood, and after a while he found that he was enjoying himself. Tomorrow, Yurula told him, all the fine crafts would be on display. The traders would have things that the Sumar-ka wanted, and after another feast tomorrow night the Traveling People would be on their way to another village.

Paris briefly thought that that was a pretty damned good life. You brought stuff that made people happy, got in exchange things that made you happy, and ate like a king for two nights in a row. No, it was not a bad job at all.

He found himself watching Trima, even as he laughed and ate and made humorous attempts to communicate through gesture. She seemed solemn, even for her. At one point, she spoke in low tones with Weymar. They both looked solemn after that.

Midway through the feast, Paris looked up and noticed that Trima had quietly left. Where had she gone? Sudden, illogical fear rushed through him. Maybe something bad had happened. He rose and looked around the happily eating and laughing crowd, ascertaining that she really was gone and not just off talking with someone else.

As unobtrusively as possible, he excused himself and went to look for her. He was not foolish enough not to realize that sometimes young lovers wanted privacy, but Trima, like Matroci before her, had remained most definitely unpaired. He wondered if that was part of the requirements of a Culil or simply an individual choice.

There was light coming from her hut. He rapped on the door. "Trima? It's Tom. May I come in?"

He heard scuffling noises from within. "Just a moment," Trima called in English. When she opened the door, she looked harried. "What do you want?"

"Are you all right? You left the party and I just wondered . . . ." His voice trailed off. He shouldn't have come. Trima was Culil of the village, its spiritual head. She could take care of herself.

But Matroci hadn't been able to.

Her stern expression softened. "Yes, I am all right. Thank you for your concern. It's just, well, I received some bad news and I wished to be alone. To meditate on it," she added hastily.

"What bad news?"

She hesitated, then relented. "Everyone will know about it by tomorrow anyway. I might as well tell you now." She stepped back and indicated that he might enter. She poured them both a cup of tea. Paris sipped, tasting the earthy herbs.

"Weymar was saddened to see that I, not Matroci, stood to greet him as Sumar-ka's Culil. But he wasn't surprised." She looked into her cup, as if she could glean information from the leaves floating there. "You see, it was not the first time the Traveling People had

89

come to a village to learn that the Culil had died. It has happened before—in five of the eight villages they have visited this season. All under strange circumstances."

She lifted her blue eyes to Tom's. "The Traveling People fear that someone is murdering the Culils. And I fear that they are right."

He took a chance. "Matroci didn't die from inhaling the smoke of the Sacred Plant, did he?"

Trima straightened, and the mask descended on her pretty features. "Of course he did."

"Okay, yes, that's what eventually killed him, but you dressed the body, Trima. You saw what I saw. A dark blue mark, right on the abdomen."

Trima rose and busied herself clearing away the dishes. She almost snatched his cup from his hand, never mind that he had only taken a few sips. "Perhaps you ought to leave."

"It was the mark of a directed energy weapon," he persisted. "Someone stunned him, so that he wouldn't be in any position to fight. And someone is killing the other Culils. Trima, if you know anything about this, you have to tell me."

"Why?" She whirled, anger suffusing her pale blue face. "You are a Stranger. How do I know that you didn't kill him? Or Chakotay?"

Paris thought fast. "Because I know that Matroci confiscated our weapons. And you know that, too."

She wilted before his very eyes. Her hands stopped their busy movements. "I do," she confessed. "But I did not kill Matroci. He was a good, kind man. Everyone loved him. I never had any desire to become Culil." She sat down, slowly, as if she had suddenly aged. "It is good, to talk of this with someone at last. Have you ever kept a secret, Paris? Have you ever lied for a long, long time?"

Tom thought about the lies he had spun to keep himself out of prison. Lies that to this day haunted him. "Yes," he said quietly. "And it's not a good feeling."

"No, it's not. Not even when you think you are doing good by telling these lies." Finally, she looked up at him. There were tears in her blue eyes. "What I am about to tell you, you must promise not to reveal to anyone unless I say so."

He stared at her, caught up in the depths of her eyes. "I promise."

She swallowed hard. "I am Culil of Sumar-ka. I was trained to become this from a young age, when I wandered into the village lost and seemingly broken. I underwent the Ordeal at age ten, Paris. I know what you went through. After that, the Sumar-ka adopted me when I told them of my parents' tragic deaths in the jungle. Except it was a lie. It was all a lie. My name is Trima, and I was born Culilann, but that is the only truth here."

She licked her lips and continued. "I was raised Alilann. My family left me to be taken by the Crafters shortly after I was born. You see, I had a deformed mouth and no tongue. I would not be able to speak."

"Then—the Crafters are real!" It was surprising, but it went along with the theory he had proposed to Chakotay, that the Crafters were advanced aliens who appeared as gods to these people.

Trima shook her head. "No. The Alilann take the babies left on the sacred mountain. They recover them, heal their deformities, and raise them as Alilann. Except some they send back to the villages. To spy on the people who abandoned them. I am one such. My code name is The Silent One, because I could not speak. My task is to report to the Alilann on the very people who trust me the most. I tell them when Strangers have come, so that they may Recover them. I tell them when babies are left on the sacred mountain, so that they may rescue them."

Tom didn't know what to say. "It sounds like you're doing good things," he said lamely. "You're helping the Alilann save lives."

"By betraying my own people!" Tears now began to trickle down her round, blue cheeks. She wiped at them angrily.

"But you're Alilann."

"For the first ten years of my life, yes. But ever since then, I've lived here. I am neither, Tom. I am somewhere in the middle. I am The Silent One, and I am Trima, Culil of Sumar-ka. I think some of the things the Culilann do are barbaric, awful. But I love how they live, how they create without even thinking it's anything special. The Alilann abhor things made by hand. They scorn music, and art, and growing their own food. At some point I will be called back, and I don't know if I can live that way anymore."

Tom was silent, listening. There was nothing he could say to comfort this woman. Now he knew why she had tried so hard to appear icy and distant. She was wrestling with her emotions, her Culilann and Alilann halves. Better to not form attachments.

"It was easier when I was just the Sa-Culil. But then Matroci was murdered, and I don't know what to do now. I don't know if it's something that the Alilann have deliberately done, or if it's just a rogue acting on his own. But my people are in danger. *I* am in danger. And I just don't know what to do."

She buried her face in her hands and wept softly. Not

knowing what else to do, Paris rose and went to her. Gently, he put his arm around her and guided her head to his chest. Her long, pale blue hair fell around them, covering them both. He let her weep. Trima had been strong for so long, keeping an enormous secret and trying to do what she thought was best for both her peoples. She deserved a few moments of simple, cleansing crying.

"I'll do what I can to help you," he whispered; "and it will all work out somehow. I promise."

CHAPTER

8

CAPTAIN'S LOG, SUPPLEMENTAL. WE HAVE RETURNED TO
*our quest with a renewed sense of urgency, now
that we know the true depths of the danger we
face. It is staggering in its scope. Our minds can
barely comprehend the vastness of our own universe, let alone the tens of millions which are con-
ceivably coexisting with it. The thought of all that
destroyed, gone, is barely imaginable. But there is
no reason to doubt Telek's statement, or Tialin's.*

*Not for the first time, I wish we had the luxury
of a trained ship's counselor. But even if we did, I
do not think we could spare the time from this
task to consult one. All the shifts have work to do,
and they are all competent individuals. The fact
that we have such a personal stake in the outcome
serves as excellent motivation.*

Engineering is operating at maximum capacity. There is dark matter everywhere, it seems. It is a good thing that we are not alone in this quest, that Tialin and her kind are also working toward this end. Our little ship couldn't hope to get it all.

Janeway paused and leaned back in her chair. "End entry to captain's log. Call up captain's personal log."

"Personal log awaiting entry."

"I really didn't expect it of Ulaahn," Janeway said quietly, her eyes seeing not the computer console in front of her but Ulaahn's last, determined look. *See that you succeed.* "He was arrogant, short-tempered, rude . . . and yet he believed us. He gave up his freedom, probably for the rest of his life, in order that we could go about accomplishing something that must seem incredibly far-fetched. And there's no way to prove to his council that he was right. If we succeed, his world will keep turning as it always has. And if we fail, well, no one will be around to gloat. The universe owes this man a great, great debt. Thank you, Ulaahn."

She turned around and regarded the stars streaking past in a graceful, silent ballet. A yawn caught her by surprise. It was late; she needed the rest. Janeway knew that she had a bad habit of driving herself too hard, and was not always the best judge of when to rest and when to push just a little bit more. But she'd said it herself in her log—she had a capable crew who knew exactly what was at stake, and exactly what to do about it. No captain could ask for more than that.

She yawned again, instructed the computer to lower the lights, and dressed for bed. Crawling in between the cool, crisp sheets, Janeway smiled a little to herself. They would succeed. Failure was not an option.

Alone in his quarters, Telek was feverishly entering his own thoughts into his personal log. Most of this he had already recounted, at the mockery of a hearing and to Janeway's senior staff. But he had to make certain he recorded it all. It would be vital for his Statement, when the time came.

"The Shepherds came into existence shortly after the dark matter itself," he said, speaking quickly and forcefully. "They realized what awesome power it had in forming and shaping the universes. Once they saw all the wondrous things that came into being, they realized that, knowing what they did, they could not be responsible for these things blinking out of existence. So they began guarding the dark matter, making certain that all the universes stayed at the critical balance, which we call the Omega balance.

"But Lhiau and others like him thought that this was foolish. What did they care about what pitiful creatures evolved, or were destroyed? They were safe in their third spaces, in their own universes that were not impacted by the presence or lack of dark matter. Perhaps they were not doing good after all. Perhaps they were interfering by making sure the universes stayed in perfect balance. The natural state of the universe is chaotic, and they decided to take it upon themselves to restore that chaotic state."

By duping foolish Romulans, and who knows how many other greedy, gullible races. By offering conquest as fleeting as a raindrop, conquest which will lead to the destruction of literally everything. My only hope is that there are wise heads who are daring to stand up to

Lhiau. Surely they must realize by now that the dark-matter cloaks are dangerous!

Telek did not underestimate the role he himself had unwittingly played. Thanks to his wormholes, the mutated dark matter had spewed into this quadrant like so much sewage. Now *Voyager* was racing to repair the damage, with the highest stakes imaginable.

He took a deep breath, and called up his Statement. His mind was too active for him to sleep. He might as well keep working.

"We had no way of knowing the information I have just cited, but Lhiau did. He and the other Shepherds have spent eons manipulating dark matter, and they understand its nature very, very well. We know how the Shepherds' apparatus works. It gathers particles of dark matter directly to it, like a magnet attracts metal. We do not understand *why* the apparatus works, but our best minds are hard at work at deciphering this mystery. It is better to not be in debt to anyone. We Romulans know that."

I am a Romulan, he thought fiercely, *and I will die like one if I must.*

Harry Kim was absolutely beat. He'd worked well into the second shift, helping Seven up in Astrometrics to graph out all sectors in which the dark matter had been detected. It was a task that was not going to be accomplished in any short period of time. With every yellow spot that showed up on the screens, Kim's spirits dipped lower and lower. How were they expected to get it all? How could anyone, anything?

"You are in distress," Seven had observed crisply.

"Yeah," said Harry. "Look at that. There's no way we're going to be able to gather it all up. It just goes on forever."

"A typical emotional exaggeration. We know that the universes are finite. Therefore, anything in the universe is finite, including mutated dark matter. Although," she added, "I admit it is a daunting task." Her blue eyes flickered to his. "You are projecting your own emotions onto the task at hand."

"What do you mean?" he asked, then wished he hadn't.

"Your inability to consummate your relationship with Khala due to your cultural differences is distressing you. You view it as hopeless. Therefore, you see the task at hand as hopeless."

Harry felt his face grow hot. "Oh, great, so my failed romance is the talk of the ship."

"Of course not," Seven replied. "Just of Engineering."

"Oh, that's just—"

But Seven was smiling. "I am utilizing humor to defuse a tense situation."

He relaxed, just a little, but was still uncomfortably self-conscious. "Well, maybe you need to do a little more research to determine the topic you want to joke about. Some things aren't appropriate."

"But Mr. Paris used to call this—" She paused, searching for the word. "Kidding," she said finally.

That bothered him too. "I'm sure that wherever Tom is, he still does call it kidding," Harry said, a touch too harshly. "I'm not thinking clearly, Seven. I'm going to call it a night."

"Ensign Kim," said Seven as he turned to leave. "I had no desire to cause offense with my comments. You are not a topic of idle gossip. Your friends are concerned about you, that is all."

Harry managed a smile. "Thanks," he said, with genuine warmth. "That's nice to know."

He had just stepped into the turbolift when his combadge chirped. "Ensign Kim," came Neelix's voice. "Could you stop by the mess hall for a moment?"

Neelix's chipper, upbeat attitude was the last thing Kim wanted to encounter at this moment. He was hurt, tired, scared and just wanted to collapse into sleep. "Neelix, I know we've been bugging you about working on that coffee substitute, but I'm heading to bed. I don't need caffeine right now."

"Oh, it's not about that," said Neelix. "Please, just for a moment."

"All right," sighed Kim. To the turbolift he said, "Mess hall."

As the door hissed open, he said, "Okay, Neelix, this better be—"

There were no lights, save for a small candelabra on a single table. Music wafted through the air; a soft, soothing melody played on an ancient instrument called the harp. Something delicious was cooking.

"Neelix?" asked Kim, in a less demanding voice.

"Neelix went to his quarters after he finished helping me cook a late supper," came Khala's soft voice. Kim's heart sped up a little. She stepped forward, into the candlelight. As ever, Kim found her utterly gorgeous.

But he also knew when things had gone as far as they could. "Khala," he began, "I think the differences are just too great. I appreciate your—" He broke off. "Did you say 'cook'?"

She nodded. She looked just like a kid with a great big secret. "Yes," she said excitedly. "We went to the aeroponics bay and picked out some fruits and vegetables. Then he showed me how to make bread. Look! I can't get the dough out from under my fingernails!"

Khala stuck out her fingers. Sure enough, there were little crescents of white beneath her nails. "It'll come off in the sonic shower, of course, but I think of it as kind of a trophy. And I went through the ship's computers, trying to find some music."

"Khala—"

"And there are all kinds! And they all sound *different!* And that's just Earth's history of music. I can't wait to start listening to Vulcan lute music, or Bolian—"

"Khala!" She stopped in midsentence, blinking at the volume of his voice. He gentled it at once. "This is very sweet of you, and don't think I don't appreciate it. I know how unpleasant it must have been for you to cook and listen to music, and I'm flattered that you did it to make me feel better."

She was smiling now, a mysterious, sweet smile that made him feel fifteen years old again. "But you don't want me to make myself into someone I'm not just to please you, right?"

"Exactly. You're an Alilann. These are things you despise, even though they are things I love." He ran a hand through his hair, struggling for the right words. "I really care about you, but it's obvious we're too different to make this work."

She was still smiling, even though he had delivered bad news. What was going on?

Slowly, Khala walked toward him and placed a gentle hand on his arm. He knew he should pull away, not encourage her any more, not when he had decided that no matter how much he wanted this to work it never could, but he didn't. He didn't want to.

"Harry," she said softly, "I'll admit that when I came to Neelix and asked him to help me learn about the things you loved, I did so because I thought it would make you care for me more. And that first sandwich was just awful."

She wrinkled her cute little nose and Harry's heart broke a little more.

"But then, we moved on to other foods and began cooking them. I got interested in the chemical changes that took place in the process of cooking. And the smells as they cooked were just wonderful. I've smelled a prepared meal from a replicator and enjoyed it, but there's something about the fragrances the foods emit during cooking that—mmmm! The next thing I knew I was eating fruit right off the vine and loving it. Not because you did, but because it was good! Do you see?"

He thought he did. Oh, God, he hoped he did.

"Then I began listening to samples of music in my quarters after my shifts. At first they were so strange, but then I detected the mathematical precision to music, and I began to like that too. My favorite was something called 'Jingle Bells.' Do you know it?"

"Yes," Kim managed. His chest felt oddly full.

"It made me want to laugh and move my body in a strange way. I went to the Doctor and he said this desire to move to music was called 'dancing.' I liked it. I liked all of these things, and not for you, Harry—for *me*. For the first time in my life, I had a glimpse into the mind of a Culilann, and I understood how those primitive things they do give them pleasure. Because they were giving *me* pleasure."

Her fingers curled around his forearm, and she glanced away. Even in the dim light, he saw her cheeks flush blue.

"So I just wanted to thank you, tonight. For opening my eyes to something that I found I enjoyed so very much. I never would have tried to learn about these things otherwise, and I would be much poorer. Please don't think you owe me anything. I understand that this is probably too late to—"

She didn't say anything more, because Harry had pulled her into his arms and was kissing her deeply. Her arms crept around his shoulders and she kissed him back.

Janeway stepped onto the bridge at 0755. Tuvok and Jenkins were already at their stations. Stephen Murphy, the young ensign who had captained the vessel during the night shift, snapped smartly to attention.

"Good morning, Mr. Murphy. How passed the night?"

"Uneventfully, save we recovered more dark matter." A blond lock of hair fell into his eyes, and for a second he reminded her painfully of Tom Paris, when she had first encountered him at the penal colony in New Zealand. Her heart hurt for an instant, as she fixed his face and Chakotay's in her mind, then let them go. She extended a hand for his report and slipped into the command chair.

They'd purged two uninhabited planets and a nebula last night, though probably the lower life-forms they'd had to disassemble and reassemble were still in a bit of shock from the experience.

"Excellent, Ensign. Dismissed."

As Murphy trotted for the turbolift, it hissed open. "Good morning, Mr. Kim," said Janeway. She'd slept unusually well and, after the successes last night, to her it was a very good morning. She raised an eyebrow in surprise as Khala, too, stepped out of the turbolift.

"Khala, is something wrong?"

"No, Captain. At least, I hope not." The young

woman blushed blue. Harry, standing beside her, reddened. Janeway smothered a smile. It didn't take a genius to figure this one out.

"Captain," began Kim, "may we speak with you in private for a few moments?"

"Certainly. Tuvok, you have the bridge." She indicated that the young ensign and his friend should proceed her into the ready room. The doors hissed shut behind them, and Janeway waved for the two to have a seat on the sofa while she went to the replicator.

"Captain, we—"

Janeway flung up a commanding hand. "We don't say anything to our captain until she has had at least a sip or two of coffee," she remonstrated jokingly. "Would you two care for anything?"

"No, thank you," said Harry.

"Nothing for me either, Captain," said Khala.

Janeway nodded. "Computer: Coffee. Hot. Black." She picked up the warm mug, inhaled the scent, and took a sip. "Now," she said, sitting down on the couch beside Harry, "you may proceed."

More than she cared to admit, Janeway sometimes felt like a mother to this crew. She'd never had children of her own, and probably would not now. These were her children, her crew. And who would say she was wrong to think that way? Who could have asked for a finer son than Ensign Harry Kim, he of the honesty and talent and skill and sheer likability that had made him a favorite with nearly everyone on the ship? Or who could have been more proud of a flesh-and-blood daughter than Janeway was of Khala, who had come from who knew where to a culture very alien to her, to pitch in with unwavering enthusiasm, energy, and knowledge?

"We have come to formally request authorization to pursue an intimate relationship," stated Kim. He smiled a little. "I want to do everything right this time. By the book."

"I'm delighted to hear it." Janeway allowed herself a smile in return, glancing from one young person to the other. "Though I have to say this comes as no surprise. Khala, you've been a valuable addition to this crew. I don't know where this relationship will take you, but if you decide to stay aboard *Voyager,* you could only be an asset. You'd be most welcome."

"Thank you, Captain."

"Have you thought about staying on? We haven't had time to try to locate your homeworld, but once we have solved the dark-matter problem that would be our top priority."

Khala thought for a moment before she answered. "I do miss my home," she admitted. "My family. I was close to them and I'm certain they wonder what's happened to me. But I've changed since I've been aboard *Voyager,* and it's not just my attraction to Harry." She smiled at him, and he visibly blossomed under her gaze. "I've opened my mind to so many things that as an Alilann were completely alien to me, even negative. I couldn't really go back, not even if I wanted to. I don't want to live like the Culilann, out in the elements with no technology, but no Alilann would understand my newfound enjoyment of the arts, of eating fresh foods. I'd be outcast, passively if not literally. So no, I suppose I don't want to go home."

Janeway nodded her comprehension. "You do understand, I hope, that this is not a mere formality. You're both going to have to get clearance from the Doctor as well as from me. And if he finds any reason why you two should not, er, continue, then I must forbid it. And

I will admit to some concern about that scrambled DNA of yours."

"We of the Alilann have similar regulations, Captain," replied Khala. "Certainly, unwise interaction between species almost decimated my people once. I understand that these rules have developed for the safety of all individuals and species involved."

"But even with Khala's DNA, the Doctor didn't find any reason to quarantine Khala," interjected Kim hastily.

Janeway raised an eyebrow. "True," she said, "but that was for casual contact only. What you two are looking at—well, I think you realize that's a whole new ballgame. I'll tell you what. We seem to have things pretty well in hand. Why don't both of you go see the Doctor right now? If we need you, we'll call."

They rose, their hands reaching and clasping. "Thank you, Captain. We'll report to sickbay immediately."

Janeway returned to her chair feeling happier than she had in a long time. They were utilizing every means at their disposal to retrieve the dark matter, and doing so as efficiently as possible. Harry Kim had found someone to care for, who cared for him, and whom he didn't have to lie about seeing. She hoped the Doctor would find nothing to prevent these two people from forming a more intimate, and perhaps permanent, bond.

As captain, she had the right to perform weddings aboard her ship. And thus far on this amazing adventure, she hadn't had the opportunity. Now that she thought about it, Khala and Harry would make a lovely bride and groom.

Harry was terrified. It had taken all his courage to go in and talk to his captain with Khala, after the incident with Tal. He had loved Tal, but that romance had had a heady, dangerous edge to it that had gotten him into a lot of trouble and had damaged his credibility in the eyes of his captain and chief medical officer. Even so, he did not regret it. He could not find it in himself to regret something he had done for love.

But his feelings for Khala were different. No less real, or passionate, but with a deep sincerity and a sense of rightness about it, as right as his relationship with Tal had been, in so many ways, wrong. In a way, his feelings for Khala reminded him of those he had held for Libby, the fiancée from whom he had been torn over six years ago. Khala was brilliant, and sweet, and thoughtful, and passionate about what mattered to her. The joy she was taking in discovering her passion for creativity resonated in Harry's soul, and he tightened his grip on her hand as they stepped into the turbolift.

"Harry, I'm scared," said Khala, voicing Harry's own feelings.

"It's half over," he reassured her. Reassured himself. "It was getting the captain's approval that I was nervous about." A half truth. "The Doctor's just a formality."

She looked up at him with those blue eyes in a blue face. "But what if he finds something?" she asked in a quavering voice. "What if there's some physical reason we can't—be together?"

"Then," he said, turning toward her and taking both her hands in his, "we will turn the not inconsiderable talents of every member of this crew toward finding a way for us to overcome it. It'll work out. What I'm worried about is that you'll decide to leave me and go home one of these days." There, he had said it. All of his fears were now laid out on the table, naked for her to see.

By contrast, her brow unfurrowed and a soft smile spread across her face. "Oh, Harry," she whispered, "where you are is my home."

Tears prickled his eyes and he kissed her. They did not hear the soft hiss that indicated that the turbolift door had opened, and an uncomfortable cough made them spring apart like guilty children. Ensign Lyssa Campbell grinned broadly at them, enjoying Harry's discomfiture.

"Nice catch, Khala," Campbell said as they left and she stepped into the turbolift.

"I don't know about you, but I'm getting tired of blushing," said Harry.

"Me too!" said Khala heartily.

"We all did this to Tom and B'Elanna when they started seeing each other," said Kim. "I guess it's our turn now." Her fingers were so warm, where they entwined with his own.

"Ah, the two young lovebirds, awaiting permission to build a nest," said the Doctor, smiling with superior benevolence at them as they entered sickbay.

"Okay, okay," said Harry, lifting his hands in a gesture of surrender. "Don't I get a break for following procedure?"

"No," said the Doctor cheerily, picking up his medical tricorder. "We'll start with Khala, since I have all the medical information I need on Mr. Kim."

Obediently Khala lay on the diagnostic bed. Two metal halves of a semicircle emerged and closed over her torso. Kim leaned over and planted a kiss on her forehead.

"Enough nookie, Mr. Kim. With luck you'll have ample opportunity to get to know Khala better later, in private," the Doctor chided. Then, abruptly, he said,

"You realize that I can already tell you that you will not be able to have children."

"What?" said Kim.

The Doctor's dark eyes flickered briefly from his tricorder to Harry, then back again. "I would have thought that had already occurred to you. Khala's DNA sequence is the direct opposite of yours. They are completely incompatible."

"Oh," said Khala.

"Is that a problem?" asked the Doctor. "It's better to discover now if it is." He stepped toward his office, to download the information and cross-reference it, or whatever it was he did.

"Is it a problem, love?" asked Harry gently.

"Family has always been important to me," said Khala. "My parents and my brother—we've always been very close." She laughed, a little bitterly. "I won't miss Alilann society one bit, but I'll miss them. What about you?"

Harry was silent. He was an only child, but he recalled hordes of cousins, aunts, uncles, grandparents around him at all major functions in his life. "I never really gave it much thought," he said. "Though I guess family's pretty important to me too."

"There are other ways of having children than conceiving them," said Khala. "If that's what we want. The Alilann are always eager to adopt the Culilann children they Recover. There are always homes for them, and they are as loved as if they were their parents' natural children."

"Couples have faced not being able to conceive before," said Kim, making his decision. "If it's acceptable to you, I say let's cross that bridge when we come to it."

"It sounds wonderful to me," said Khala.

"Then that's settled," Kim stated.

"I'm afraid not." The Doctor had emerged from his office, and Kim's heart felt like a rock in his chest at the expression on his face. "It's much more complex than that. I'm afraid I have some very, very bad news."

CHAPTER

9

JEKRI DREW BREATH TO SCREAM, TO GIVE VOICE TO HER horror and despair, but Verrak was swifter and stronger. He quickly covered her mouth with his hand and wrestled her to the floor. His lips moved to her ear.

"For love of your freedom, do not scream! I am here to help you!"

She didn't believe him. Why not scream? They were going to send her back, back to that *areinnye*-hole, and leave her to die. She felt something press against her arm and heard a hiss; then her body, against the raging will of her mind, went limp. Even her eyelids closed.

"We have to work quickly." Jekri recognized the voice of the female doctor who had conducted such barbarous, painful tests on her.

Who had implanted the energy cell into her wrist.

"The infection looks bad." Verrak. His voice sounded

full of concern. What was going on here? Jekri heard more movements, felt herself being lifted and placed on a table of some kind. More hypos were injected into her body. She felt a warmth all along her left hand. The agonizing pain in her wrist began to fade.

Healing her, to enact more torture.

"That's because it is bad," said the doctor crisply. "You were supposed to be out of here with her by now."

Out of here?

"I know, but in her state she'd just attract more attention. Jekri, listen to me." She felt him take her right hand in both of his. She wanted to snatch it away, spit at him, flee from whatever new torture he was improvising. "This is going to be difficult for you to believe, but you must. You will only succeed in getting us both sent back there if you try to fight me. I grieve for what you underwent, but I had no choice. I had to make the Senate believe that I was turning you over to them, or else I would not have been able to remain free. By feigning betrayal, I was able to serve you still."

What kind of new lie was this?

"Dr. T'Lar is also one of us. One of those who believe that Lhiau has taken over the Empress's mind and is leading us down a path that will end in disaster. I know you believe this too, and there are more people than you think who were willing to help you. We had to keep up the pretense of torture, but it worked to your advantage. Had I tried to transport the energy cell with the food as I did the other materials, it would have been detected. Dr. T'Lar's transports of you to and from the examination rooms were not supervised, so she could manage what I could not. We inserted the cell inside your body, where you could easily remove it."

Jekri thought of the pain digging around in her wrist had caused, and did not think it easily removed.

"She is treating your injuries right now and rehydrating you."

Slowly, Jekri became aware that her body's movements were returning to her control. She opened her eyes and gazed at Verrak.

"Jekri," breathed Verrak. The emotion in his face was almost painful to behold. His strong, angular face was soft with passion and grief. Jekri was embarrassed for him.

"I am so sorry for what you went through. I do not dare hope you will ever forgive me, but perhaps you will understand. I have procured a ship for you. The commander is prepared to defect in order that you may achieve your goal. He thinks that once you have done so, the Senate and the Praetor will listen to you. You will have exposed Lhiau's evil and perhaps saved the Romulan people. You will most certainly get your title back. In the meantime, please. Trust me. Come with me."

She licked her lips. "I will come." There was no alternative. Perhaps it was a trap, but to what end? They had already gotten her, were able to do what they wanted to her. Unless Lhiau wanted her to dance to his tune again, and for a shot at freedom, at bringing the *fvai* as low as she could, at recovering the Empress's sanity, she would trust the President of the Federation herself.

Verrak's face broke into a smile, and he pressed his forehead to her small hand. "I know you do not trust me yet, but you soon will. This, I swear to you."

He eased her up, and she moved carefully, mildly surprised not to be in pain anymore. She turned to the doctor, who regarded her as coolly as Verrak did with heat in his gaze.

"How did you find me?" asked Jekri.

"The energy cell was more complicated than it appeared," replied Dr. T'Lar. "It emitted a certain signal. No one else would have detected it unless they were specifically searching for it."

"That's how we knew which tunnel you were in," said Verrak.

"Subcommander, the two of you must leave now." The doctor wasted no words. "Kaleh, you are as healed as I can make you at this moment. Change into these and with luck I will be able to walk the both of you right out the door."

Hastily Jekri slipped into the impersonal uniform worn by the doctors. She was glad to shed herself of the last physical remnants of her time in prison. Verrak, she noticed, was already wearing the off-white pants and tunic with the medical-officer insignia on the left breast. Quickly and efficiently, T'Lar handed them their props to complete the charade. A medical tricorder to peek out of one of the tunic's pockets. A padd with charts and patients' names on it.

Jekri looked around and realized for the first time that they were in a storage area. She had been treated while lying not on a table but on a box of stacked bins.

T'Lar picked up a small box of some sort of medical supplies, opened the door, and peered out. She turned to face them, nodded, then flung the door open and strode out. Verrak followed, then, taking a deep breath, so did Jekri.

The doctor was an accomplished actress, it would seem. Nothing about her body posture gave her away. She spoke as they strode down the corridor.

"How are those tests coming on the camanovirus

toxicology estimates?" she asked. Two other doctors, deep in conversation, were approaching them.

Verrak looked at the padd. Jekri looked at it too, ducking her head to keep her face from being seen. "It's highly effective, but that's just in the first round of tests," said Verrak. "The symptoms are exactly what we anticipated. Lesions, liquefaction of tissue, all predicted. We're on track."

"Excellent," said T'Lar. They came abreast of the two doctors, heard something about "immunological defects"; then they were past and their conversation lost.

It took Jekri several seconds to comprehend what their false conversation had been about. Dr. T'Lar had been discussing using the nearly ninety-eight-percent lethal camanovirus, which had only recently jumped species from *hlai* to Romulan, as a biological weapon. She stumbled slightly.

Verrak quickly caught her elbow and propelled her forward. "Keep moving," he hissed.

She had not known about this. And anger rose inside her as she realized she, the chairman of the Tal Shiar, ought to have known. They were experimenting on their prisoners. Anger, relief, and terror flooded her system as she realized how fortunate she had been. Dr. T'Lar's ministrations had been far from tender, but Jekri had just been granted a brief glimpse into exactly how badly her imprisonment could have gone. The knowledge strengthened her trust in both T'Lar and Verrak.

They headed for the turbolift. "Exit," said T'Lar. She turned to face them. "When you reach the exit, keep walking. I've erased the identification marks of your predecessors and substituted your ID signatures. It's the usual, fingers, eyes, DNA scan." Her gaze flickered to Jekri. "I'm sure you're familiar with it."

"I am," replied Jekri. This woman might have been part of the mission to rescue her, but she had enjoyed her task of causing Jekri torment far too much for the Little Dagger to like her. "I assume our predecessors won't cause trouble?"

"They have been eliminated. The ruse will be detected soon enough, probably within the hour. But that should be enough time to get to the rendezvous point."

Jekri nodded her comprehension. Two doctors had been quietly killed, their identifying genetic markers switched with those of Jekri and Verrak. For a moment, she felt a stirring of regret that innocent lives had been lost, but then she recalled what the doctors here did. None of them could truly be called innocent.

"Time is precious," said T'Lar. "The guard you killed could be discovered at any moment. I would make haste, but be careful. Do not draw attention to yourself."

Jekri felt an expression of annoyance flit over her face. As if the chairman of the Tal Shiar—

No. She was no longer the chairman. She was something better, something that had been strong enough to survive when the chairman had fallen. She was the Little Dagger, and the Little Dagger understood covert operations better than anyone.

The door hissed open. They were in a small antechamber, only a few steps away from the green luminescence of a forcefield. On the wall at about eye level were two purple squares. Casually, Jekri and Verrak each placed their hands on the grid. The system "recognized" them and the field deactivated. They stepped forward into a second tiny antechamber.

For just a moment, Jekri felt claustrophobic. The walls were a similar color to those of her cell. She licked her lips and kept going. Not looking at one another, they placed their faces up to a small glassed window. A light scanned their retinas, identified them, and the second field deactivated.

Jekri's heart was beating rapidly. One more test to freedom. The third antechamber had holes in the wall. Again, they inserted their hands. Jekri felt cold metal against her palm, felt a slight tickling sensation as the mechanism painlessly extracted a DNA sample for analysis. On the other side, Verrak did likewise.

The machine hummed. Jekri was sweating. She hoped they did not pass too close to anyone; her stench would give her away. Dr. T'Lar might have been able to clothe her in a doctor's garb and heal her injuries, but there had been no time for a sonic shower. She wondered if her face was dirty. Surely the grime beneath her gnawed nails would reveal her as no doctor should anyone chance to glance at them.

A hum, a click. The forcefield shut down. After the small confines of the security antechambers, the room that yawned ahead of them seemed cavernous. They were in a large area, patrolled by bored-looking security guards who glanced up disinterestedly at them. Jekri sniffed. No proper centurions here. *Her* people would have been more alert.

Her people. No, they were not her people. Was anyone, anymore?

Verrak leaned over and began chatting about Test Subject 10928-Alpha and the reaction he had had to the drugs, which merely confirmed their theories. Jekri nodded at appropriate times, but did not dare speak.

A wail rose in the air. Jekri's heart lurched to a stop, then resumed beating with a painful rhythm. The lights dimmed to a dull red. The lethargic guards snapped to attention, listening to messages on their combadges.

Their heads came up and they stared at the two "doctors."

Verrak inhaled swiftly. "Keep going," said Jekri in a low voice. "You run now, you'll give us both away."

Verrak nodded, but nonetheless quickened his step. Jekri supposed he couldn't help it. She fished in her pocket for the padd. She'd have to risk speaking.

"Yes, I understand," she said to the phantom on the other side of her combadge. "We're on our way. Yes, I have the information right here." She glanced up at Verrak. "Code Alpha-Gamma-Theta, Doctor. Let's go."

Now she broke into a run, head held high. Not the frantic flight of a prisoner, no, but the assured, purposeful trot of a professional hastening to an emergency.

A guard stepped right in their path as they were a mere meter from the door. "I'm sorry, Doctors, but we have a Code Red here."

Jekri didn't hesitate for a second. "And I have a very special patient with an emergency," she snapped, waving the padd in his face. "Code Gamma-Theta." She stood, trying to convey a certainty that he would let her pass.

He looked suspicious. "I'm not familiar with that code."

"Of course you're not," said Verrak. He wore an expression of supercilious anger. "Though your superior would be. The content is classified. Let us through or there will be trouble."

The guard looked as though he wanted to believe them, but was afraid to. "I apologize, but our orders are very clear on this point. With an escaped prisoner loose, all exits are to be sealed."

Jekri laughed harshly. "So, is that what you plan to tell the Praetor's widow?"

The guard's eyes widened. "The P-Praetor?"

"Our patient. We are his personal physicians."

The guard paled before the steely glare in Jekri's eyes. Cursing, he hit the controls and the door slid open. They darted through and continued moving quickly.

"You were brilliant," said Verrak as they strode across the deceptively pleasant grassy area behind the palace.

"I did what was necessary. Where is our beam-out site?"

"Just over by the—" The distinctive sound of disruptors being fired cut him off. As one, they broke into a run.

"Apparently I wasn't that brilliant," Jekri gasped. Her fingernails. She had waved the padd in front of the guard, moved her fingers over the keys. He'd seen them but hadn't really understood what he was seeing, until now.

Verrak pulled out a small device and pressed a button on it. At once the world around them shimmered. When Jekri could see again, she was standing on the darkened bridge of a top-of-the-line warbird. Jekri looked around wildly. She glimpsed someone in a command chair, a conn, active stations, and a viewscreen with Romulus filling every square centimeter.

"Shields up! Activate cloak!" someone was ordering in a deep, booming voice. "Set coordinates for the rendezvous point!"

"Done, sir!"

"Let's get there, then. Warp nine!"

The image of Romulus vanished, to be replaced by the familiar, distinctive streak of stars as they hurtled through space at warp nine. Jekri stumbled to the railing and leaned on it, catching her breath. It would seem she was not fully recovered.

The commander of this vessel rose. Jekri stared in surprise and pleasure. "Commander Idran," she said, her voice warm.

He saluted her smartly. "Chairman, we are honored by your presence aboard the *Para'tar.* She, her crew, and her commander are yours to command."

Jekri gathered strength and forced herself to stand erect. She took a deep breath and levelly regarded the crew that had committed treason to assist in her rescue.

"In times of darkness, old friends are the truest," she said, including Verrak in her sweeping gaze. "I thank you for your part in my rescue. Rest assured that I will do everything I can to see that you are rewarded, not punished, for your actions here today. Status report."

"Your vessel, the *Tektral,* waits to rendezvous with us," said Idran. "We will be able to take on what crew wishes to accompany us, as well as the vital information we need to carry out our mission."

"And what mission is that?" challenged Jekri. She thought she knew, but wanted to make certain.

Idran, grizzled and elderly veteran that he was, grinned like a Klingon. He knew exactly what he was doing. And to Jekri's immense pleasure and relief, he told her.

INTERLUDE

THE ENTITY HAD KNOWN THAT AT SOME POINT IT WOULD run across them. But it did not wish the contact. It did not wish it at all, but it had a duty to perform.

The Borg cube was all but destroyed. Holes gaped in its side, through which open space was visible. Sparks flew, lights flickered, and it tumbled through space with a randomness and wildness that would have appalled its makers, had they been able to express such a thing.

The Entity hesitated, ruminating. The Borg were implacable in their purpose: to assimilate and plunder the knowledge of other species. Such a single-mindedness—and the term, with them, was quite literal—had made them almost invincible. Almost. Though on occasion, wit and courage and determination had foiled them.

There was no doubt in the Entity's mind, if such it had, that if the bad things, the mutated dark matter, had found one Borg cube, it had infiltrated all of them. To one degree or another, every Borg ship in the quadrant, or even elsewhere, would be affected at this point. What the Entity was now regarding was merely an infected ship in the later stages.

If it were only the destruction of the Borg that was at stake here, the Entity knew, its decision to help them would be a harder one to make. But there was so much more. Certainly, the Borg would be destroyed, but the dark matter that had been their downfall would linger on, waiting for something more innocent to infect, perverting even the space in which it existed. It would eat away at the fabric of this universe. No matter who benefited, it must needs be contained.

So the Entity descended upon the hurtling Borg cube, enveloping it into itself with a care the ruthless creatures did not deserve. It felt the hive mind trying to assimilate it even now, their multiple thoughts condensed into one powerful demand: We are the Borg. Resistance is futile. Prepare to be assimilated.

But the Entity was unique, and knew it, and far beyond even their frightening comprehension. It brushed aside their attempts to make it one of them almost as an afterthought, a distraction to its true task, which was to purge them of the wrong things that would have been their ruination.

Through its connection with the ship, it knew where the other cubes were, and departed. Again and again it enveloped a cube, purged it, and moved on. Their numbers were almost uncountable, but the Entity partially existed outside time and space and the vast distances were nothing to it.

It was done. The Borg were cured. They would not contaminate others they assimilated with the mutated dark matter, though some might feel that Borg assimilation was something worse. It was not the Entity's place to decide such things. It merely had a task, a task far greater than any single individual's needs: a task that would save or doom everything, from the smallest microbe to beings nearly as vast as itself.

The Borg were cured, free to pursue their own task. It did not sit well with the Entity, and it puzzled over the moral dilemma as it drifted to the next place where the wrong things dwelt.

CHAPTER
10

THE DOOR TO CHAKOTAY'S QUARTERS BUZZED ANGRILY.
Quickly he stepped to answer it, wincing at the annoying
sound.

"You're prompt," he told Ezbai.

"Promptness is a virtue," the young Interceptor replied.

"I'm almost ready. Have a seat." Chakotay indicated
a utilitarian stool while he sat on the edge of the bed to
put on his boots.

"You've had nothing to eat or drink since last night?"
asked Ezbai.

"Not a drop nor a crumb."

Ezbai smiled, relieved. "Oh, good. Our doctors are very
adamant about that. Food and hydration alter the baseline
chemical makeup of your system, and if you'd had anything I'd be in the Implementer's office in a heartbeat."

Chakotay stepped down on his boot to fit it snugly

123

onto his foot. "I've noticed that. He comes down pretty hard on you."

Ezbai flushed blue. "Oh, no, not really. He's that way with everyone. He's exacting, that's all. By the way, please let me apologize for the testing you underwent. With the hand sensor. From what I understand about your customs, you probably considered it rude. It's just our way, we do it to everyone."

"I understood," said Chakotay. "You think it's a necessary precaution. Every culture has its ways and traditions." *Like the Culilann,* he thought, his own choice of words vividly recalling images and faces. He glanced down at the young man walking beside him as they traveled through the labyrinth of dark corridors. Ezbai seemed a little scattered, but sincere. Unlike the Implementer, Ezbai struck Chakotay as someone he could talk to.

"Tell me how the Culilann and the Alilann came to be so separate," he asked, and Ezbai did. He spoke of an ancient people who were nearly decimated by beings from another world, and how there had been two reactions to the disaster. One branch felt that it was divine punishment for forsaking the ways of the ancestors. Their response was to renew their dedication to the old ways. They became the Culilann, the "seekers of things of the world." Another group wished never to be vulnerable to such attacks again, and redoubled their efforts to advance their technology. Thus were born the Alilann, the "seekers of things unmade." Both of them showed how deeply the alien attack had scarred them, despite their naturally friendly natures. The Culilann had the Ordeal, and the Alilann had their truth-tester and array of defensive weapons. They were more alike than they wanted to think, and this division both saddened and angered Chakotay.

And now there was evidence of murder prompted by this division. He almost wished he hadn't come bringing the news of the mutated dark matter. The Implementer, rather than face the unpleasant reality that someone among the Alilann was taking intolerance to a new and violent level, had latched on to the dark matter as a perfect scapegoat. Chakotay had a bad feeling that things were going to get worse before they got better.

"So Ezbai, do you personally disapprove of the Culilann's way of life?"

"Of course!" he replied, and inwardly Chakotay flinched. Ezbai said it with pride, as if it was the only right way to feel. "I know how they treat Strangers, and their own malformed children. I know that many of them die from injuries or illnesses that could be cured in a matter of seconds if they'd only let us help them. I know they spend their days wasting their time doing useless things, like making pots and weaving blankets."

"Pots to hold food," Chakotay said gently as they stepped into a turbolift. "Blankets to please the eye even as they cover a sick person."

Ezbai looked at him with pity. "It seems we Recovered you just in time. This happens, sometimes. The aliens live too long among the Culilann. They don't recognize the foolishness of their ways."

"When there was the division between the Culilann and the Alilann," said Chakotay, "who left whom? Did the Culilann originate in the jungles of this planet?"

"Well, no," said Ezbai. "We lived all over the face of the planet. There are temperate regions as well as tropical. We have polar ice caps as well."

A terrible suspicion began to occur to Chakotay. He chose his words carefully. Whatever happened, it certainly hadn't been Ezbai's fault. The division had occurred hundreds of years ago. Although perhaps the young Interceptor was at least partially responsible for maintaining the situation.

"Are there still Culilann villages located all over the planet?" he inquired.

The turbolift stopped and they exited. Ezbai led him down yet another corridor that looked exactly like any one of a dozen they had already negotiated.

"Well, not really. They live mostly in the deserts, the ice caps, and along the equator. We have our domed cities in the more temperate areas. This is actually something of a far-flung outpost. We're roughing it here. Thanks to transporter technology, though, nothing's really remote anymore."

"Why do you think someone wants to kill the Culils?" Chakotay asked, abruptly changing the topic.

Ezbai blinked, startled by the bluntness of the question. "Why, you yourself provided the explanation, Chakotay. It's the dark matter."

"You don't think," said Chakotay slowly, turning to look at Ezbai as they walked, "that perhaps this separateness between your people might have caused some hatred? Has there never been a Culilann uprising, or an attempt to eliminate a village?"

"Well," stammered Ezbai, "of course, but—well, we don't like to talk about that much. I mean, of course the Culils—the smarter ones among them anyway, the ones intelligent enough to realize what they're missing—of course they resent us. Not that we don't stand ready to welcome any of them who want to join us."

"Really?" Chakotay continued to gaze steadily at Ezbai. "Do you really welcome them, as Culilann? Or do you insist that they abandon everything that makes them who they are and embrace only what your culture tells them is right? If a Culilann showed up right here, right now, and wanted to learn Alilann ways, would you let him have a garden?"

"Of course not! What a waste of resources!"

"Or paint. Suppose he said, 'I want to paint a scene of my village's life on this wall.' What would you do?"

"Chakotay, this argument makes no sense!" said Ezbai, and by that Chakotay had his answer. It made him even sadder. He said nothing more and they continued on in awkward silence.

Finally, they reached the medical center. This, too, required negotiating, but after what seemed like an eternity Chakotay was checked in and lying on a diagnostic bed in a large room in which a great deal of activity seemed to be occurring. The light was bright, comparable to sunlight, and the tools, trays, and furnishings sparkled. All spoke of cleanliness and efficiency, of clinical detachment and coldness. And Chakotay thought of the warm affection and nurturing atmosphere of Soliss's hut, and found himself missing it.

"I'll be by to pick you up and escort you back to your quarters when you're done here," said Ezbai, not meeting Chakotay's eyes. He hastened off. Chakotay realized that their conversation had upset the young Interceptor. He regretted the necessity that had driven him to it, but was not sorry he had pushed Ezbai to really look hard at his culture. Everyone needed to do that from time to time.

"Sector?" said the doctor in a flat, bored voice. He picked up a padd and began to peruse it. He hadn't even introduced himself.

"I'm not sure," said Chakotay. "I was Recovered from the village of Sumar-ka, if that helps."

"It doesn't," replied the doctor, sounding as if he wished he were anywhere but here. "Ah, here it is. All right. Male, species called human, no known illnesses, recovering from that barbaric Ordeal they always put aliens through. We're going to do a full examination on you, standard procedure." He shot Chakotay a look. "You haven't had anything to eat or drink since retiring last night, have you?" The question was almost an accusation.

"Not a thing," Chakotay replied. He was itching to get out of here. He wondered how anyone who was actually ill recovered in a place like this.

"Good." Without wasting breath on further conversation, the doctor and a bevy of assistants began poking and prodding Chakotay. They ran instruments over him which hummed, whistled, and beeped, took samples, and rushed through the examination with efficiency and detachment. Chakotay was hard-pressed to recall a time when he felt less like a living, sentient being. Once or twice he tried to make conversation, but it was answered so brusquely that he gave it up as a bad idea.

Then, all at once, the doctor stopped dead in his tracks. His blue eyes widened and he leaned against the chair for support. "This can't be," he breathed. "It just can't!"

"What—"

But before Chakotay could even finish the question the doctor had rushed off. Chakotay sat up on the biobed, startled by the outburst and a lack of explanation. Though he was in a huge room with dozens of people, no one responded when he asked for assistance. So he sat, and waited, and wondered what the unnamed doctor had found.

Probably the dark matter, he thought. They wouldn't know what it was, and he supposed it had been foolish of him to think the Implementer had already gotten around to informing his people of the problem. Though it would have saved them time and effort if he had. This was a society that was drowning in its bureaucracy, and Chakotay wondered if his request to search for *Voyager* would even be acknowledged unless it was submitted in triplicate, with the proper footnotes and addressed to just the right people.

Something stirred beneath the bed. Frowning, Chakotay bent over and peered beneath the metal frame.

Crouched underneath, his tail wagging and his pink tongue lolling, was Coyote.

Chakotay gasped and sat back up. He closed his eyes, calmed himself, and again looked under the bed. Nothing. He realized he was shaking. Something must be going wrong if he was starting to see Coyote with his waking eyes.

Finally the doctor returned. With him, their gazes impersonal and yet intimidating, were three guards. "I have just spoken with the Implementer," said the doctor. "He insists on seeing you immediately."

"If you'll just tell me what's going on, perhaps I can help you with your diagnosis."

But the doctor was not interested, and was already moving on to another bed, another body to treat as if it were devoid of personality.

"Please come with us," said one of the guards in the same flat voice the doctor had first used. Chakotay sighed and surrendered to the irritating absurdity of the situation. A situation that clearly delighted Coyote.

He found himself in the same room he had visited last night, but now the Implementer and Ezbai were the only ones present. The Implementer's face was unreadable as he gestured for Chakotay to have a seat. With a wave of a hand, he dismissed the guards.

"We have to stop meeting like this," said Chakotay. Ezbai and the Implementer exchanged glances, not getting the ancient joke. "Sorry. A bit of human humor."

"There's nothing funny about why I asked you here." The Implementer jerked his head in Ezbai's direction. Belatedly Chakotay realized that Ezbai looked awful. He was pale and seemed to be fighting to control terror and tears. "I asked Interceptor Ezbai to join us because I believe this affects him as well."

The doors opened and the doctor who had examined Chakotay entered and took a seat. He looked anxious and out of breath and clutched a small padd in a tight grip.

"I'll come straight to the point," the Implementer continued. "There's something wrong with you, Chakotay."

"Let me guess," said Chakotay. "There's a peculiar substance in my body that you can't identify, and it's growing at an exponential rate. It's targeting some specific system—the adrenal system, or the brain, or the pulmonary system." He sat back, crossed his arms, and waited for them to verify what he had said.

"No," said the doctor, whose name Chakotay never had learned. "It's something much stranger. Commander Chakotay, your DNA sequencing is all backward. Strand by strand, it is precisely the opposite of ours."

Chakotay felt a chill run down his spine. A memory stirred. Hadn't the Doctor spoken about something like this with Khala? He hadn't gone into detail, but he had said something about how the tricorder must have been damaged by the dark matter to give such backward readings. But apparently the tricorder had been operating perfectly.

"When we found Khala," Chakotay said slowly, "our doctor noticed something amiss with her as well.

Something similar. I don't remember the details, and then the passage opened."

"The same passage which you said my sister claimed she stepped through," said Ezbai. "I remember. I saw it. White light appearing, engulfing her, then disappearing—taking her with it."

"Logic would indicate that something took you from your world and Khala from ours," said the Implementer.

"I thought we had already determined that," said Chakotay.

"But there's more," said the doctor. "Something is happening to you. It's slow, but it's certain. Various cells in your body are simply disappearing."

Chakotay remembered the Romulan scouts, lying in sickbay in terrible pain as parts of their bodies disappeared and reappeared. The Doctor had no idea where those parts went to when they vanished. Now, the same thing was happening to him, cell by cell.

"It's the dark matter. It's got to be. We saw something similar to this on the ship."

The doctor was clearly getting irritated with Chakotay's insistence on the dark matter being the culprit. "No, Commander, there is no trace of anything like that in your system at all. There is no foreign agent. This is a natural occurrence. And I would imagine that the same thing is happening to Khala."

"Natural?" cried Chakotay. "How can you say that my cells disappearing one by one is natural?"

"Because," said the Implementer, "your body is returning home. Piece by piece, to where it truly belongs. According to Dr. Reksis, you are not from this universe."

In his mind, even as he stared at the Implementer, Chakotay heard Coyote, the Trickster, laughing.

* * *

The rain fell in sheets. Ioni and her companions were drenched, and had been for some time. Nonetheless, they slogged on determinedly. There was something important waiting for them at the end of their quest.

It was in the large, hollowed center of an ancient, fallen tree. This village had a sacred tree instead of a sacred mountain. As always, the anger rose inside Ioni as she beheld the helpless infant. Kaminor reached and picked it up. She couldn't even see what was wrong with this one until her Recovery team leader held it up, to get a full view. A twining birthmark. To superstitious eyes, it could resemble a snake. Therefore, the poor infant must be cursed. Alilann doctors wouldn't even bother treating this one. There was nothing wrong with it.

"Hush, little one," soothed Shamraa Kaminor, his big, powerful body at odds with the soft voice and gentle handling of the child. "You'll be in loving arms soon."

"Blasphemy!"

The team whirled to behold a young woman. She was crying, but outrage shone on her wet face. "You blaspheme the Crafters by stealing the child that they have marked for their own!" The woman, probably the baby's mother, stooped to pick up a stone.

For a moment, they all stood still. This had never before happened to a Recovery team. They had gotten careless, failed to monitor their instruments to see if there were any Culilann lurking nearby. Sometimes that happened. Sometimes someone, usually the parents, wanted to behold with their own eyes the Crafters taking their child. All that could be done in such situations was wait and hope the parents would grow weary of their vigil. Sometimes, and Ioni had seen it happen, the child had died before the parents left. Ioni wondered what the Culil of the village told a distraught mother at such times.

The woman pulled back her arm to fling the stone, and Ioni's weapon came up. She fired, two quick shots that ripped through the woman's torso. The Culilann woman fell without a sound, her belly blackened and smoking.

"Kilaa Ioni!" Kaminor's shout cracked loudly in the stunned silence. "What have you done?"

Ioni regarded the dead body that a few seconds before had been a living, breathing woman. She felt no flicker of remorse.

"The right thing," she said.

CHAPTER

11

IT SEEMED LIKE AN ETERNITY PASSED BEFORE JANEWAY reached sickbay. After his ominous pronouncement, the Doctor had refused to say anything more until the captain was present.

Finally, the door hissed open. "What is it, Doctor?"

The hologram looked as distressed as Kim had ever seen him. Kim tightened his grip on Khala's hand, and she squeezed back.

"I hardly know where to begin," said the Doctor. "You all remember when we first brought Khala on board. We determined that her molecular structure was unlike anything we had ever seen, and you, Khala, were equally surprised by our molecular structure."

"I remember," said Khala softly, stoically.

"I believe I have determined the reason for that. When I sat down to analyze the results of my examination, I noticed something distressingly familiar." He handed Janeway a padd.

"It's like what happened to the Romulan scouts," said Janeway, passing the padd on to Kim and Khala. Kim felt cold when he looked at the Doctor's analysis. The same thing was happening to Khala that had happened to the Romulan stowaways. One by one, slowly, not quickly enough for Khala to have experienced pain or even noticed it at all, her cells were simply vanishing.

"But this doesn't make sense!" said Kim, his voice rising in his anger and frustration. "There's no dark matter in Khala's system, none at all!"

"I am aware of that, Mr. Kim," said the Doctor, a touch sternly. Kim bit his lip. "But it is precisely the same thing. I had no idea what was happening to the two centurions when pieces of their bodies flickered in and out of existence. I now know a great deal more about how this dark matter works, and what Lhiau's nefarious purpose was in causing it to mutate. I suspect that what was going on with the Romulans, and is presently going on with you, is parts of the body are slipping out of existence in this universe and manifesting in another one. With the centurions, the dark matter was forcing it to happen. With Khala, it's happening naturally."

"How can this be natural?" said Kim.

"Because," said the Doctor, looking at him levelly with dark brown eyes, "Khala does not belong in this universe. She originated in the Shadow universe. The Shepherds brought her here, into ours, to help maintain the balance of matter that Lhiau was manipulating. By the same token, Tom and Chakotay ended up in Khala's universe."

"Then you think the same thing is happening to them?" asked Janeway. "That they're—dissolving somehow, as their cells attempt to cross back over into their proper universe?"

"I do," said the Doctor solemnly. "Khala, you are in no immediate danger, and I believe I can give you something that will slow this process down. But somehow, we need to find a way to eventually return you to the Shadow universe, and recover Commander Chakotay and Ensign Paris. Unless you return, you will die."

Khala turned her face up to Harry's, and he could almost hear the sound of her heart breaking. He sure as hell knew his was. This couldn't be happening. It simply wasn't fair. He'd finally found a soulmate, someone who understood and loved him with a steadiness that embraced and yet overwhelmed mere passion.

The Shadow universe. He'd heard it theorized, but it had never been proved. It was one of the more entertaining theories espoused by scientists more often known for dull, boring conjecture. The theory was that there was a Shadow universe entwined with the universe he knew and inhabited. Shadow people, shadow stones, even shadow planets passed through them without ever interacting. They were mixed together, combined so completely that separation was inconceivable.

"We were mixed, blended thoroughly together," said Janeway, as if reading Harry's thoughts. "Our universe and yours, Khala. Mixed supposedly inextricably, like tint added to white paint."

"Exactly," said the Doctor. "Except now, thanks to Lhiau's disruption and the Shepherds' attempts to counteract that disruption, both universes are unraveling. Some things from the Shadow universe are appearing here, and some things from here are manifesting in the Shadow universe. Now they're no longer blending, to use your analogy, Captain, like tint into paint. They are being juxtaposed, like threads of yarn woven into a rug."

" 'Things fall apart,' " said Janeway. Harry recognized the quote; it was from Yeats. " 'The center cannot hold.' " She searched Kim's eyes for a moment, then Khala's. "Doctor, a word with you."

She and the Doctor stepped away a few paces, spoke in soft tones; then Janeway quirked a finger at Harry. Obediently he left Khala and came to her.

"Captain."

Her face was soft with compassion as she spoke. "Harry, I'm so sorry. But Khala's life depends on her returning to the Shadow universe."

"I understand that, Captain." He understood all too well.

She hesitated before speaking. "Harry—there seems to be no physical reason why you and Khala shouldn't continue to . . . be together until it's time for her to leave. I realize you wanted something more permanent."

Strangely, he felt no embarrassment at the conversation. His pain went too deep for that. "I understand what you're saying, Captain. And I thank you."

She smiled, squeezed his shoulder, and left. The Doctor, too, had discreetly left to work at his desk. Khala sat alone on the biobed, her feet dangling, and Harry was suddenly, swiftly reminded of the first time he'd seen her. It was here, in sickbay, and the Doctor had asked for his assistance in examining Khala since Paris had disappeared.

Swallowing hard, he went over to her. He knelt in front of her, like a gallant knight of old, and placed his head in her lap. Khala ran gentle fingers through his thick, black hair. He lifted his head and gazed at her.

"Will you come to my quarters?" he asked, softly.

She nodded, her eyes bright with tears.

Janeway stepped onto her bridge in a melancholy mood. Poor Harry. Poor Khala. She'd enjoyed watching the romance blossom, but now she felt that she and the Doctor had come along with shears to nip it in the bud. But Khala's very life was at stake, and by extrapolation, the lives of Tom and Chakotay.

Until now, recovering her two lost crewmen and returning Khala to her home planet had been a lower priority. First had been to carry out the Shepherds' quest of gathering up the dark matter. But Janeway wondered now if she was going to be asked to sacrifice three lives to accomplish that laudable goal. If so, then it was three lives too many.

"Bridge to Engineering. Status report?"

"And good morning to you too, Captain," said B'Elanna. Janeway realized that all the good humor she'd arrived on the bridge with this morning had evaporated like morning mist under an unkind sun.

"Good morning. Status," she repeated.

"During the night, we've been able to recover still more dark matter. I don't want to jinx anything, but this is starting to become almost routine."

"Sounds like we're due for a little routine after what we've been through. By the way, don't worry that Khala's not there. She'll show up later. If you need her, report to me and I'll determine priority."

"I see." B'Elanna's voice was warm with humor. Janeway felt a pang. *You'll see soon enough, B'Elanna.*

Khala lay in Kim's arms. What ought to have been a moment of languid joy was instead transformed into a heavy sorrow. He tried to burn this moment into his memory: the gentle weight of her head on his chest, the fall of her blue hair, the exquisite softness of her skin.

"What are we going to do?" she said, breaking the silence.

"What we have to do. We have to find a way to get you home."

"But Harry, it's not home anymore." Khala shifted her weight and folded her hands across his chest, peering into his eyes from only inches away. "I belong here. With you."

"Apparently your cellular structure disagrees with you."

"Your doctor is so clever. I'm certain he can find something . . . ." Her voice trailed off. They gazed at one another, acknowledging the inevitable even as they tried to deny it.

Khala sighed and sat up. "I can't stand this. I have to do something."

"Khala, you're not sorry, are you?"

She looked at him, and a smile spread softly across her face. "Oh, no, Harry. No, I'm glad. But it's awful, isn't it, to be together when we know we're going to have to part?"

Harry knew exactly what she meant. It was bittersweet, lying in the dim light together when they knew it was not a real beginning but only the beginning of the end. He, too, desperately needed distraction, needed to feel useful. Harry, too, rose, pulled Khala to him, and kissed her.

"Come on," he said, cupping her face with his hands. "I think we can both fit in the sonic shower if we try."

"I am going to give Harry such a hard time," Torres chuckled as she ran a diagnostic on the warp core.

"You are exacting revenge upon Ensign Kim for his teasing of you and Ensign Paris, when you began your romantic union," stated Seven.

"Precisely."

"Revenge is irrelevant."

"Seven, you've come a long way since you left the collective," said Torres, glancing over at Seven and grinning, "But you still have a lot to—" She broke off in midsentence. Every morning since this whole crazy thing began, she had started her shift with a routine diagnostic on the status of the warp core and the small universe housed within. Every morning, she had found that the bubble was holding stable.

Not this morning.

"What is it?" asked Telek, stepping beside her and looking at the readings.

"I—don't know," B'Elanna managed. "It seems to be fine one minute, then—there. Look at that."

Seven did not say anything, nor did she move to join Torres and R'Mor. But Torres knew her well enough to know that she was calling up the same thing on her console.

The small warp-shell bubble they had created, the mini-universe that was safely holding all the dark matter they had gathered up to this point, fluctuated. Torres thought her heart would stop.

"The shell is weakening somehow," said R'Mor.

"How much dark matter is inside now?" asked Khala. B'Elanna was surprised. She hadn't even heard the woman enter. Khala was lucky. B'Elanna's teasing mood had evaporated.

"Eight point five four grams," stated Seven.

"That doesn't seem like a lot," said Khala, frowning. "Seven, you had mentioned something about an attempt to create a stable warp-bubble universe aboard the *Enterprise*. What happened to it?"

"Dr. Beverly Crusher was inadvertently trapped inside," said Seven. "When the shell began to dissipate, her universe shrank proportionately. She thought she was aboard her ship. Yet when she reported a drastic reduction in the number of crewmen, her captain thought she was mentally damaged in some way. Piece by piece, the ship's crew and the size of the vessel grew smaller, until Crusher was trapped alone."

"This does not bode well," said Telek.

"Dr. R'Mor, you have a gift for understatement." As Torres watched, the shell flickered again. *Please don't collapse. Please don't collapse.*

She tapped her combadge. "Torres to Janeway. We've got a situation."

Ten minutes later, the senior staff had assembled in the meeting room. Janeway listened intently to Torres's bad news. "Options?" she asked.

"Well, we're going to see if we can't create another bubble universe and transfer the dark matter into that one. I don't know. It's never been done before. And if the dark matter is released all at once on this ship—"

"I understand," said Janeway briskly, before her imagination could take the dreadful thought any further. "Is there time to run any scenarios on the holodeck?"

"I would not suggest it," said Telek R'Mor, surprising her. "When we ran scenarios earlier, when we were trying to unlock the key to the Shepherds' technology, they proved to be almost useless to us. In each scenario, we failed somehow. Yet when we actually attempted a transfer, it was successful. We are dealing with things so far beyond what your holodeck and your science can comprehend, Captain, that there seems little point. And we do not have a great deal of time. The warp shell is destabilizing far too quickly for comfort."

"I understand. One more thing." She glanced quickly at Harry. "We have learned something new about our visitor, Khala. The Doctor has determined that her molecular structure is so different from ours because she comes from another universe."

Her crew was too well trained to gasp, but everyone was startled.

"We suspect that Commander Chakotay and Ensign Paris are now presently in Khala's universe, as she is in ours. All three of them need to return to their proper universes or else they won't survive. Similar to what happened with the two Romulans, cells in Khala's body are disappearing, in all likelihood destabilizing in this universe and reappearing in her own. The Doctor is working on preparing something for Khala to retard the progress of the disintegration. Dismissed."

Her senior staff was unusually quiet as they left to take up their various positions. Janeway sank into her chair and announced to anyone who would listen, "You know, just once I'd like to be really, thoroughly, and completely bored. No lives at stake, no shore leave for excitement, just good old-fashioned boredom."

"We do appear to have more than our share of events," acknowledged Tuvok.

"And we've got one right now," said Kim. "There's a wormhole opening at coordinates seven zero three mark eight. It's huge, Captain."

"On screen," snapped Janeway, fully alert. There it was, another giant wormhole. Telek R'Mor, who had not yet left, moved to a console without Janeway having to utter a word.

"It's one of mine," he said, referring to the technology the Shepherds had given him back in the Alpha quadrant to increase the efficacy of his wormholes.

"Red alert. Shields up," ordered Janeway. If a wormhole with Shepherd technology was opening right in front of them, it could mean one of two things: a Romulan attack, or the appearance of Tialin and her benevolent Shepherds. Janeway didn't dare hope for the latter.

"Ships are coming through," said Kim.

"Four warbirds—" Tuvok broke off and looked over at R'Mor. "Four warbirds and Dr. R'Mor's vessel, the *Talvath*."

Even as he spoke, the ships emerged from the wormhole, which closed without a trace behind them. They were not cloaked, not this time, and loomed before *Voyager* in all their proud, lambent green glory.

"We're being hailed," Kim said.

"Put them on, Ensign," said Janeway, puzzled as to why the warbirds were so flaunting their presence. The last time they'd appeared, they had been cloaked and refused to even talk to *Voyager*.

The face of a Romulan female, who would have been beautiful had she not been so thin and haggard-looking, filled the viewscreen. Janeway recognized that face, and so did Telek R'Mor, who stood stiffly at his post.

"Captain Janeway," said the woman. "My name is Jekri Kaleh."

CHAPTER

12

JEKRI WAS FEELING ALMOST—ALMOST—ROMULAN AGAIN. Dr. T'Lar had given her supplements that had made her feel stronger almost immediately, and the friend/foe had also healed all of Jekri's many festering injuries. Still, it had taken a shower and an enormous helping of *viinnerine* before Jekri felt even a shadow of her old self.

Idran was an old and trusted friend, back in the days when Jekri had believed herself to have old and trusted friends. Like Verrak, Idran had come through for her, for what she was fighting for, and Jekri was more grateful than she ever would have imagined.

She ate hungrily in Idran's quarters while Verrak and Idran told her the plan. Things were worse than she had feared. Without Jekri Kaleh watching him, Lhiau had been free to move unencumbered, and move he had.

"We will likely be striking within the next forty-eight to seventy-two hours," Idran told her solemnly. "The fleet is beginning to gather. We must hasten if we are to rendezvous with the *Tektral* and appear in our appointed position on time."

"Where? How many?" Jekri asked, reaching for a glass of fresh, cold water and gulping it down eagerly. She had thought nothing of water a few weeks ago. Now, she marveled at how refreshing, how precious a fluid it was. She would never take water for granted again.

Idran rose and activated a viewscreen. "Here, here, and here," he said, indicating three key positions along the Neutral Zone. "We have a total of over four thousand vessels."

Jekri almost choked. It was the largest fleet she had ever heard of being assembled.

"The Federation has colonies in these five systems," continued Idran. "We will be in a position to explode from the Neutral Zone and destroy those colonies in moments. This would put an end to any spy missions that might be encamped there."

"Lhiau has commandeered the *Talvath* and its wormhole technology as well," said Verrak.

"I am not surprised," said Jekri, knowing with a sick knot in her belly where this was leading.

"Once the battle is under way, we will allow a few hours for the Federation to respond to the crisis at the colonies," said Verrak. "At that point, we will open several dozen wormholes, one right after the other. Their targets will be—"

"Earth, of course," said Jekri. "Vulcan, Bolaris IX, Starbases 12 and probably 74 and 212, at the very least. You frighten me, gentlemen, with this news of war. It seems that we would win."

"But the dark matter is not wholesome, Jekri," said Verrak, leaning in earnestly. "Lhiau has done everything to cast suspicion on Telek R'Mor, but I have called in a few favors and had some testing done in secret. We do not know much, but we know this: the dark matter is dangerous. And by arming so many vessels, and using so many wormholes, Lhiau is causing us to create more and more of it."

Jekri's hunger was sated, for the moment. She knew she should eat more, build up her strength, but her mind was working on the problems and she did not want to eat. Pushing the *viinnerine* aside, she thought back to the disastrous battle with *Voyager.*

"Thirteen warbirds against one Federation starship," she said, voicing her thoughts aloud as they occurred to her for the benefit of her comrades. "Even with *Voyager*'s advantage of twenty years of advanced technology, we ought to have won that battle."

"But the ships seemed to help destroy themselves," said Idran. "We saw."

Impulsively, Jekri reached out a hand to the heavyset, gravelly-voiced commander. "Glad I am that you were not on one of those ships, Idran."

"As am I," the old warrior admitted, "though at the time I thought it an insult."

"May we all have such insults," said Jekri, and for the first time in she couldn't remember how long, she chuckled. Then she sobered. "But I have every reason to believe that that disaster could happen again."

"Except that instead of thirteen warbirds, we would be speaking of thousands," said Verrak.

"Which is why your plan is the only one," said Idran. "Jekri, when I wear my formal regalia, my chest is crowded with medals. I have been dubbed a hero of the

Empire. I never thought there would come a day when I would disobey orders, especially direct orders to go to war."

"Only a *veruul* would fight a war such as this one," said Jekri, "and such is what Lhiau must think us. Verrak, you have been free to listen. What have you learned? Is the Empress his?"

Verrak looked uncomfortable. Jekri had deliberately left unsaid the reason that he had been free to listen—because he had pretended to betray her. Knowing what she knew now, she approved of his decision and held no grudge. It was the wisest, indeed, the only logical, avenue he could have pursued. But clearly, Verrak was still wrestling with guilt.

"It is the worst scandal that has been seen in decades," said Verrak with obvious reluctance. "She makes no attempts at disguising her infatuation with that *fvai.*"

"A little charity, my friend," said Jekri. "The Empress's mind is not her own. I doubt she breathes without Lhiau's express instructions."

"But why did he not attempt to infiltrate your mind, or mine?" asked Verrak.

"We were lesser targets, and he did attack me mentally." She smiled slyly. "Did you really have me followed?"

Verrak blushed. "Have you followed? No. Follow you myself? Yes."

"More ammunition with which to frame me?"

"It was out of concern!" cried Verrak. "I thought you might be walking into a trap, I—"

Jekri held up a hand. "Enough. I believe you. Are those people in any danger?"

"I do not believe so. There was no follow-up, once you had been sentenced."

"Good. I would not have them come to harm on my account." Idran was scowling, not knowing what they were talking about. Jekri thought about enlightening him, but decided against it. Not everyone was ready for the concept that the former chairman of the Tal Shiar fought against the mental attacks of an enemy with Vulcan mental control.

"These battles, in the Neutral Zone and at the various homeworlds, must not be permitted to happen," she stated, hearing in her voice again the assurance of old. "It would ruin the Empire. I do not know why Lhiau hates our people so much that he wishes our obliteration, nor do I know why he is so intent that we ourselves be the vessels of our own destruction."

Verrak frowned. "When he first came to us, he asked for our help in defeating his enemies. How can destroying our people accomplish such a goal?"

"Lhiau speaks in riddles, he twists words, he never reveals himself," said Jekri. "He cannot be trusted to simply state something." She leaned back and folded her arms across her lean chest, absently noting the sharpness of the bones. She had lost a great deal of weight during her ordeal.

Verrak had raised an excellent point, one that needed to be understood if they were to truly defeat Lhiau. How could the Romulans help Lhiau defeat his enemies if they were destroyed?

Unless destroying the Romulans would somehow harm his enemies.

She brooded on this thought for a moment, then sighed. "We do not have all the information we need in order to solve this puzzle. The successful completion of my plan is therefore even more vital. Idran, you said we were to rendezvous with the *Tektral*. What then?"

"Then we must report to our position in the front line and await orders to attack." He grinned savagely. "We will attack, but not the way they think. They have their prize; we will have ours."

Under Jekri's leadership, the *Tektral* had been a smoothly operating machine. When she materialized on the bridge of her vessel, she found chaos. There had been an uprising upon news of her imprisonment. Some aboard were loyal to the chairman of the Tal Shiar, and when Jekri no longer held that position, she no longer held their loyalty. They were content to simply wait until they were notified as to who the new chairman might be and serve him or her as they had served the Little Dagger.

But there were others to whom loyalty was a much more personal thing. They followed Jekri, and continued to follow her even as they watched her carefully orchestrated downfall. Lhiau's trumped-up charges had been seen by everyone for what they were. But few had dared protest, because the unspoken message was *This can happen to you.*

Among those few were some stalwart souls aboard the *Tektral* who, like Verrak, had pretended to cooperate but who were all the while still Jekri's people. Verrak, who had captained the vessel until such time as a new chairman could be officially appointed, had known whom to trust, and when he had given them the word they had risen up against their enemies and retaken the ship. There was no brig aboard this vessel, but a small cargo bay was now crammed full of so-called Imperial loyalists. When Verrak had given her a list of all those who had turned against her, Jekri's heart had ached. Among their number were some that she might have called friends, if the chairman of the Tal Shiar could be permitted to have something as intimate as a friendship.

Those who had chosen Jekri and her struggle against Lhiau were permitted to join the crew of the *Para'tar*. Jekri graciously welcomed everyone individually, thanking them personally and assuring them of eventual victory.

"What do you wish to do with the loyalists?" Verrak asked. Jekri had opened her mouth to reply when Idran interrupted.

"Leave them on the *Tektral*," he said bluntly. "Destroy it. That is what we do to traitors."

Once, and not that long ago, Jekri would have been the one to issue that order. Now, she realized she did not want to execute over thirty people with the single push of a button.

"They do not yet understand," she said to Idran. "Take them prisoner. Your brig will certainly accommodate them. Besides, I do not want to see my ship destroyed."

"If we win, the Empress will give you a better ship— a dozen, probably, if you like. If we lose, you will have no need of a vessel, no matter where you go. They are traitors as far as we are concerned, and that is what happens to traitors."

The image of Dammik, of young Tarya, appeared in Jekri's mind. Neither of them would have approved of this. It was not necessary. It would have been had they been forced to simply leave the loyalists in charge of the *Tektral*. But there was a place to keep them until this was settled one way or another. She simply couldn't shake the feeling that this was wrong.

"No," Jekri said firmly. "We will take them with us. You are operating on faith, old friend, and for that I am more grateful than you can know. Verrak knows Lhiau, knows what he has done. These people were not permitted aboard the *Talvath*, they do not yet appreciate the danger. I will not have their blood on my hands if it is not necessary."

Idran lifted a slanted eyebrow. "Perhaps Verrak was wrong," he mused. "Perhaps they did break you in prison. You've gone soft, Jekri."

Before Idran could even blink, Jekri had drawn her weapon and shoved it under the old warrior's chin. "Soft? I? I do not think so, considering who has the weapon and who has the weapon at his throat. You said this ship and her crew were mine to command when you beamed me on board. Are you going back on your word?"

"No," said Idran, carefully. "The ship is yours, Chairman."

"I told you, I do not have that title." Jekri resheathed her weapon and Idran's hand went to his neck, as if to make certain it was still whole. "You may call me the Little Dagger." Once, the name had been shameful to own. Now she claimed it proudly, more honored by that title than that of chairman. "Beam them into your brig, and let us make all haste to the rendezvous point. I would not wish to draw attention by arriving late."

It took traveling at warp nine to reach the rendezvous point at the edge of the Neutral Zone, but they managed. Idran had been given a precise set of coordinates at which to position the *Para'tar*, and they moved slowly to take up their ordered position.

Jekri was now dressed as a low-ranking bridge officer. While her name was known, and her former title feared, because of the nature of her position her face was not immediately recognizable. She had wanted to be on the bridge and though there was a risk of someone speaking with Idran identifying her, it was a slight one. She managed to keep her shock from showing, but she was flooded with disbelief and not a little apprehension as the *Para'tar* moved toward its position.

She had never seen so many ships in one place in her entire life. They stretched for thousands of kilometers along the Neutral Zone. The *Para'tar* threaded its way delicately, slowly moving past ship after ship after ship in a languid dance that might have been beautiful had not its significance been so deadly. Finally, they were in position.

Jekri tapped up a map on the screen. There was their target—the *Talvath*, positioned several hundred kilometers away. It was dwarfed by the mighty warbirds that surrounded it, yet it was perhaps the beating heart of the entire invasion plan. It was the only vessel that had been equipped with Shepherd technology to augment Telek R'Mor's own; the only way that the wormholes could be opened. Without that tiny ship, the invasion would be crippled.

She swallowed hard. They would succeed. They had to. She did not know precisely what hinged on their victory, but she knew it was awesome in its magnitude.

Kelleh Taklarin had replaced the traitorous Sharibor, and while he was not as adept as his predecessor, he was good, and he was loyal. Presently, Jekri knew, he was hard at work intercepting messages, breaking codes, and creating new, false messages of his own.

The first one flashed across the screen. It was allegedly from the third-highest commander of the invasion. "Para'tar *and* Khalvur *exchange positions.*" To divert attention, Kelleh had several other ships exchange positions as well. Slowly, the mighty warbird moved into position. This single move closed the distance between the *Para'tar* and the *Talvath* by nearly three-quarters.

They waited. Jekri thought the seconds crawled by like hours. Another message came from Kelleh, this one ostensibly from the Praetor to all vessels: *"Prior to the implementation of the invasion, Subcommander Verrak will assume position as commander of the* Talvath. *Nonessential personnel aboard the vessel shall prepare to be transported to the* Para'tar *until such time as Subcommander Verrak deems it safe for them to return. The* Talvath *is a science vessel, not a warship."*

Even as she marveled at its brilliance, she caught her breath at its daring. With one order, the *Para'tar* would pull into position beside the *Talvath,* Verrak would secure it, and they would capture all personnel—for Jekri did not think for one moment that, granted the opportunity, Idran would not beam everyone over and put them into the brig. The *Talvath* was a small ship, meant to be crewed by only one person. Under her command, there had been six crammed into the tiny space: herself, Verrak, and four lesser officers. And Lhiau, but he did not require quarters.

She wondered if Lhiau was aboard. There was no way to tell. Any scan to see if he was present would seem to confirm it, as the *Talvath* was crammed to the gills with Shepherd technology. She desperately hoped he was not. Things were difficult enough as it was.

She cursed how slowly they had to move in order to not give the appearance of haste. Any moment now, someone would realize that these messages had been forged. The mighty warbird settled into position alongside the *Talvath.* Jekri, Verrak, and two of her most trusted men hurried to the transporter.

The young woman at the transporter gave her a brief but sincere salute. "Good luck, Honored Chairman. We will see you on the other side."

Jekri, Verrak, and the two officers materialized inside the *Talvath*. She stifled an instinct to contact Idran. Their communications would be monitored. She had to leave that to Verrak, whose confirmation of a safe transport would not arouse suspicion.

"Subcommander Verrak to *Para'tar*," said Verrak, slipping into a chair at the console. His voice was utterly calm, almost bored-sounding. "I have assumed command of the *Talvath*."

"Nonessential personnel have arrived safely," responded Idran, sounding as neutral as Verrak. *I hope they enjoy their stay in the brig,* Jekri thought.

Verrak thumbed the channel closed and turned to her. "Six minutes before the order to attack is scheduled to be given," he said.

"Do you remember how to do this?" she asked with a half-smile.

"I burned it into my brain," Verrak replied. Together, they set the coordinates. There would be no more conversation with Idran. There was no need. The commander would know what to do when the time came.

"Coordinates set," said Verrak, and his voice trembled ever so slightly.

Jekri took a deep breath. They would have to move fast from here on in. With a deft touch, Jekri activated the Shepherd device.

"Commander Stahl to the *Talvath*. Why have you activated the wormhole technology? Stand down and prepare to be boarded."

"He's fast," muttered Verrak. "Hurry."

Jekri needed no urging. She tapped in the controls and at once a purplish cloud swirled in front of them. The wormhole yawned open.

"Let's go!" cried Jekri, and the *Talvath* surged forward at full speed. Behind them, so close as to almost touch, was the *Para'tar.*

And behind them, swooping through just as the wormhole closed behind them, were three other warbirds.

INTERLUDE

THE PLANET'S SURFACE WAS HARSH, UGLY, AND FILLED THE Entity with a sudden, unpleasant shock of remembrance. It had been here, and the experience had been a difficult one. But what? What was that experience?

It floated swiftly along the planet's surface, seeking out the dark matter that called to it. In the earth, in crops that had been ominously left untended, in some of the tough creatures that managed to find food, creatures that seemed almost as bad as the mutated dark matter itself.

The carnivorous kal *plants. The "sand that eats," which were more than simple quicksand, but actual living creatures. The Xians, whose complex brains were geared toward harsh survival and who reveled in brutality.*

Had the Entity possessed a corporeal body, it would have shuddered.

Yet nothing was completely evil, not even here. There

were more benevolent beings as well, though they were being affected by the dark matter and were sometimes behaving in as cruel a fashion as the Xians.

It was pulled to the pain of one such species, the kakkiks, small, gentle, and oh so intelligent. The dark matter had not corrupted them, not these little beings, but it was killing them. As the Entity floated along the surface, it grieved at the number of small, winged bodies that were rotting on the earth.

They sensed the Entity at once. Of course they would. They flocked to it like a moth to fire, seeking its benevolent aid. They knew it would help. Their large, soft, dark eyes held a world full of torment, and they beat their wings frantically, hovering, sending messages that the Entity could understand all too clearly: Something is wrong. Something is terribly wrong, and we do not know how to stop it. Help us. Save us. Save this place.

It sent back thoughts as full of love as it could manage as it gathered up the dark matter from their beleaguered bodies. Their little hearts calmed, and they fluttered away, singing joyfully as their bodies were purged of the evil that had been destroying their entire species.

On to the other beings. It knew their names, too; had known them ere now. They were wise and good, though their fearsome, ursine bodies belied such statements and their minds had been ravaged by dark matter. They would grieve over what they had done, the fear that had wrapped them in its cold cloak and forced them to turn on one another, turn on their greatest friend—

The Entity felt knowledge surging through it, so powerful it was almost overwhelming. The great ally.

It had spoken to this being, told him once that he could choose to be the great ally or the great enemy. That he could turn his long life toward helping others instead of imprisoning them, that he could find comfort and richness in his interaction with the Sshoush-shin. And so he had, until the dark matter had come.

And now, he would again.

As it had done before, it entered into the very cells of the ancient being who called himself Aren Yashar. It trembled along his nerves, coasted through his veins, planted warm affection in his brain. Once, Aren had demanded love from the Entity it could not give. Now, there was nothing it could not love, and it sent that love to the Rhulani.

All is not lost. The healing can begin again. You will find that the Sshoush-shin welcome your aid. Forgive them, as I have forgiven you, and you will know love and belonging once more.

Tall and still handsome, as the Entity remembered, but thin and worn and consumed with fear and hate, Aren Yashar shuddered as he felt the Entity's healing presence. He fell to his knees, alone in the cave that had become his dwelling place, and gasped. His hands came up to his hearts and pressed hard on his chest, as if he could touch those aches and calm the pain inside them. The Entity tasted the bittersweet joy that flooded him.

"You," he whispered.

CHAPTER
13

PERSONAL LOG, STARDATE WHENEVER. I REGRET TO SAY THAT Trima and I have been avoiding one another ever since her confession a couple of nights ago. She's probably sorry she told me, and I am at a total loss as to what to say or do. I don't envy her one bit. Her role as Culil would be difficult under any circumstances, and to have obtained it the way she did, and to be what she is—a woman divided—well, all I can say is I'm glad it's not me.

Tom realized that the words he had just written were all squiggly. His hand was shaking. He swallowed hard and forced himself to continue.

On the other hand, Trima appears to be well, something I most certainly am not. Soliss can't explain it. It's nothing I've eaten, I don't think I've been bitten by any nasty little insect, and it doesn't seem to be any one of the eighty-three or so fevers he's familiar with. I'm tired, and weak. It almost feels as though I'm recovering from an injury or something, like I've lost a lot of blood. I'm craving meat on the rarer side these days.

That was enough. The words were almost too shaky to read, so he abandoned his log for the day. He hated this. He couldn't contribute any more, and did not want to feel like a charity case. His mind made up, he rose, rather unsteadily, and made his way to Trima's hut. They had to do something.

Tentatively, Paris knocked on the door. "Enter," she called in her cool voice.

He did so, and gave her a faint smile. Her pale blue brows came together in a frown of concern. "Paris, you do not look at all well."

"Yeah, so Soliss tells me. But I can't stand any more tree-bark tea, so I thought I'd come while away some time with you."

She glanced down. She had not risen, but had remained seated on the soft floor cushions. "What is it you require?"

"A trip home." He sat down, quickly, before he fell down. "I know you said you don't like to contact the Alilann frequently, but we both thought they'd have come for me by now."

She nodded. "I have received no more messages. I do not understand what's happening."

Tom thought he might. Contrary to what he had just said, he asked for a cup of tea before he began. He'd need it to keep his throat wet through what was certain to be a long story. He took a sip, and then began. He told Trima everything, from Telek R'Mor's unexpected contacting of the ship to the discovery of the dreadful nature of the mutated dark matter to his arrival in this place. Her eyes widened when he mentioned Khala, but she remained silent until he had finished.

"I think that may be what's wrong with me," he said at last, draining his cup. "I think your planet has dark matter in it somewhere and it's starting to affect me. It may have already affected your contact people."

"It may be responsible for Matroci's murder," said Trima softly. "This is a frightening tale you weave, Tom Paris."

"If only it were just that—a tale. But it's the truth."

She gave him a cold look, as if doubting him, then smiled. Tom thought it was like the sun coming out from under a cloud, and that thought frightened him more than the thought of dark matter in his body. He was terribly afraid he was starting to fall for Trima. He really, really wished that Chakotay had been able to drag B'Elanna along with them through the portal. Tom was not particularly good at resisting temptation. He never had been.

"It would serve you nothing to make up so complicated a story," she said. "Of course I believe you. And you are right. Much as I hate to do this, it is clear to me that you are ill. Soliss has done wonders as a healer and I respect him, but I also respect the Alilann doctors and their science."

She rose and with a slight rustling of her long robes went to a carved wooden chest. Gracefully she opened it, and to Tom's surprise, removed a false bottom.

"Hey, my phaser and communicator!" he said, moving over to sit beside her. She hesitated, then slowly picked up his possessions and handed them to him.

"These do belong to you," she said. "Please, keep them concealed. We are not supposed to return technological devices to Strangers who become part of the village."

"Gotcha," said Paris, already in the process of hunting for a place in his clothes to secrete them.

"Your communication devices are quite beautiful," said Trima. "If any of the Sumar-ka saw them, they would be after a jeweler to make replicas for them."

Tom looked at her closely. Yes, it was definitely humor. He allowed himself a smile in return.

Trima removed another device. After all this time not seeing advanced technology, to Paris the thing looked dark, alien, and sinister in her hand. One corner of it blinked green.

Trima thumbed a control, then shook her head. "No messages. I had hoped they would have left one. I check every night before bed, just in case."

She had been kneeling beside the chest. Now she extended her legs, long and muscular, crossed them, and settled the device in her lap. Quickly, she tapped in a message. "There," she said.

"What did you say?"

"The Stranger Paris is ill. Send Recovery team as soon as possible. The Silent One."

"Short and sweet," said Paris, thinking that he'd warranted something a little more eloquent.

"Brevity is best," said Trima, seeming to agree with him.

A thought occurred to him. He reached into the chest, removed Chakotay's combadge, and handed it to Trima. "You should wear this," he said.

She recoiled, and again Paris felt a rush of sympathy for her. Part of her still reviled technology, even as she realized how useful it was.

"Listen, there is someone out there killing Culils," he said intently. "We don't know how high up this goes. It could be one person acting on his own or this could be the new, improved Alilann policy toward the Culilann. You've told me that you're only known as The Silent One. They don't know you're Trima, the Culil of Sumar-ka. Right now, you're in as much danger as Matroci was. At least if you have this hidden on you somewhere you'll be able to contact me if something happens."

She stared at the device, then slowly, reluctantly, closed her fingers around it. Paris felt a rush of relief.

"You too," she said. "If something happens and you need help—you can contact me."

"I couldn't," he replied. "The combadge makes kind of a chirping noise. It would give you away."

She lifted her chin and her eyes flashed. God, but she was beautiful. "If you are in danger, then it is my duty as Culil—and as your friend—to help you. Regardless of what sacrifice it might entail. I trust you to use it only in a life-threatening situation, Paris, but use it you will, if you need me."

He swallowed hard. "Okay," he said. "You've got yourself a deal."

He felt better when he left. It had been strange to be without a weapon on this planet, and downright unsettling to be without a combadge. A dozen times a day he'd find himself tapping his chest, trying futilely to communicate with someone. It had gotten so that the children teased him, lifting their right hands and touching their left breasts when they saw him.

And he was glad he'd persuaded Trima to take the combadge. He knew she hadn't wanted to, and frankly, he was furious that there was a need for her to do so. The Culilann ought to be safe. They were hurting no one. Grimly, Paris thought of his talk with Chakotay, about Earth's Ghost Dance and the fact that the more technologically advanced group had felt so threatened by a less technologically advanced one that they had to round them up and, on occasion, kill them for good measure.

He was very much afraid that he was about to see the same thing happen here.

It was about then that he passed out.

"You've got to send a Recovery team after Paris right away," said Chakotay over his shoulder as the doctor and Ezbai were leading him out.

"That will be considered," said the Implementer.

"Considered? He's got no access to proper medical care, he can't even get the treatment I'm going to get. You've got to Recover him at once!"

"Implementer," said Ezbai, "I would be willing to lead a team—"

"What, and miss Paris a second time?" Chakotay saw Ezbai cringe at the criticism and his heart went out to the young man. It hadn't been Ezbai's fault that Paris was off in the jungle when the Recovery team had arrived.

"Chakotay is right," said Ezbai. He looked as surprised as the rest of them at his assertiveness, but continued. "We don't know how fast this cellular—I don't know what you'd call it, cellular transfer or whatever—is progressing. He is a stranger on our world and he may be dying."

"We can't get a team together," said the Implementer, "and besides—"

A strange beeping noise interrupted him. Grunting, he thumbed a control. There on one of the screens was the same black-and-white lettering as before, again translated for Chakotay's benefit: *The Stranger Paris is ill. Send Recovery Team as soon as possible. The Silent One.*

The Implementer's ugly face looked even uglier in annoyance. "See?" yelped Ezbai. "Even our spy wants him gone!"

The Implementer sighed. "I suppose you are right, for once. Still, there is no time to get a proper team assembled. Everyone is on assignment."

"I'll go with him," said Chakotay.

"Absolutely not!"

"Let me check in with your doctors and see what they can do for me," Chakotay persisted. "Then let me go with Shamraa Ezbai. I know the Sumar-ka. They won't suspect anything if they see me. Perhaps I can fabricate a way for Paris to leave the village and then we can both depart."

Something seemed to break in the Implementer. He sighed heavily and ran his hands over his balding head. "We had order, we had structure. Now you come, Chakotay, bearing tales of dark matter and madness. We've got a missing Shamraa and a sick stranger and someone or a group of someones out there murdering Culils. It's all but spiraling out of control. Go, then. Take whatever and whomever you need, but return here as quickly as possible. There's too much going on for teams to be out now. Do you understand?"

Ezbai nodded. "Yes, Implementer."

"Thank you," said Chakotay. But the moment of honesty and softness had vanished, and the Implementer merely growled and waved a dismissive hand.

"There are a couple of people who were in the last patrol who might be willing to go out again," said Ezbai. "I'll see if I can locate them. You report to the doctor, and let him do what he can for you."

There was an intensity, a determination, about Ezbai

that Chakotay had never seen before, and he thought he knew the reason for it.

"This isn't about Tom, is it?" said Chakotay softly. "It's about Khala."

Ezbai nodded jerkily. "It's foolish, but somehow I think that if I work hard to save you and Paris, then someone will be working hard to keep Khala alive until we figure out how to get her back home safely."

Chakotay smiled. "It's not foolish, Ezbai," he said. "It's not foolish at all."

Three hours later, Chakotay, Ezbai, and four others had donned appropriate gear and were striding through the rain forest. The transporter had cut kilometers off their trip, but there was still something called the "no-transport zone" that had to be honored. Chakotay was glad of the supplements the doctor had given him. Even so, he felt weaker than usual, and could not help but wonder how Tom was faring.

For a while, they simply hiked. Sweat pooled beneath their protective gear. Chakotay thought these people, intelligent and advanced as they were, still had a lot to learn about dressing for the tropics. He was not altogether happy with the team Ezbai had been able to cobble together, but he supposed beggars couldn't be choosers. In particular, he was sorry to see the bigoted Ioni among their number. He had taken a strong and instant dislike to the woman and regretted that she was part of this team. But for the moment, she was silent, keeping her prejudices to herself.

"I've been doing a lot of thinking, Chakotay," said Ezbai quietly. They were some distance ahead of the others, but Ezbai's voice was pitched so that only Chakotay could hear. "About what you said earlier."

"About the division between the Culilann and the Alilann?" said Chakotay in an equally soft voice. The last thing he wanted was for Ioni to overhear. Hope began to seep through him. Sometimes, all things needed in order to change was one good man, and with all his failings, Ezbai was a good man.

Ezbai nodded, keeping his eyes on the trail. Mud sucked at their boots. "They are the ones who rely on the soil for their food, and yet somehow they've ended up in places where the most extreme weather systems on our planet occur. I don't know how that happened. But I still think we are being tolerant in taking their children, giving them continued life and homes with loving parents."

From under a large frond, a long muzzle poked. Chakotay caught a glimpse of bright yellow eyes. He blinked, and it was gone. But it had left an answer in his brain.

Now he understood why his subconscious had begun conjuring Coyote. Coyote symbolized something from another culture, a Native American culture, but one in which Chakotay had not been raised. Coyote was not his tribe's totem animal, but that of other Indians, among them a nation called the Navajo. The lesson Chakotay needed to recall was that of the Navajo, of Coyote's people. He could almost sense the spirit creature leaping joyfully as it realized that Chakotay finally understood.

"Yes, you bring them in, and heal them, and feed them, and teach them your culture," he said, choosing his words with care. "And considering the alternative is a cruel death by exposure, I wholeheartedly give you full credit for that. That tells me that you have a great deal of compassion."

Ezbai seemed pleased at the acknowledgment, but also realized that Chakotay had more to say.

"Many years ago, my people were the Culilann," Chakotay continued. "And my planet's version of the Alilann, the Anglos, decided that they wanted to live where the Culilann lived. So they rounded them up and forced them into the least habitable places in the hemisphere. Said these places were 'reserved' for the Culilann, for the Indian. The children were given a way off these reservations, but at a cost. They were forbidden to speak or write in their native tongue, or practice their traditional faith. A whole generation of children from one tribe, the Navajo, was taken from their families and forced to attend Anglo schools. They were punished if they spoke Navajo. The culture was almost lost."

Ezbai looked wretched, and Chakotay suspected that it was not from the weather. "But why is that bad? Why does a—a backward culture need to survive?"

"Because ties with your past teach you how to be truly alive. Ezbai, you—the Alilann—you are doing to the Culilann what the Anglo culture did to my people," he said softly, without rancor. "It took centuries before it was realized that by trying to stamp out another culture, the Anglos were cheating themselves too. The Vulcans figured it out long before Earth did: Infinite Diversity in Infinite Combinations. Without that kind of tolerance, it all comes down to hate. And fear."

"I don't hate the Culilann," said Ezbai.

"Perhaps not personally, but as a culture, you do. You hate the Culilann, and believe me, they hate you right back. You're not a killer, Ezbai. But someone is. There is some Alilann out there, or perhaps a group of them, who are killing the Culils of the villages because they hate what they symbolize."

"I can imagine hating someone, an individual, enough to kill him," said Ezbai, with obvious reluctance. "If they tried to kill you, or hurt your family. But wanting to kill someone just because they're different?" He shook his head, not comprehending.

"And that is what makes you a good man, Ezbai," said Chakotay, placing a hand on the younger man's shoulder. He said no more. Ezbai needed time to think, to digest what had been said. This situation had taken thousands of years to evolve. Change would not come overnight.

After a few more moments, Ezbai consulted his instruments, then lifted a hand to signal a halt. More hand gestures; Chakotay guessed that they were within hearing range of a Culilann or the village itself. Adrenaline began to spurt through his system, and he was alert at once.

They had discussed the plan. Chakotay was wearing a replication of the traditional Culilann clothes he had worn when he had first been Recovered. He would be wearing a communication device hidden in his clothing, and when he was alone he would report to the Recovery team his and Paris's status. Chakotay suspected that the Sumar-ka would let him and Tom leave, especially if Paris was ill, but also suspected they would want to give them the Culilann equivalent of a going-away party. The Recovery team would in all likelihood have to wait until the still of the night, as they had before.

Chakotay was a little nervous as he made for the village. What if he was wrong? What if they wouldn't let him leave, set a guard on him? What if Paris was already too ill for the Alilann doctors to help?

But the delighted cry that left Yurula's lips when he appeared at the outskirts of the village set his mind at ease.

"Chakotay!" she cried, running to him and embracing him. "We feared the worst! Are you all right?"

"Yes and no," he said, hugging her back. "It's a long story. How is Tom?"

She sobered. "Not well. Soliss has done everything, yet he continues poorly."

"I've no doubt that Soliss has cared well for him," said Chakotay. "Take me to—" He almost said Trima, then realized that knowing about Matroci's death would reveal too much. "To Matroci," he said, hoping he hadn't hesitated too long.

"Matroci is dead," said Yurula as they turned and headed for the Culil's hut. "He went to join the Crafters, by inhaling the smoke from the Sacred Plant as his predecessor did. Trima is our advisor now."

"I'm so sorry," said Chakotay, and this he did not have to feign. "When did this happen?"

"The night you left," said Yurula. "It was a bad time for Sumar-ka. Paris had gotten treed by a mother *iislak,* and we feared that you had not been spared by her. It is a delight to me to see you again, Chakotay." Her smile was radiant, genuine, and Chakotay bitterly regretted the falsehoods he was being forced to feed her.

"I'm all right, for now. My people found me and they want to take me and Tom back home with them. We're ill from living here, Yurula. If we don't leave, we'll die." This much, at least, was no falsehood.

"Truly?" Her eyes searched his and he nodded. She looked down. "We will miss you. You will leave behind those who love you—both of you."

"I know," said Chakotay, "but the alternative—"

"Cannot be contemplated. Trima is—" Soliss rushed up to them, cutting off her words.

"Chakotay! Yurula! You must help me with Paris. I went to check on him and found him unconscious in his hut!"

They all began to run. Chakotay's heart sank. *Don't*

die, Tom. B'Elanna would never forgive me. And frankly I'd never forgive myself.

But Paris was sitting up by the time they reached him, and managed a weak smile of genuine pleasure. "Chakotay! A sight for sore eyes." He tried to stand, but swayed. Chakotay caught him just in time. He picked Paris up and laid him on the bed.

"This place is just not good for me," Paris gasped.

"You're more right than you know," said Chakotay. He turned to Soliss and Yurula. "May I have a few moments with him in private? I'll come out and speak with both of you and Culil Trima as well."

They nodded their understanding and withdrew. Chakotay turned to Paris and spoke in a hurried, low voice.

"I've got a lot to tell you, Tom."

"And I've got something to tell you, too. Me first, I'm sicker." Chakotay had to grin at that. Tom had lost none of his spirit. "The Alilann have a spy planted here."

"I know. The Silent One."

"Yeah. It's Trima."

"What?" Of everyone in the village, Trima was quite literally the last one Chakotay would have expected to be the spy.

"They Recovered her as an infant and healed her. Then they sent her here in deep cover at the age of ten. She's very conflicted, Chakotay, but she's chosen to confide in me. Matroci's dead."

"I know."

"He didn't commit suicide, he was murdered. By one of the Alilann."

"I know that, too."

Paris frowned, annoyed. "I'm worried about Trima."

"I understand. The Alilann came for us both, but they

missed you. I hear you had an up-close and personal encounter with a mother *iislak.*"

"Yeah, and Junior too. Not one of my finest moments."

"There's a Recovery team waiting to take us back, and from that point our top priority has to be returning to *Voyager.* We're dying, Tom." There was no way to put it other than bluntly. Paris could take it. "We're not from this universe. We're in the Shadow universe and our bodies are rebelling, trying to go home a cell at a time."

Paris stared at him, but Chakotay knew the ensign believed him. "When do you think we'll be able to leave?"

"You know the Sumar-ka. Any excuse for a party."

"I was afraid of that. We'll have to play up your illness, see if we can't have that farewell dinner tonight."

Paris grimaced. "We won't have to play it up all that much."

Chakotay had been right. The Sumar-ka were caring people, and they believed Chakotay's story about returning to his ship. They could see that Paris was ill, could even see signs of weakness in Chakotay. They were left alone in their hut to rest and dress for the ceremony, which would be held after nightfall. Chakotay contacted the Recovery team and informed them of the situation.

Paris hadn't wanted to sleep, but it came for both him and Chakotay regardless. He woke, hot and sweating, as the twilight shadows were beginning to fill the hut with a soft light. He woke Chakotay and they splashed cool water on their faces and changed into clean robes.

Trima came for them as soon as dark had settled fully. She looked like an incarnation of twilight herself, with her blue skin and purple-gray robes. Her normally poised demeanor was gone, and she looked small and lost inside the formal dress of her office.

"Hi," said Paris, his voice sounding awkward in his own ears. "I didn't know you'd come get us."

She smiled, but it did not reach her eyes. "It is my privilege, as Culil. I have been notified about the Recovery team waiting for you." She paused, then said, "I will miss you, Tom Paris. It has been good, having someone to confide in."

"Yeah," he said. He couldn't think of anything else to say, and was acutely aware of Chakotay's gaze boring into his back.

Trima did something entirely unexpected. She stepped forward and kissed him quickly on the cheek. The place where her lips had touched seemed to tingle.

"Let us go," she said, and just that quickly, she ceased being the insecure Silent One and became Trima, Culil of Sumar-ka, with important duties to perform. His face still burning from her kiss, Paris followed. Chakotay brought up the rear.

The celebration was similar to that with which the Sumar-ka had initiated them into their bosom, except it was more subdued. Paris started feeling slightly unwell again and just wanted the thing to be over with. He was ready to go, Trima had kissed him, dammit, which was a bit of a problem, and he wanted to be gone, to be home with B'Elanna, which was where he knew he belonged.

They came, one by one or in pairs or family units, to say farewell. There were no trinkets or offerings this time; the villagers seemed to know that Paris and Chakotay would not wish to be laden with gifts. The food was delicious, as always, and Paris knew that this was certainly one of the things he would miss most about this place.

Trima sat away from them after she had performed her ritual role. She gleamed in the moonlight, but not like an Ice Princess, not anymore. Paris knew her now, and despite the coolness of her demeanor he knew her great beauty disguised the warm heart of a confused, caring woman. He was going to miss her, too.

At last it was over, and Chakotay rose, as they had agreed he would.

"My people have no wish to disturb the peace of Sumar-ka," he began. He smiled a little as he added, "Nor do they wish to endure your Ordeal, necessary though we all know it to be." Answering smiles went around the small circle. "So we shall take our leave now, but we will carry forever in our hearts the memories we have shared with you."

Paris rose now, too, somewhat unsteadily, and he and Chakotay gave the threefold salute common among the Sumar-ka, touching temples, throat, and abdomen. There was a shuffling sound as every single member of the village rose and did likewise. Then there were no more words. Paris cast a last, quick look at Trima. Surely it was a trick of the moonlight that made her eyes gleam, as if with tears.

They turned and left.

After a few moments, Paris said in a low voice, "I'm going to miss these people."

"Me too," Chakotay said. They said nothing more until they met up with the Recovery crew.

"Did it go well? Did they suspect?" The young man who rushed forward to greet them looked slightly familiar to Paris, which he knew was impossible.

174

"Not a thing," said Chakotay. "Tom, this is Shamraa Ezbai Remilkansuur. He's Khala's brother."

"That's why you look familiar," said Paris. "Khala's in good hands."

Ezbai nodded, a rapid movement. "Let's go. The sooner we get past the no transport zone, the sooner our doctors can begin treating you."

Paris found himself wishing he'd brought his staff, the lovely one they had made for him when he was ill the last time. It was a shame, really. He knew that whatever pleasure he had found here, he was always going to associate this place with being sick or injured. They hiked for a bit, their going slow in the thick jungle foliage and hampered by lack of light. From time to time they would rest, and then they'd keep going. Tom lost track of how long they had been hiking. It seemed like forever.

Suddenly Ezbai paused. "We've lost some people," he said, glancing around. "Ioni, Kelmor, Travya—"

At that precise moment, Paris's combadge chirped. He felt himself grow weak, for he knew that signified only one thing.

Trima was in danger.

CHAPTER
14

"CHAIRMAN KALEH," SAID JANEWAY CRISPLY. "I REMEMBER you from our last encounter." She had heard Tuvok issue the orders to put up their shields and sound a red alert. "We do not wish to fight you, but—"

"Nor do we wish to fight you," said Jekri hurriedly, surprising Janeway. "Help us."

Utterly confused, Janeway opened her mouth to ask more questions when suddenly the reason for the request became clear. Jekri's image disappeared, replaced by the image of the ships on the screen. One of the warbirds had maneuvered itself between the *Talvath* and the other warbirds. Now the other three began to open fire: one targeted the warbird protecting the *Talvath* and the other two swooped in on *Voyager*.

The ship rocked from the impact. "Harry," cried Janeway, "any sign of dark matter in those vessels?"

"Not yet, but—there they go." Sure enough, as he spoke the two attacking warbirds slowly disappeared.

"Target engines and weapons systems, Tuvok. Mr. Kim, get the chairman back."

"Captain," said R'Mor.

"Not now, Telek."

"Captain!" Janeway gave him an angry glance at his direct defiance. Telek barreled on. "You must protect the *Talvath!* It has the wormhole technology aboard— the Shepherd augmentation of my own efforts. It could be your way home!"

Janeway stared, all the anger suddenly gone. *It could be your way home.* She had not even considered it. She had been so completely focused on retrieving the dark matter that the fact that Telek, in conjunction with the Shepherds, would know exactly how to send them home, to their proper place and proper time, had simply never come up.

"I've got her, Captain," said Kim, interrupting Janeway's sudden flood of hopeful thoughts.

"On screen," ordered Janeway.

Again the image of the chairman of the Tal Shiar filled *Voyager's* screen. Before either woman could speak, both ships were attacked by the three hostile warbirds.

"Captain!" cried Jekri, clutching a console in a desperate attempt to keep her balance. "The *Para'tar* and I seek your assistance! Destroy the other three warbirds!" Although she was beseeching Janeway for a favor, Jekri Kaleh spoke almost as if giving an order. Janeway opted to ignore the other woman's attitude. There would be time to hash things out with Kaleh and the commander of the currently friendly warbird once the other three had been subdued.

Jekri was aboard the *Talvath,* of course, throwing a

wrench even deeper into the works. And she and the single warbird who had chosen to protect the little science vessel were as clearly targets of the other ships as was *Voyager*. It was a puzzle, but Janeway would have time for puzzle solving later. Now she had to act.

"Chairman—"

"No longer," growled the small woman. Janeway was surprised and suspected a lie, but continued.

"We will attempt to extend our shields to cover your vessel. The *Para'tar* is too large for such protection, but we will continue to defend it. If you approach at your slowest speed, you should be able to penetrate our shields without forcing us to lower them."

"At my slowest speed, I shall be dead before I reach your shields!" snapped the Romulan.

Janeway lifted an eyebrow. "Have it your way," she replied coolly.

The woman at the controls of the *Talvath* fixed Janeway with a cold, hostile stare that unnerved the captain totally. And that didn't happen all that often. She could understand why Jekri Kaleh, despite her youth and small stature, had made such a formidable chairman of so dark an organization as the Tal Shiar. But Janeway merely lifted her own chin in a subtle gesture of defiance.

"End communication," she told Kim. At once, the screen again filled with the image of battling warbirds. The ship rocked and this time the lights flickered briefly. Janeway could smell the acrid scent of burning.

"A direct hit," said Tuvok in his usual calm voice. "The warp core is offline. We are venting plasma from the starboard nacelle. Injury reports are coming in from decks seven, twelve, fourteen, and ten."

Janeway heard a sharp intake of breath. It came from the conn, and as her gaze flickered to Ensign Jenkins, she saw that the young woman was clutching a burned hand. Janeway could see bones through strips of blackened flesh.

"Get to sickbay, Jenkins," Janeway ordered, rising and coming down to the conn.

"Captain, no, you need someone—" Jenkins's voice was tight, fighting pain, and she steadfastly blinked back tears of agony.

"You're no use as a conn officer with a burned hand," said Janeway, not softening the words. "Get to sickbay. That's an order."

"Aye, Captain." Reluctantly, Jenkins rose and headed for the turbolift. Janeway moved from her captain's chair to man the conn herself.

Another blow. Again, the vessel shuddered. Something Tuvok said lingered in Janeway's mind. Something about the damage. What was it?

The warp core was offline.

And the dark matter was stored in a fragile little universe inside that warp core, a fragile little universe that Torres had reported had already begun to disintegrate.

"Oh, God," said Torres. "Not now, not now . . . ." As if there was ever a *good* time for the warp core to be offline. But now, right in the middle of a battle with Romulans, when the warp-bubble universe was already showing signs of rapidly increasing instability, was quite possibly the very worst time the warp core could have chosen to go offline.

She knew that Janeway would want warp drive back immediately, but right now getting that warp-bubble universe stable again was the most important priority. Without it, having warp drive wouldn't matter one damn bit.

"Seven, how are you coming on creating that second shell?"

"I am making progress," began the former Borg. At that moment, the ship rocked again. Her console began spitting sparks. "This console is damaged. I will have to start from the beginning." As if that didn't matter to her at all, Seven calmly strode to a second console and began tapping in equations.

Torres admired Seven's cool even as it frustrated the hell out of her. She made a decision. "We don't have time. Keep working on it anyway, Seven, we may need a backup. Khala, Vorik, give me a hand here. We've got to see if we can't create some kind of field around this thing."

Something that would halt the destabilization of the miniature universe. Something that would not halt a transport of dark matter from That Damned Ball into said miniature universe.

There were moments when being chief engineer on *Voyager* made being a Maquis look like an afternoon in the park.

"Shield," said Khala softly. Her pretty brow furrowed in concentration.

"Sometime today, Khala, if you don't mind," barked Torres.

"Wait a minute, B'Elanna. I have an idea." Khala tapped her combadge. "Khala to the Doctor."

Despite Jekri Kaleh's haughty attitude, Janeway noticed that the *Talvath* was heading straight for the protection that *Voyager* had offered. The battle continued, with Janeway now manning the conn. *Voyager* and the Romulan warbird that defended the science vessel were outnumbered three to two. It was an odd little dance.

Janeway was not issuing orders to destroy the ships, merely cripple them. She knew, as the Romulans could not, how they had been duped and how closely they were skirting death. The warbirds, for their part, were also firing carefully on the Federation ship. Janeway realized that they still wanted *Voyager* as a spoil of war.

However, the *Para'tar* seemed to have no such compunctions. It was firing to kill, and the other warbirds attacked it with equal vigor.

"Come on, Kaleh," said Janeway under her breath. The vessel's approach was agonizingly slow. But it needed to be, she reminded herself.

One of the enemy ships suddenly became aware of the *Talvath's* snail-like progress. It ceased firing on *Voyager* and redirected its efforts on the smaller vessel, landing a direct hit. The ship careened off course, badly damaged.

"Target and fire," Janeway ordered. She knew the Romulans must be baffled that she could see them so accurately with their supposedly flawless shields erected. Tuvok obeyed, and the warbird took heavy damage. It turned slowly, then stopped.

"That one's out of the battle," said Kim.

"I hope you're right," said Janeway. "What's the status on the buildup of dark matter in the area?"

"It's increasing with every moment that their shields are activated," Kim reported. "There's also a high concentration that was discharged by the wormhole."

"They're killing themselves and they cannot even see it," said Telek. "The more they utilize Lhiau's Shepherd technology, either with the cloaks or the wormholes, the more dark matter they spew forth."

The ship shook again. "Our ship is responding to the barrage of dark matter. Our shields are down thirty-four percent. Weapons systems are offline," Tuvok reported.

"Is the warp core still offline?" Janeway asked. If they couldn't fight, they would have to flee, with, she hoped, the *Talvath* in tow. They needed at least one defense option or Romulan shock troops from the remaining two hostile warbirds would be aboard *Voyager* before they knew it.

"Affirmative," said Tuvok.

"Captain," said Kim, "Torres reports that they are still having trouble with the Shepherd technology. She says they've got to fix that before they dare engage in warp drive."

Janeway nodded her comprehension and made her decision. "Fire at will, Commander Tuvok."

"Aye, Captain," acknowledged the Vulcan.

Seated at the conn, Janeway badly wanted to utilize her ship's quick movements to defend herself, but she couldn't, not yet. The small science vessel had recovered from the nearly devastating attack and was again heading straight for them. To make the ship dip and dive now would be to lose the *Talvath*.

"How close is the *Talvath?*" she asked.

"Almost here," said Paris.

She could see it on the screen, a visible David among the cloaked Goliaths, moving with steady purpose toward safety. Again Janeway wondered what was going on. There was the distinct possibility, almost a likelihood, that this was part of a trap. But if so, were the Romulans really willing to nearly destroy the only vessel equipped with wormhole technology simply to make the fight look believable? To destroy themselves? Something about this rang true, and Janeway had seen enough to trust her gut. She still had her suspicions, though. One did not deal with the chairman of the Tal Shiar without having suspicions.

Even a former chairman, if Jekri Kaleh was to be believed.

Another direct hit. Janeway fell forward and hit her head on the conn. For an awful moment, the world went gray. When she recovered, everything had a slight halo around it. A mild concussion. She gritted her teeth and willed herself to stay conscious. Neither she nor her vessel could take much more of this.

Suddenly there was a bright explosion. For a brief, wild second Janeway wondered if this was some strange manifestation of her head injury, then realized that one of their photon torpedoes had landed a direct hit on a warbird—and utterly destroyed it. This was becoming far too familiar, this vulnerability of dark-matter-cloaked warbirds, but seeing it repeated did nothing to lessen the pain and regret Janeway experienced at the sight.

"Any life signs?" she asked.

"Negative," said Kim. Even as he spoke, the first warbird, the one that had been put "out of the battle," as Kim had phrased it earlier, also exploded.

"Dammit, why did we fire on a crippled ship?" cried Janeway, blinking in a frantic attempt to make the halo go away.

"We did not," Tuvok replied. "It either self-destructed or the dark matter destroyed it."

"Open a channel to the remaining warbird," she said. Even as she uttered the words, she knew they were futile. It was déjà vu. How many times must this ghastly scenario reenact itself before the stubborn, proud Romulans would listen to reason?

"Open, Captain," Kim replied.

"This is Captain Kathryn Janeway of the Federation starship—"

"We know who you are, Captain," came a harsh,

183

masculine voice. No visual, not yet. "Stand down and prepare to be boarded."

"The *Talvath* is safely within our shields," Kim said. Janeway nodded her acknowledgment. One good thing, anyway.

"You are harboring a traitor to the Romulan Empire," the commander of the Romulan vessel continued. "Return the ship before we board you and you will be treated with more leniency."

"I have no intention of returning the *Talvath* or of letting your crew board *Voyager*," Janeway snapped. "We have no desire to continue this conflict. If you will stand down, we have information about weaknesses in your dark-matter cloaks which—"

"Federation lies," snarled the Romulan. "Federation tricks."

Romulan lies, Romulan tricks. Klingon lies, Klingon tricks. Janeway wondered how long racial fears would be a part of relations between species. Probably forever, she thought sadly.

"Kim, get me a visual. Commander, please show your face. See mine."

After a long moment, a Romulan visage appeared on the screen. The man was thickly built, with a large, jowly face and sunken, suspicious eyes.

"Surrender," he said, "or—" His eyes widened as his gaze fell on Telek R'Mor. "It is a good day for me," he said. "I have captured the traitors Telek R'Mor and Jekri Kaleh. I have recovered the *Talvath* and *Voyager* as well."

"Don't rest on your laurels yet," Janeway said. "Haven't you wondered why your mighty warbirds were destroyed so easily the last time the Romulans came after us? And this time as well?"

"You have some sort of technological advantage over

us, Captain," the Romulan answered haughtily. "But soon, you shall have it no more. Our sensors indicate that your ship is badly damaged. Surrender, and there will be no more loss of life." He straightened in his chair. "I give you my word."

"Do you know, Commander, I am inclined to believe you," said Janeway, "but I'm not surrendering my ship. Let Dr. R'Mor transmit the information we have gleaned. It's the dark matter that the Shepherd Lhiau has given you. It's damaging your ships, and your crew. Please. Let us have a cease-fire while you examine this material. I'm sure you have capable crewmen aboard who can verify its authenticity."

She expected the standard rebuttal, but the Romulan captain hesitated. He seemed to be seriously considering her offer. Hope rose inside Janeway. There had been no question in her mind that if she could just get someone to see Telek's data, they would believe it. It was getting the other Romulans to trust that was the hard part.

Finally, the Romulan commander seemed to make a decision. He opened his mouth to speak.

At that precise moment, flames erupted on his bridge. The connection was severed. Janeway stared, appalled, at an enormous fireball where the Romulan warbird had been. The *Para'tar* had taken this moment, when the other commander was distracted, to fire and destroy the other ship. But its attack on the other warbird proved to be its death blow. No sooner had it fired than it itself exploded. Janeway stared for a brief moment at two blinding, roiling blasts of multicolored light. Seconds later, there was nothing but turning debris where two mighty vessels had been.

"No," whispered Janeway, tears of compassion and horror springing to her blue eyes. They had almost had open communication. She had seen it in the commander's eyes. He was on the verge of believing her. And he had probably died thinking she had lulled him into carelessness.

Federation lies. Federation tricks.

Janeway slammed a fist impotently on the conn, then summoned control. She blinked the tears back angrily. She had enough trouble seeing already.

"We are being hailed," said Kim in a subdued voice.

"On screen." She was relieved her voice didn't crack.

The visage of Jekri Kaleh appeared. The younger woman was smiling, even though green blood trickled from a nasty-looking cut on her head.

"You are a brilliant tactician, Captain Janeway. Your conversation with Commander Shurvik distracted him sufficiently for Idran to get in the decisive blow."

"We were serious about our discussion," said Janeway. Cold fury roiled in her gut, but she ignored it. "Your enemies are dead, Jekri Kaleh. What do you want from us?"

The young Romulan, her features gaunt and almost skeletal, leaned forward. Her silver eyes snapped with intensity. Blood dripped onto the console.

"I want to save my people," she said, "and I believe you can show me how."

Then the compelling silver eyes rolled back into her skull and Jekri Kaleh collapsed.

CHAPTER
15

"WE'VE GOT TO GO BACK!" PARIS CRIED. "I GAVE TRIMA my combadge. If she's using it, she's in terrible danger! She wouldn't risk giving herself away otherwise!"

"Danger? From what? Give what away?" asked Ezbai, but comprehension spread across Chakotay's dark face.

"Tom, hurry! They're here!" said Trima's voice, issuing from the combadge. A scream, then nothing.

"She's The Silent One," Chakotay said, drawing his weapon. "And Ioni and the others went back to kill her."

"Now, wait, Ioni may be a little harsh, but—" Ezbai began, but Paris and Chakotay ignored him. They set off at a dead run the way they had come, and Ezbai and his crew had no choice but to follow.

Paris felt his body threatening to betray him with every step, every painful, gasping breath he drew. *You listen to me,* he told his body firmly. *Get me to Trima and I'll feed you, massage you, bathe you, and relax you when we get home. Just stay together long enough to get me to Trima!*

They heard the screaming soon afterward. It seemed to take forever, but they finally burst through the underbrush to a scene of absolute chaos.

Nearly all the little huts, some of which Tom and Chakotay had helped build with their own sweat, were on fire. Paris caught glimpses of bodies lying still in the grass. He hoped desperately they were unconscious, not dead, but Matroci had been shown no such mercy. Whoever it was who had killed him, and it was beginning to look as though the murderers were members of Ezbai's team, had come back for more.

Much more.

The smoke stung his eyes and he blinked, trying desperately to focus. Over the cries of fear and the crackling of the flames came another sound, one he had never expected to hear in this quiet little place: the unmistakable, singing sound of a directed energy weapon being fired.

"Oh, God," Paris whispered, and forced his protesting body to run toward the sound. His own phaser, set on stun, was already in his hand. Behind him, he heard Chakotay shouting orders.

More weapons fire. Tom tripped over something and went flying. He hit the ground hard, and gasped as he got to his hands and feet.

He had tripped over the prone form of a villager. Every cell in his body was screaming for him to find Trima, but in a way each person here was dear to Tom. He quickly flipped the prone form over, and realized it was Yurula. He felt for a pulse. Relief washed over him. There it was. She was injured, but she would not die.

He clambered to his feet. Not a second later, a figure jumped out of nowhere. A rifle of some sort was pointed right at him. Paris didn't hesitate. He fired, and the figure tumbled. Paris jumped over it and kept running. He would have to remember to thank his body later for its cooperation.

He was disoriented by the thick, black smoke and the licking orange and red flames of the inferno. Which way was Trima's hut? Was it even still standing, or had Ioni and her followers burned it, with Trima inside, to the earth?

"I don't like where that thought's going," he muttered to himself. But dammit, where was it?

Screams came from the nearest hut. Children's screams. Paris's blood ran cold. He'd always thought that was a cliché, but at the awful sound he felt he had ice water in his veins. The hut was ablaze, its thatch already twisting as if with a life of its own, curling into dark wisps as it burned. At any moment, the whole structure would go.

Covering his face as best he could, Paris charged the burning hut. Three children were inside, two girls about ages twelve and three and an infant. The older girl clutched the baby in her arms.

"Come on!" Paris cried. Although it was too smoky for them to be able to see him, they would recognize his English and know it was either him or Chakotay: a friend. He grabbed the youngest girl, flung her over his shoulder, and herded the older girl out before him.

"Mother!" cried the older girl. Dammit. The mother was probably unconscious from the smoke. The girl handed the infant to her sister and prepared to charge back in.

"You stay!" yelled Tom. "I'll get her."

He didn't think he would. He thought it very likely that the hut would collapse on both of them and he would die, right here, burned to a crisp like one of Neelix's failed soufflés. He also knew he had no other choice.

He gulped a breath of air into seared lungs and raced back in. Paris couldn't see, so he groped frantically. His hands closed on a leg and he reached along the torso, gathering the woman in his arms. He turned and ran for the exit.

Paris had taken two steps before the hut collapsed into an inferno.

"Mama!" the girls shrieked, and rushed to her. Coughing, the woman sat up. She had been so close to the flames that her hair and clothing were singed, but she was alive.

"Tom?" she rasped. He realized that it was Winnif, whose child had recently been abandoned to the care of the Crafters. To the care of the Alilann.

He smiled, turned, and kept going. Trima. He had to find Trima.

Suddenly something hard struck him in the center of his back. Paris stumbled and almost fell. A second hard thing whizzed by his ear.

"Betrayers!" screamed a woman's raw voice.

"Yurula?" Tom turned around and was barely able to duck in time as she threw something at him. This time, he could figure out what it was. It was a stone.

"You brought them here! You led them to us!" Stumbling on shaky legs, still weak from the attack that had rendered her unconscious, she looked around for more ammunition.

Something twisted in Tom's gut. She hated him. She thought this whole thing had been planned, that the

Alilann wanted to kill them, and that he and Chakotay had been part of a plan to exterminate Sumar-ka.

He turned and kept running. He hoped there would be time for explanations later.

More sound of weapons fire, but when he rounded a flaming pile that had once been Resul's pottery shed, he skidded to a halt.

Trima stood proudly, alone. Her garb had been torn and burned, but she appeared uninjured. Her hair was loose and hung in a tangle down almost to the ground itself, and her eyes gleamed wildly in the red light of the burning homes. She grasped Chakotay's phaser, the one Tom had left behind, and stood in a bare area encircled by several fallen bodies.

"Trima!" he cried in relief. She swung around, pointing the weapon at him. Instinctively he raised his hands. He hoped to God the setting hadn't accidentally been set to kill.

"Tom," she breathed. As he watched, the anger, fear, and feralness bled from her. "Oh, Tom. It's over."

He wondered how she could say that when there were still cries that filled the night, still houses that burned, but then he realized that she wasn't talking about tonight's disaster.

Paris walked toward her and held out his hand for the weapon. Wordlessly, she gave it to him. He checked the phaser and relief washed over him. It was still set to stun. Trima hadn't killed these people. She'd be glad of that. At least he hoped she'd be glad.

Shapes ran at them out of the darkness. They moved in a precise military trot, and beside Tom, Trima tensed.

"Shoot them! Shoot them!" she cried, seizing Paris's arm and shaking it.

"It's okay," said Tom. "These are the good guys."

It was Chakotay, Ezbai, and the others who had not allied with Ioni. "We found and neutralized three of them," gasped Ezbai, "but Ioni is still missing."

Out of the darkness came a rock. It struck Ezbai on the side of the head and he sank down at once.

Paris whirled, targeted, fired. It was instinct. Yurula might be armed only with rocks, but properly thrown, a rock could kill as surely as a phaser. Yurula went down without a sound.

"Ezbai!" cried Chakotay.

Ezbai moaned, but he was conscious. "Find . . . Ioni," he gasped. "Have to stop . . . the killing . . . our fault. You were right, Chakotay. Fear, and hate . . . kill us all."

"It's not just your fault," came a voice from the darkness. Soliss stepped forward and knelt to examine his wife. He looked up at Paris, at the weapon the young man held, and then turned to regard Ezbai. "It's the Culilann's fault as well."

"We'll argue about who's at fault later," said Chakotay. "Tom, you're with me."

"But Trima's the target," Paris protested.

"I was the target," said Trima, "but now the whole village is. Stop whoever is doing this, Tom. Stop them right now."

He looked into her eyes, saw the determination there, and nodded. She would be all right. For the moment.

"No rocks at Trima," Paris told Soliss. The man smiled, sadly.

"No rocks at anyone," he assured Tom.

Chakotay and Paris moved swiftly in the darkness, in search of a killer. Inwardly, Chakotay grieved. Why did it always seem to have to come down to this? If only he could believe what the Implementer so clearly had chosen to believe, that dark matter was at the heart of the conflict.

But it wasn't. Hate was.

Instinct told him to move silently, stealthily. But the overwhelming roar of the blazing village would drown out any noise he could possibly make other than a shout, and the false, wild shadows of the flickering flames would do as much to disguise him from another's eyes as reveal him.

Ioni was the only one at large now. The Recovery team had found and stopped her compatriots. Whatever loyalty they had had toward her had disappeared under Chakotay's angry interrogations, and they had all been quick to agree that she had been the ringleader. Chakotay privately did not doubt it, but he would let Ezbai and the Implementer reserve judgment until after a fair trial.

Paris moved quietly behind him, his shadow. Soot and sweat were the most notable parts of his features now, and his clothing had been burned. Chakotay knew how weak the ensign was, but also knew that Tom had an inner strength that he was calling upon and that would not fail him until this final task was done.

Carefully, they moved from hut to hut, from pool of shadow to pool of shadow, searching for movement, a flash of pale blue skin showing white in the night. One by one the huts were collapsing, becoming so much tinder. There was a chance, a good one, that Ioni had already fled into the shelter of the surrounding jungle. It would hide her and her trespasses, and she had a weapon to defend herself against the other beasts that dwelt there.

But something told him she wouldn't. Ioni acted out of arrogance and hate, and such motivations seldom allowed for fleeing into the night. She would be here, and she would kill or be killed.

Glance into the hut, see if there was anyone, murderer or victim, inside, move on. Chakotay's mouth was parched from the smoke and he knew Tom wasn't feeling any better.

There were only a few more huts remaining. Chakotay tensed for the confrontation.

Ioni's skin was almost blistering before her eyes. How had it gone so wrong? They were several armed Alilann against a slumbering, unarmed village. It ought to have been ease itself to wipe this place off the map.

The huts would catch so quickly the occupants wouldn't even awaken as they burned to death. The only one who might be a problem was the Culil, who might be awake praying to their false gods, and who would rouse the others. Ioni had killed enough of them to be able to identify their huts by now. She had dispatched the former Culil easily enough; his replacement ought to be no problem at all.

Except the Culil's replacement *had* been a problem. An enormous problem, a deadly problem. She had met Ioni at the door with some kind of weapon of her own. Ioni barely had time to dive to the side before the younger woman fired. What was a Culil doing with so technologically advanced a weapon? Ioni tucked and rolled and came up shooting.

"I don't want to hurt you!" the Culil was crying. As if Ioni would believe such a thing. The Culilann hated the Alilann as much as the Alilann hated the Culilann. This particular battle lost, and badly too, Ioni had fled into the night to kill what she could, burn what she could, and wonder how things had gone so wrong.

She had still thought they could escape and rejoin the others until Chakotay and Paris had come bursting through the jungle, with that idiot Ezbai hard on their heels. And that was when Ioni realized it was all over, all but the dying. For she would not go back and face trial, face condemnation and punishment, for doing the right thing: killing Culilann barbarians.

It was hard to breathe, now. She felt faint and wondered if she would lose consciousness before the flames claimed her. She set her teeth. She would die like a soldier, awake, conscious, tasting the pain.

Tears filled her eyes and poured down her cheeks. She couldn't see. Was it just the roiling smoke, or were there figures in the black hole that was the doorway?

"Ioni!" It was Chakotay. "Come out! This hut's about to go!"

She scuttled backward, ignoring the heat, the pain. She did not reply, but thought, *Let it burn.*

Her weapon was hot in her hands, but she lifted it and fired. Her aim was off and from their voices she knew she had missed both of them. It was so hard to see, so hard to breathe—

"I'm coming in for you," called Chakotay.

"No! You'll die if you do!" she screamed, her voice raw.

"You'll die if I don't," he replied.

Ioni propped her weapon up on her knees, settling it in the valley between them. It was so hot she couldn't hold it anymore, and it kept slipping.

The shadow in the doorway moved closer.

Ioni fired.

INTERLUDE

WHEN THE PRESENCE APPEARED AGAIN, THE ENTITY WEL-
comed it. The benevolent, alien Presence permeated the
Entity, told it that it had succeeded in its quest, and that
it was time to safely put away the dark matter it had
gathered. Soon, the Presence would come to claim it.

The Entity expressed its gratitude for the experiences
it had undergone while gathering the dark matter. It had
been enriching, and had completed the Entity. For now
it understood so much of what had been strange to it.
Memories were recovered. Holes were filled. Wounds
it had not realized it had were healed, and all because it
had helped the Presence help every universe that had
ever existed.

When the Presence informed the Entity of its destination, the Entity was overjoyed. Full circle, it would
come now. It sped off to surrender the dark matter to

those who were also engaged in a quest to gather it. Eventually, it would all be harvested by the Presence, but for now, the Entity had a destination.

It had a name. A place which had once been its home, to which it now rushed aflame with delight at once again seeing those it had loved so dearly.

Voyager.

CHAPTER

16

Janeway rose and strode down to the screen. Kaleh had not cut off communications, but the screen showed only beeping, flashing consoles and the interior of the ship.

"Kaleh!" she cried. There was no response. Janeway whirled to look at Tuvok, the question plain on her face.

"Sensors indicate there are only two life signs aboard the *Talvath*. Both are unconscious and weakening."

"Beam them to sickbay. Janeway to the Doctor. You've got a pair of Romulan patients."

"Now is not a good time," came the Doctor's irritated voice. "I'm presently in Engineering, assisting Lieutenant Torres with erecting a forcefield around the disintegrating warp-bubble universe."

"Doctor, can't the engineers handle Engineering?"

"Not when it involves the same delicate technology I

am using to erect a forcefield around Khala," he said. "I'll return to sickbay the moment I'm through."

"We do need him, Captain."

The Doctor wasn't available. Paris was gone, and she couldn't spare Kim. Janeway's mind went back to when they had discovered the Romulans on board. The Doctor had requested a hand with the autopsy, but she couldn't spare any of her senior staff.

"I'll have Ensign Campbell assist you," she had said.

"She's the transporter officer!" the Doctor had complained.

"She's got two good ears, she can learn," Janeway had replied.

Now she tapped her combadge. "Ensign Campbell, report to sickbay. You'll be in charge of welcoming our visitors." She turned to Telek. "They need you down in Engineering, Dr. R'Mor."

He nodded and hurried into the turbolift.

Ensign Lyssa Campbell did not want to be the only one in sickbay when a pair of severely injured Romulans materialized. Like everyone else on the ship, she had of course undergone the rudimentary emergency field medical training required of all cadets at the Academy. And sure, she'd helped the Doctor out once or twice before.

Key word: "helped."

As the doors hissed open and she strode into sickbay, she saw that her patients had already arrived and were lying unconscious on the beds. They both looked bad. The male had burns on his hands and face and what looked to be a deep wound in the abdomen. The female—God, she looked fragile—was bleeding copiously from a large cut on her ridged forehead. Green blood. Lyssa had never seen that.

"Okay," she told herself, needing to hear a voice, even her own. "Okay, this guy looks the worst. Medical tricorder, medical tricorder—here it is."

She found it and began analyzing the patient.

And then she crumpled to the floor.

Swaying slightly, Jekri Kaleh surveyed the body of the blond young human female. Knowledge of the Vulcan nerve pinch was proving to be very useful.

She spared a moment for Verrak, critically surveying his wound. The burns could be treated with a dermal regenerator. The wound in his abdomen looked bad at first, but a quick examination revealed that the cut, although bloody, was shallow and did not affect any vital organs. The blood was already slowing; he would not lose much more. He would survive.

She had to move quickly. How to find her quarry? Her gaze fell on the limp form of the ensign. On her left breast was what Jekri recognized as a communication device. Romulans had voice-activated computer systems. Did the Federation?

Jekri again knelt and tentatively touched the badge. "Computer," she said cautiously.

"Awaiting request," came a cool, crisp female voice.

Jekri smiled. "Locate Telek R'Mor."

"Telek R'Mor is in the turbolift."

"What is his destination?"

"Engineering."

"On which deck is sickbay located?"

"Deck five."

"Which level is Main Engineering?"

"Main Engineering is located on deck eleven."

Jekri sprinted out the door.

* * *

Jekri's heart was racing from the exertion, but she forced her breathing to slow as she flattened herself against a bulkhead. The turbolift door hissed open, and Telek R'Mor emerged.

She sprang quickly, pinning one arm painfully behind his back and locking the other one around his throat.

"You are coming with me, Dr. R'Mor. I confess it would be easier if you were conscious, but I can carry you if I have to. Do you understand?"

He nodded as best he could. She released him, but remained tense. He outweighed her, and she was injured from the recent battle and weakened by her time in prison, but she knew she could take him down if he fled or fought.

R'Mor gazed into her eyes, and saw her confidence. Recognized it. "They probably already know you are not in sickbay," he said.

"Then we must make haste. Let's go."

She had ascertained the quickest way to get to the nearest transporter room. Placing one hand on Telek's back, within easy reach of his shoulder and neck area, she walked him back into the turbolift.

"We are on the same side, Kaleh," he said. "We both wish to save our people."

"You are the key, R'Mor. If I bring you back with me, the Empress will listen."

"She already listens to the chairman of the Tal Shiar."

"I am no such person." She glanced up at him. "You can see."

He nodded, taking in her gaunt features, her bony body. He saw. He knew.

The doors hissed open. They raced down the corridor and headed into the transporter room.

"Get on the pad," she told him. He obeyed. Jekri

stared at the console. She could not decipher it. She pressed first one button, then another. Finally she swore in frustration and pounded her fist on the console.

"Your chances of successfully beaming off the ship would have been better had you not rendered the transporter officer unconscious with a Vulcan nerve pinch," came a calm, masculine voice.

Jekri looked up to see a tall, dark-skinned Vulcan. He pointed a phaser directly at her, and to either side were two men also clad in mustard and black.

Despite her chagrin at being thwarted, Jekri could not suppress a sudden, quick rush of pleasure. A Vulcan. If only there were time for discussion. There were so many questions she wished to ask.

"You will accompany us to sickbay. The captain has many questions for you."

"I think it's working," said B'Elanna, cautiously. It was an interesting conundrum. She could program the Doctor, but there were some things he could program better than she could.

"It's getting the resonance correct that's the tricky part," he said, running a tricorder over Khala. It had all been the alien woman's idea. She had theorized that, just as her cells were dematerializing in this universe, so was the warp-bubble universe. A shield around her would trap the cells, for the time being at least; a shield around the warp-bubble universe might render it more stable.

The thought that she would have to go around with a shield over her body from now until who knew when obviously depressed Khala. Torres could understand. To be in love, and not be able to touch one's beloved, possibly not even to say goodbye—that was something Torres wouldn't wish on anyone.

The field around Khala was invisible, and wrapped around her almost as tightly as a garment. She could continue to move objects, input data. The field was holding, as far as the Doctor was able to tell. Now to test it on the warp-bubble universe.

Torres took a deep breath, forcing knotted muscles to relax, as the Doctor turned toward the warp core. His holographic fingers moved deftly over the controls. There was a sharp, crackling sound, and for a wild instant Torres thought, *That's it, it's over, this is the end.*

"Please confirm," said the Doctor, his dark eyes on the warp core.

Torres checked, and for a moment felt weak with relief. "It's back to normal." She turned and favored the Doctor with a grin. "Well done. You make a passable engineer, for a doctor."

He preened, just a little, then headed to sickbay.

Janeway had briefed the Doctor while he was in the turbolift as to the escape. His captain was there, arms folded, when the Doctor entered. An embarrassed-looking Campbell was busy running the medical tricorder over the male Romulan, who was just now regaining consciousness.

"Are you all right, Ensign?" asked the Doctor, taking the tricorder from her.

"Nothing bruised but the ego," she managed, smiling ruefully.

"No one expected a Romulan to know a Vulcan attack method," said the Doctor. Even as he spoke, the door hissed open and Tuvok entered, escorting their wayward Romulan.

"Jekri Kaleh," said Janeway crisply. "And here I thought we could talk like civilized people."

Weak and injured as she was, the other woman shot her a look of such hauteur that Janeway was impressed. She had spirit, that much was for certain.

Tuvok assisted Jekri onto the bed. The woman snatched her hand away and clambered on by herself.

"Why did you try to kidnap Telek R'Mor?" Janeway asked.

The woman did not reply at first. Finally, she seemed to reach a decision.

"I will tell you all, Captain Janeway of the Federation. If I am wrong in my trust of you, then soon nothing will matter. I was once the chairman of the Tal Shiar. In that office, it was my duty to attempt to retrieve your vessel and the presumed traitor, Telek R'Mor. Since the time when he—disappeared, I have learned a great deal about a being who calls himself a Shepherd. His name is—"

"Lhiau," interrupted Janeway. "And let me guess. You began to suspect that he wasn't what he seemed. That he was not helping your people, he was using them to further his own ends."

Only a slight widening of silver eyes conveyed Jekri's surprise. She nodded her dark head and winced at the pain the movement engendered.

"Don't do that," the Doctor remonstrated. He began to treat her lacerated scalp.

"Correct, Captain. After our last encounter with you, which destroyed thirteen warbirds, I began to suspect that there was something dangerous involved. Lhiau tried to blame Dr. R'Mor, but I wondered. The more I learned, the more obstacles were flung up in my path. Finally, I must have learned too much, or have been close to stumbling upon something. I became a target of the Family of the Blade."

At Janeway's lifted eyebrow, Telek explained, "Formally trained assassins. They do not exist, if you understand what I am saying."

"I do," said Janeway, grimly. "Go on."

"I thwarted the assassination attempt by using—" Jekri stopped abruptly. She looked over at Tuvok. "There are people on my planet who believe that reunification with the Vulcan people is desirable. I studied Vulcan meditation techniques from one such woman. That is where I learned the nerve pinch, as well as ways to block my thoughts from being influenced by Lhiau. He could not corrupt me mentally, so he arranged for me to be branded a traitor. I was imprisoned, but thanks to Verrak and some others whom I do not know, I escaped."

Janeway must have looked skeptical, because Telek R'Mor, who had no cause to love Jekri Kaleh, said, "Look well at her, Captain. Look at her body, her face. She has been tortured." He smiled without humor. "I recognize the signs."

Surprised by Telek's words, Janeway again regarded Kaleh. The woman flushed green, but did not look away. Now that Janeway looked, she saw. Telek was right. Granted, she would not put it past the Romulans to torture one of their own to make a lie seem more convincing, but what would be the point? And the last Janeway heard, studying to learn Vulcan mental disciplines—or the ever-useful nerve pinch—would have been enough grounds for a high-ranking Romulan to be interrogated.

"Our Empress was not as fortunate. She is utterly his pawn now. But there are others, who mistrust Lhiau, who were willing to follow where I would lead." Jekri looked at the floor. "Captain Idran was a good friend. The *Para'tar* was a noble ship." When she looked up again, her silver eyes almost glowed with intensity. "Their deaths must count for something."

"Your suspicions were right," Janeway said. "Lhiau's purpose isn't to help the Romulans. It's to make you destroy yourselves, and take the whole universe along with you. The more dark matter the Romulans use, the more the balance tips. It's my understanding that we are pretty close to the end right now. We've been trying to harness the dark matter, render it harmless. We've met the other side, the good Shepherds. It seems that they have been guarding the balance that keeps the universes—all of them—intact. Lhiau wants to tip the balance and destroy everything."

Jekri seemed to believe Janeway. "But why? Why destroy everything? Wouldn't he die as well?"

"And if he had the power to do such things," put in Jekri's companion, now sitting up, "why would he try to trick us into doing it for him?"

"All good questions," came a melodious voice that made Janeway's skin prickle and her heart speed up. A warm, purple glow filled sickbay, faint at first, then growing in intensity until Janeway had to shield her eyes. When at last the glow faded, Janeway knew whom she would see.

Tialin stood, smiling with that heart-calming benevolence. Janeway felt the tension ebb from her body.

"Questions," Tialin continued, "that it is time for me to answer."

CHAPTER
17

"WHO ARE YOU?" KALEH DEMANDED. "YOU CANNOT BE Dammik R'Kel, though you wear her face and form."

"My name is Tialin. I am of Lhiau's people, and I wish to stop his terrible deeds as much as, nay, more than, you do."

She fell silent, and Jekri Kaleh's face suddenly went blank. Then she shook her head, as if waking from a dream. New respect was on her face as she regarded Tialin.

"I understand," she said, and so did Janeway. Tialin had telepathically informed Jekri of everything that had happened to date. Janeway wished that the Shepherd had shown such consideration with them earlier, but let it go. No doubt Tialin had her reasons.

"Time grows short. Lhiau is, when all is said and done, a Shepherd, though a renegade. He will not violate the Oath that we all took, back when the universes were young. He will not actively destroy life. But he can trick others into destroying themselves."

"I have been," said Jekri firmly, "a *veruul.*"

"No," said the other Romulan. While they had been talking, the Doctor had been busy healing their visitors' wounds. Now the Romulan male, a handsome young man, rose and went to Kaleh, though Janeway noticed he stopped short of actually touching her. "You have been wise, Jekri."

"As have all of you," said Tialin. She cocked her head, her eyes unfocused, as if listening and watching something Janeway could not see or hear. A faint smile curved her lips. "It is time you have arrived, my friend," she said, softly, with great love.

The Entity rushed toward Voyager *filled with joy such as she had never known. What a precious thing it would be, to come home to the people who had freed her, then loved her, then let her fly to her true destiny. How fulfilling it would be to, for a time at least, assume that small, female form into which she had been born, and speak with them of all the marvels she had witnessed.*

She had lacked control, the last time she had been with them. Her powers were overwhelming her. They were the master, not she. Now, she was complete. She had attained mastery. She had the vast comprehension that this transformation had granted her, and, thanks to Tialin's Presence, she had gone on this quest not only to recover the traces of the dangerous dark matter but also to remember her own identity. She knew who she was, at last.

How satisfying it would be to say hello and then farewell, but not forever, to people whom she had not been able to before. She envisioned chatting with the

Doctor, sharing her medical knowledge; eating Neelix's food and simply loving his sweet presence. And Captain Janeway, her mother and friend. Now, she could thank this remarkable human.

There it was! Oh, sweet home, forgotten and remembered with new poignancy. The Entity swept down, penetrating shields and metal alike with carefree ease, flying through corridors down which she had once walked. They were in sickbay, a place she knew, she knew! In she came, and—

The Entity's joy turned to icy horror as the gentle tendrils she had sent forth found something dreadful.

They would not welcome her. They would fear her. They would be afraid that she would come filled with fury as she had once before, to march through the ship leaving death in her wake. No, no, this was not she! She loved these people. She would never harm them!

You would not, *came Tialin's thoughts.* But another you would. And has.

And then the Entity understood. There were universes upon universes, and there was more than one destiny for every being. This was not her Voyager, her Janeway, her Neelix, her Tuvok. This was a Voyager from another universe, one in which she, the Entity, had not ascended to a greater height of knowledge and compassion, but had descended to depths of terror, pain, and rage. In this universe, when she returned, she had come with vengeance in her heart.

It was bitter, but the Entity understood. She understood so much, now. She would not be granted the sought-after reunion, not be welcomed and embraced and fueled with love.

I am sorry for your pain, dear one, *said Tialin in her*

mind, but who better to help these people in their quest than one who loves them so?

Had she assumed a mortal form again, she would have blinked back tears from large blue eyes. But she had no form, and would not, not yet, not here. Even through the sorrow that the other incarnation had caused, the Entity knew she would not have shirked this duty had she known.

There was time to fulfill her duty without hurting them further. Or so she thought. Certainly Janeway, the Doctor, and the other humans present did not notice the Entity's presence. But even as she swept from sickbay, she saw Tuvok's head come up, saw his eyes narrow. Ah, she ought to have known. She could not hide it from him. Unable to help herself, she brushed his regulated Vulcan thoughts with sad, sweet affection, then reluctantly left for Engineering.

Tuvok blinked. He must have been in error. It could not be. But Tialin was smiling, holding his gaze with her own, and he knew he had not been mistaken.

He said softly, to himself, "Kes."

The shield was holding. Which was a good thing on many counts.

"We've got to start gathering up the dark matter stirred up from that last battle," said Torres. This was beginning to become all too familiar.

"Lieutenant," said Seven. "The warp-bubble universe is expanding."

Torres ran to Seven's console to look. Sure enough, it was growing, right before their eyes.

"There's twice as much dark matter in there as before—no, three times—" Torres fell silent. It was as if the warp-bubble universe was a jar, and someone was filling it right to the brim. More and more dark matter poured into the bubble, and it kept growing, changing size to accommodate the sudden inflow.

"What the hell is going on?" Torres cried.

Suddenly That Damned Ball emitted a terrible sound. It had been loud before, but now Torres thought her eardrums might burst from the dreadful screeching. Light filled Engineering, terrible, blinding light, and then it was gone.

"Lieutenant Torres," said Seven, "the orb has disappeared."

Torres blinked, frantically forcing her eyes to adjust. Seven was right.

"So has the warp-bubble universe," said Khala worriedly.

Oh God, oh God, thought Torres frantically. "Engineering to Janeway!"

"Relax, B'Elanna," came her captain's voice. "The warp-bubble universe has disappeared, but all the dark matter's safely in the orb. Tialin has come to take it back."

Janeway thought she had never seen anything as beautiful as the orb, held safely in Tialin's capable hands. Even though she knew what was at stake, and how fragile this balance between existence and nonexistence was, Janeway felt they had a fighting chance now.

Reading her thoughts, Tialin said, "All our energy had been taken up in attempting to undo the damage that Lhiau has caused." She hesitated, then said, "Even we made mistakes, Captain Janeway. But you are right. There is still a chance."

"Mistakes?" Janeway smiled thinly. "I can't imagine you making mistakes."

All at once, Tialin looked haunted. "We are not omnipotent, as I told your Tom Paris once before. We made our mistakes. Even as we tried to undo wrongs, we caused such wrongs ourselves. You were witness, Captain, to the first time we tried to correct the imbalance by transferring matter from one universe into another."

For a moment, Janeway had no idea what Tialin was talking about. Then her eyes widened with horror as she understood. Her mind's eye filled with the image of the planet on which she had first met Tialin. It had once been a Class M planet, with oceans and clouds and a population of two billion humanoids. She remembered seeing it wink first out of, then back into, existence. She remembered the volcanoes, the radiation, staring at bodies of pale purple-skinned humanoids who died in the instant from one step to another. They had called it the Ghost Planet.

Tialin nodded sadly. "We thought that if we could move the entire planet safely into another universe, it would counter the imbalance more quickly. We did not know what destruction our well-meaning gesture would bring. Thus it was that we learned, to our terrible regret, that we could only move a small amount of matter from one universe into the other at any given time."

"Khala, Chakotay, and Paris," said Janeway, her throat tight. She was filled with rage at Tialin. Two billion people! And yet she knew that it had been an accident. A horrible, soul-chilling one, but an accident nonetheless. What Lhiau was planning was nothing short of murder. And he would not stop with a mere two billion lives.

Tialin nodded again. "And even they will not be safe

in their new universes forever, as you have discovered. All depends upon the Romulans halting themselves. If they persist, then everything is doomed."

She turned to the three Romulans. They all stood straight and tall, giving Tialin their full attention. For a moment, Janeway thought how similar they looked. Fit bodies, pointed ears, ridged foreheads, sleek, short, black hair. Similar in mind-set too, to a certain degree. The Romulan Empire was all to each of them. But how different they were, too. She had not spoken much to the male Romulan who had arrived with Kaleh, but she knew that Telek and Kaleh were as different as night and day.

Individuals. In the end, no matter how the mind tried to lump people into categories, they persisted in being individuals.

"It is time for the three of you to travel back to your own space and time," said Tialin. "I will assist you when the time is right. Make your farewells, and then prepare to open the wormhole to the Alpha Quadrant one last time."

She turned again to Janeway. "Captain, I understand how distressed you must be. You had hoped that Telek R'Mor's wormhole technology would be able to send you and your crew home, to *your* rightful space and time. I regret having taken this hope away. But the wormhole technology is in truth largely powered by Shepherd technology. Every time it opens—"

"More mutated dark matter is created," Janeway finished. "I understand." She lifted her chin and narrowed her eyes. "Don't worry about us. We'll find our way home, one day."

Tialin smiled mysteriously, but said nothing.

Telek R'Mor stepped over to Janeway. They gazed

into one another's eyes for a moment, neither saying anything. It was Telek who first broke the silence.

"Captain Kathryn Janeway of the United Federation of Planets," he said slowly, with great respect, "it has been the honor of my life to have worked with you on this noble cause. I wish I could have been instrumental in helping you find your home."

"You helped with something much bigger than that, Telek," said Janeway softly. "It has been an honor for me, for everyone on this ship, as well. You do your people proud."

He inclined his head graciously. "As I have ever sought to do." He hesitated. "I do not know what fate awaits me. I may still die the death of a traitor. I may live to a ripe old age, and entertain you in my home one day when our two governments are allies. After what I have witnessed these last few weeks, I have come to realize that, truly, anything is possible."

Janeway's blue eyes suddenly stung. Even if Telek R'Mor was pardoned and lived out his life as if this incident had never happened, even if by some miracle the Romulans and the Federation chose to be allies in science and war, she would never have the simple delight of visiting him on Romulus. That was indeed not possible, his hopeful words to the contrary. He was a dead man, standing, living, before her. He died years ago. She would never see him again. She realized that this was much, much more than a simple goodbye.

Had he been human, she would have embraced him. But she did not know if such a gesture would be appropriate or even welcomed. So she simply stood, gazing into the dark, compassionate eyes of someone she regarded as a dear friend.

Telek extended a hand. Janeway grasped it, and brought her other hand up to hold it, briefly, in both of hers.

"I look forward to reminiscing over a cup of tea with you in a few years, Telek R'Mor," she lied with all the sincerity she could muster.

He smiled, and squeezed. Then the warmth between her hands was gone, and he stood shoulder to shoulder with the other two members of his own race.

"Convey my regards to Torres, Seven, and Khala, if you would," said Telek. "I fear I will not be able to do so myself."

"Consider it done," said Janeway. She hoped her voice did not sound as thick as it did in her own ears.

Jekri Kaleh's silver gaze flitted over them all, then she did something that utterly shocked Janeway. She lifted her right hand and spread the four fingers apart into a V. Turning to Tuvok, she said without the slightest trace of mockery, "Live long and prosper, Vulcan Tuvok."

Tuvok raised a dark eyebrow, then returned the gesture. "Peace and long life, Jekri Kaleh."

Then they were gone, all four of them—Telek, Jekri, her companion, and Tialin.

"How will we know if they succeed?" asked Ensign Campbell.

CHAPTER

18

TELEK, VERRAK, AND JEKRI FOUND THEMSELVES IN THE
small central command area of the tiny *Talvath*. For just
a moment, Jekri was caught off guard by the instanta-
neous transport, but she recovered command quickly.

"R'Mor, you should be able to trace the last wormhole coordinates. Plot them, and let us return."

"The wormhole will open right onto the front lines,"
protested Verrak.

"Do you have a better idea?" She asked the question
sarcastically, but Telek R'Mor interrupted her.

"I do," he said. "Look."

There were coordinates already entered. And a message. Jekri reached over and tapped the flashing red
light. Tialin's voice filled the close quarters.

"Follow the coordinates I have placed in your command bank," she said. "Then, when you have arrived in

216

orbit around Romulus, I will see to it that you have an audience with the Empress. Do not fear for your vessel—it will not be taken. Be prepared. Lhiau can be very persuasive."

Jekri set her jaw. She knew all about Lhiau and did not need anyone's warning. She only hoped that there was something left of the Empress she could reach.

Alone with the Empress in her luxurious throne room, Lhiau could barely restrain his excitement. In a few moments, the Empress would give the command to attack. He was feeling good about the present situation, and more than a little proud of himself for turning what could have been disaster into about-to-be-realized triumph.

As the loathed Jekri Kaleh had suspected, this was not his true form. The limited minds of these flesh-encased beings could not begin to comprehend the Shepherds in all their grandeur. They would need to evolve a great deal more before they would even have the faintest idea of what Lhiau's people were, and they were not going to get that opportunity.

Lhiau was going to make them destroy themselves.

He reached into a large, silver bowl and grasped a piece of fruit. He took a big bite, enjoying the sensuous tickle of juice on his tongue, and felt the liquid dribbling down his chin. There were benefits to assuming this form. Many benefits indeed. But now, with victory almost within his grasp, Lhiau found he was wearying of exploring the pleasures of the flesh and anxious to have the deed done.

If only he had not sworn the Oath, it would all be so much easier. And quicker.

But he had taken the Oath, and he was a Shepherd, and although Jekri Kaleh would be shocked at the notion, Lhiau had a great deal of honor. Among those who deserved honor, of course, which was his own kind. He would never break the Oath, never encourage any of the renegades who allied with him to break it.

He would make these ambitious, limited, power-hungry, pitiful mortals do it for him.

How easy it had been at first. He'd studied the nearly countless species of every universe for a long time before deciding on this little quadrant of this little universe. The Romulan hostility toward anyone not of their race was convenient indeed. Their famed cloaking technology was even handier for Lhiau's purposes. And when he had discovered that one of what passed for scientists among this species was dabbling in wormhole technology, well, Lhiau's choice had practically been made for him.

He would miss the Empress, he had to admit, but not that much. She stood, arms folded across her chest, clad in the red that became her so well, proud eyes fastened on the screen.

Suddenly the screen blipped. Lhiau frowned. The face of Stahl, commander of the invasion fleet, filled the screen of the throne room.

"Empress, I have dire news to report. The *Talvath* is gone. It opened a wormhole and disappeared. Four of our warbirds gave chase—"

"What?" shrieked the Empress. Veins stood out on her lovely, long neck. Lhiau, too, was shocked. What had happened? Without the *Talvath* to open dozens of wormholes, each one spewing forth dark matter into this universe, the balance might not be tipped far enough quickly enough. He knew, of course, that

Tialin was busily about the task of trying to stop him. Every moment that passed gave her another chance to do so.

Stahl looked wretched. "There was a transfer of personnel right before it happened. It appeared to be authorized, but now we realize that the code was falsified."

"Kaleh," snarled Lhiau. He was beside himself with fury. Curse the damned Oath! Without it, it would have been child's play to make the little chairman's heart burst with a single thought. But no, he had to waste precious time in falsifying charges, planting suspicion in the Empress's mind. Thank goodness the Praetor had obviously wanted no trouble.

The news had come a few hours earlier of Kaleh's escape. No one knew where she was. He had let it go, thinking there couldn't possibly be enough time for her to thwart him. But now, now . . . !

The Empress turned to him. "You think so?"

He nodded angrily, his thoughts racing. How to salvage this?

With a visible effort, the Empress calmed herself, though her eyes still blazed and her mouth was tight with anger. "You said four ships followed the *Talvath?*"

"Yes, Excellency," said Stahl. "Their commanders are most trustworthy. They will force the science vessel to return."

"I hope for your sake you are right," snapped the Empress. "Stand down and await my next orders. We cannot proceed without the *Talvath*. A delay will not make much difference, though I confess I am eager for battle."

"As am I, Excellency," said Stahl.

Lhiau couldn't believe what he was hearing. He had

to think fast. Delay would give Tialin the upper hand. The Romulan fleet had to strike now, had to operate their cloaks, had to fire and be destroyed and spread more dark matter into this universe before it was too late.

"Excellency," he said, hastening to the Empress and placing his hands on her shoulders. "You do not need the *Talvath*. Your mighty fleet will overwhelm the Federation without it."

She turned to him, the full force of her anger brushing aside the subtle tendrils of his telepathy. "Of course we need the *Talvath*! Do not underestimate the power of the Federation and its allies. Unless we strike with an unexpected, crushing blow at the outset, we have no chance. The Federation will recover and come after us with their full amassed forces. The Empire will be crippled and perhaps even defeated. We must see Earth and Vulcan destroyed before anything else, and the wormholes are the key to that!"

He nuzzled her neck, in the fashion he knew she liked. "You underestimate your might, Great Leader. The Romulans will crush the Federation—"

She shrugged him off. He was utterly shocked.

"I will and have sent soldiers to die, but never for a worthless cause," she snapped. "A few hours, a day, what difference does waiting make?" She turned again to Commander Stahl. "You will await my command to attack. We will wait for the return of the *Talvath*. If it does not return," she added, turning to Lhiau, "then I am certain that our good friend Ambassador Lhiau will give us another device for another ship. Dismissed."

Lhiau gaped, then grew angry again. "There is no time for this nonsense!"

"There is nothing *but* time!" cried the Empress. "You asked for help in defeating your enemies. How can we do so if we are crushed and broken?"

Lhiau had no answer. He found himself, like a careless spider, impossibly snared in the lies of his own making.

"Excellency," interrupted Stahl.

"I dismissed you, did I not?" she replied.

"Yes, but there is another problem. The ships are suffering from structural breakdowns of some sort. Systems are shorting out and even some of the crew have reported feeling ill or displaying inappropriate emotions."

"The normal glitches and tensions of a fleet before battle," said Lhiau quickly.

"I would like to take this opportunity to investigate further," Stahl barreled on, ignoring Lhiau. "I do not wish to raise false fears, but the problems we are seeing are similar to those that happened to the ships we sent after *Voyager*."

"I thought it was the wormholes that damaged the ships," said the Empress slowly, turning to regard Lhiau thoughtfully. "That's what you said—that something R'Mor had done was responsible. Something that you assured me you had corrected."

"It is the dark-matter cloaks which are causing the problems," came a male voice.

The Empress and Lhiau whirled at the same moment. Lhiau stiffened, horrified. Standing before him were the four people he wished least in this or any universe to see: Jekri Kaleh, Verrak, Telek R'Mor, and his nemesis, Tialin.

In silence, thousands of light-years away and twenty years into the future, the crew of *Voyager* stared at the viewscreen. Janeway's fists were clenched so hard her hands began to ache, but she couldn't seem to relax. The fate of all the universes was at stake. *Voyager*'s efforts had bought the time for this final scene to be played out.

She desperately hoped it would be sufficient.

The Empress quickly recovered from her shock. "How did you get in here?" she demanded.

"I brought them," Tialin said simply, as if that would answer everything. "I am Tialin, of the Shepherds. You have been duped, Your Excellency. Duped by a master of deception, the renegade Lhiau. Listen to these people, Empress. Standing before you are no traitors, but quite possibly the most loyal servants you have ever had."

The Empress narrowed her eyes. "Once, I would have believed you, stranger, but they have since turned on me."

"How?" asked Jekri, stepping forward. "Before Lhiau came, you trusted all of us implicitly. Think, Empress! Remove the cloud Lhiau has placed over your mind!"

"He asked for help in destroying his enemies, but never told you who they were," said Telek urgently. "He gave you technology, but would not permit you to analyze it. When disaster occurred, suddenly it was someone else's fault—mine, or Jekri's. Never his. We have taken his word for everything, and all we have to show for it are destroyed warbirds and dead Romulans!"

"Don't listen to the traitors!" Lhiau rushed toward the Empress. If he could touch her, he might be able to penetrate the wall that anger and logic were beginning to erect around her thoughts. But she stepped away from him. He could see doubt forming in her face.

"We, the Shepherds who have been guardians of a delicate balance, are the enemies he would have you destroy—by destroying yourselves. By destroying your entire universe," said Tialin.

The Empress blinked. "It—it does not make sense—"

"It would if he had a little hole into which he could crawl when this was done," said Jekri. "Empress, the Shepherds won't be affected. They don't live in any universe we understand. It doesn't matter to Lhiau what happens outside of that hole. He knows that it will just begin again—without any of us."

"Madness!" Lhiau implored the Empress. "They are speaking madness to you. Send the ships now, Empress. Now, before they try to stop you!"

"They are doing nothing save talking," the Empress observed. "You are the one pushing me to impulsive action. Why is that, Lhiau?"

He stared, wild-eyed, at the Empress, then at his enemies. He could not think. The lies would not come. He had one chance left. He shoved the Empress to the floor and with a thought erected an invisible but impenetrable barrier between himself and the others.

He ordered his body to shift, and it obeyed. Lhiau, now wearing the face and body of the Empress herself, stepped forward and pressed a button. The face of the commander appeared.

"Begin the invasion!" shrieked Lhiau, in the Empress's voice.

Stahl looked unhappy, but he would obey his Empress. Lhiau knew he would. At that moment, Lhiau heard a humming noise. He knew what it was and turned quickly, but not quickly enough.

Several dozen centurions materialized in the throne room. They appeared around the fallen Empress, encircling her, protecting her. One helped her to her feet even as the others fired.

Lhiau could not be harmed by the weapons, but they distracted him. His concentration slipped. Energy fire ripped through the borrowed image he wore, and he could feel the shape he had assumed shifting back and forth, from the Empress to the masculine body he had imagined for himself. Over the shriek of weapons firing, Lhiau heard Stahl screaming the Empress's name, heard the Empress's voice lifted in rage. His barrier was swept aside as if from the force of the entire Shepherd race. Invisible hands closed on his shoulders, shoving him hard to the floor. He was not able to move.

Seven of Nine, Khala, Torres, and the whole of Engineering stared at the image that was being played out as if by holograms in front of them. There was no purple light hovering in front of them anymore. Their task was done, and now they had to watch, helpless to interfere.

Oddly, Seven thought of Telek R'Mor and little Naomi Wildman. She wasn't sure why.

It happened so fast that it took Jekri precious seconds to even realize what had occurred. She had never been in battle herself, though she had orchestrated many. The noise, the sudden movements, her own frazzled nerves served to paralyze her for just a moment.

The centurions appeared, forming a protective circle around the Empress. Jekri watched, seeing everything as if in slow motion, as the Empress got to her feet, very pale and clutching one arm in an awkward position. Not only had Lhiau dared lay hands on the Empress, but he had hurt her!

Rage flooded Jekri and she surged forward. The barrier was somehow gone, but someone seized her arm, stopping her.

Snarling, she turned to look up into the face of the Praetor.

"No, Little Dagger," he said. It was only then that the firing stopped. Had the Praetor not grabbed her, Jekri would have rushed headlong right into the line of fire. She'd have been vaporized instantaneously.

She stood, breathing heavily, beside Verrak and Telek R'Mor. Lhiau was on his hands and knees, held there by the delicate-seeming Tialin.

"Excellency, are you all right?" the Praetor asked. Jekri had never been so glad to hear his high-pitched voice in her life.

Obviously shaken, still holding her arm, the Empress nodded. "Your intervention was timely, Praetor," she said, her voice admirably steady. "How fortunate." Once again, Jekri's heart swelled with love and pride for her noble Empress. She had been swayed by Lhiau's powerful mental controls, but in the end, the Empress herself had broken the spell the Shepherd had cast upon her. She was in all respects a worthy leader.

"Not as dependent upon fortune as you might think. I have been watching you, Empress."

Despite her obvious pain, the Empress straightened and frowned. "Spying on me?"

The Praetor inclined his head. "Those words are accurate, though harsh. I never trusted Lhiau. There were many who did not." Now he turned to look at Verrak,

Telek, and Jekri in turn. "I did what I could to help those who were brave enough to openly show their mistrust."

All at once, Jekri realized just how deeply the Praetor had been involved. He had warned her that night of the formal dinner, when the Empress had humiliated her. He had been the mysterious friend who had alerted her to Lhiau's assassination order before Sharibor had had the chance to act on it. He had contacted her after Sharibor's attack, sending the untraceable message culminating with her nickname, "Little Dagger." Other than Verrak, Jekri suspected she had never had a truer friend.

He saw comprehension spread across her face and nodded before returning his attention to the Empress.

"You assisted traitors?" said the Empress.

"Oh, yes," said the Praetor. "We are all technically traitors here. Telek R'Mor, with his family held hostage, still dared tell the *Voyager* crew about their danger, so that the true timeline was not polluted. Jekri had misgivings about Lhiau and was open in her suspicion. She then had the audacity to survive an assassination attempt—oh, Lhiau didn't tell you about that one, did he? When she spoke up against him, suddenly all kinds of charges were levied against her. I know they were false, because I helped make them up. Then I helped to free her. And Verrak, too, would seem to be a traitor."

"I—I do not understand," said the Empress faintly. She had turned pale at the news of the assassination attempt.

"Lhiau knew that the dark-matter cloaks were dangerous," Telek said. "The more we used the technology he gave us, the closer we stepped to annihilating our own universe. He played on our desire for conquest. If it had not been for Tialin and *Voyager,* who have been doing everything they can to gather up this mutated dark matter, Lhiau would not have been stopped."

"You keep talking as if you've stopped me." They all turned to stare at Lhiau. He was kneeling, but there was nothing submissive about him. His face was contorted with rage and he radiated defiance. "I can still bring it about. I can do it with a thought."

"Lhiau!" It was Tialin speaking, but with a different voice, higher and younger-sounding. Jekri blinked. "You have sworn the Oath." A third voice issued from her throat, this one masculine and deep. "Would you betray that Oath? Would you use your powers to destroy these worthy beings?" Still another voice. Jekri realized what was going on. All of the Shepherds were speaking through Tialin.

"We never should have interfered! It was wrong!" For the first time since Jekri had met him, Lhiau's voice was filled not with arrogance and contempt but with raw pain. Whatever he was saying, he truly believed. "There never *was* a balance! It was artificial. We created it. And then we had to keep it, just exactly right, so that these little things which had evolved under these false conditions could continue living their false lives!"

"We had a responsibility," said Tialin in her own voice.

"We never should have put ourselves in a position to *have* that responsibility!" cried Lhiau. "We should have left well enough alone. Chaos is the natural state of things, not this unnatural order that we in our arrogance have imposed!"

Tialin said nothing. Jekri realized with a sinking sense of horror that the Shepherd was listening to

Lhiau's rantings. Would she agree? Would they indeed all be destroyed?

"I was just trying to start over again," said Lhiau, his head sinking down. "Trying to start fresh. To let the universes evolve as they ought to have, since the beginning of time. Since the beginning of our interference."

"Not even we can turn back time," said Tialin gently, in the voice of the young woman. "To kill, to destroy—you would not do that, Lhiau. They have a right to be."

Lhiau's golden head rested on his chest. All the fight seemed to have left him. He looked tired, drained. "No," he said. "I would not break my Oath, even though to do so would be to right a grievous wrong."

To right a wrong. The Entity that had once been a corporeal being by the name of Kes knew all about wrongs done, and the desperate desire to right them. But what Lhiau was contemplating would only add to the wrongs, if wrongs there had been. Perhaps that was not the word. Perhaps misjudgments, errors, miscalculations. An overabundance of compassion, if there was such a thing.

The Entity did not know if it, too, would disappear if all the universes were destroyed. There were questions left still, it would seem. But it knew that people it loved would vanish, and for that it grieved, and feared, and hoped that it would not occur.

Tialin straightened. "I do not agree with Lhiau that what we did was wrong. And I certainly do not think that destroying what exists can possibly do any good. But perhaps it is time to cease our intervention. We, the Shepherds, will retire to that hole you spoke of, Jekri. We will lock ourselves in our own universe, and interfere with yours no longer. Natural chaos, not artificial order, will dictate your futures from this moment on."

She stepped back. Lhiau rose, and Tialin reached for his hand. "Let us go, old friend," she said. "Let us leave the beings of this universe alone, at last."

Lhiau nodded. They embraced, and then their forms shimmered into purple light.

They were gone, forever.

CHAPTER

19

THE EMPRESS STOOD FOR A MOMENT, THEN TURNED AND faced the screen. Commander Stahl stared back at her, his mouth open slightly.

"You will stand down," she said. "The invasion fleet is to disperse. Who else witnessed what transpired?"

"Only my bridge crew," stammered Stahl.

"That is good. This was a drill, a practice run. You shall not deviate from that story. What of the Shepherd technology?"

"It is still installed in Engineering, but it now seems to be completely inoperable."

"You will remove them from all the vessels and return them to the Praetor within two days. Give a day's leave to the crew of all the ships who participated. Thank them for an exercise completed smoothly." She narrowed her eyes. "Do you understand, Stahl?"

"Aye, Excellency." His face blipped off the screen.

The Empress turned to her guards. "I do not believe I need tell you to say nothing."

"Of what, Excellency?" the head centurion replied.

"Good. Dismissed." They left quietly. The room was in shambles from the energy fire, but Jekri knew that within a day there would be no signs of the desperate fight that had ensued.

There was no one left now but the Empress, Jekri, the Praetor, Telek, and Verrak. She turned and faced them, and Jekri grew cold inside.

"Well, well. What do I do with you? My little band of traitors." The Empress walked around them, looking them up and down. Her arm must have been causing her terrible pain, but she gave no sign of it other than to cradle it carefully.

"My Praetor, who rules this Empire perhaps even more than I do. The chairman of my Tal Shiar, who commands thousands of shadowy figures. My best scientist. All admitted traitors. It seems I must either kill all of you and invite in the unknown in many key positions . . . or pardon you."

For a moment, her regal mien slipped. "And it is not as if I, too, have not betrayed my subjects, albeit unwittingly. I cannot condemn you when you are the ones who have saved this Empire. You are pardoned. Praetor, meet me here in one hour. We have much to discuss. Dismissed."

He bowed, and left. He did not look back.

"Telek R'Mor. Why did you flee to the Federation ship?"

"I was taken against my will, Excellency. I admit I did contact them to warn them, but only to preserve the true timeline. In that timeline, the Romulan Empire is alive and well. I did not wish to risk harming it."

"I see. And your time aboard that vessel?"

"Was spent in helping stop Lhiau's spread of dark matter."

She nodded. "Your wormholes will not operate without Shepherd technology." It was a statement, not a question. "But clearly, you understand more about dark matter than anyone else in this Empire."

Telek looked uncomfortable. "True, but have we not seen the dangers dark matter can pose?"

"It was my understanding that Lhiau used mutated dark matter. Surely such power can be harvested and put to good use without damaging the vessels and those who operate them. We had a superior cloak and wormholes. I want them again. Safely, this time."

"Excellency," sputtered Telek. "The Shepherds are as far above us as we are above a *kllhe!* Much of their technology hinges upon what they themselves are, not what they can build. It would take us centuries, perhaps even millennia, before we can even grasp the basics of their technology!"

"Why then," said the Empress, a hint of a smile curving her full red lips, "you had best begin. With a larger, more advanced vessel, and as much support as you desire. I think this is the work of a lifetime, Dr. R'Mor."

Jekri understood what the Empress was saying, and so did Telek. Surprised pleasure filled his face. He saluted, and bowed. As he strode toward the door, Jekri called out, "Telek!"

"Yes?" He turned. The iciness was still there between them, despite all they had been through together, but Jekri thought she knew how to melt it.

"Your family. They live."

He looked skeptical. "The chairman of the Tal Shiar did not execute her prisoners after all?"

She shook her head. "No. Things happened too quickly . . . I never got around to it."

"Consider them freed," the Empress said. "Speak with the Praetor, and he will reunite you with your family, Dr. R'Mor."

Slowly, his face softened. Joy glowed in his eyes. "Thank you," he said, and raced out the door.

"Excellency," said Jekri, after he had gone, "you cannot speak of what happened. It must be wiped from all our record banks. No one must know how close we came to almost destroying ourselves."

"You speak words I already know, Little Dagger. Do not worry. Our own embarrassment will hold tongues." The Empress lifted her head. "I was tricked, and behaved inexcusably. I would not have my people know that. The Senate, too, was duped, and they will not wish others to know how easily they were tricked. Stahl has seen enough, too, to know the value of silence. The troops never knew exactly what was going on; to them, this will be nothing more significant than another drill, forgotten once the technology is removed. If even Dr. R'Mor cannot duplicate this technology, then I feel we are safe. No, Kaleh. Shame begets silence."

She strode toward the smaller woman. "You have suffered the most, yet were perhaps the most loyal. I have wronged you. I would have you back as my trusted chairman, and will see that your name is cleared. Speak a boon, Jekri Kaleh, and whatever it is, if it lies within the power of your Empress, it is yours."

Jekri looked full into the face of this lovely woman, saw there mortification, and pride, and power. She thought about her life up until this moment: a series of scrabbling, and fighting, and killing, and climbing.

She had changed too much. She did not want any part of that old life again.

"I cannot resume my duties, Excellency. Too much has happened. I can best serve in another way."

"Name it."

"I wish . . . to disappear."

The Empress was silent for a long moment. "I trust that, wherever it is you disappear to, you will always serve me and the Empire loyally. You shall have your wish, Little Dagger." Her voice was tinged with sorrow. "I hope your choice brings you happiness."

Jekri was certain it would, save for one thing, one person whom she would miss more than she had expected. She turned to Verrak and began to search for the proper words to say goodbye.

He interrupted her. "You shall not disappear alone, unless you wish it."

Stunned, she stared at him. "Your career," she stammered. "Your advancement after this incident is certain. You could become the new chairman."

"What does that mean to me?" His voice was raw, and the power of his emotions humbled Jekri. "I have served at your side for years. I do not care where you go, only let me follow! Perhaps you do not—you cannot feel—but I would be content simply to be with you—"

She stopped his words with a small hand on his lips. "If you come with me," she said, her voice husky and trembling, "you shall not serve. You shall be at my side always, as companion, friend . . . lover. If you choose to come with me."

He did not answer. He did not have to. Slowly, Jekri reached out and took his hand in hers, curling her small fingers gently around his strong ones. Warmth and strength was in his touch, and she no longer desired ever to be without that warmth and strength.

They bowed to their Empress. She shocked Jekri by suddenly flinging her uninjured arm around Jekri's neck. Jekri felt tears on her cheek and a quick press of lips.

"Be well, Little Dagger. You will always be in my heart."

Jekri felt tears of joy start in her own eyes. She bowed again, and turned with Verrak toward the door. Toward her new life. Toward a peacefulness she had only ever tasted once before, and was eager to feast upon now with her whole heart.

The Little Dagger was finally free.

The day dawned gray and wet, as if it wished to help put out the last few smoking embers. The inhabitants of Sumar-ka stumbled around in a daze, unable to truly comprehend the depth of what had happened. A few huts still remained, and for whatever reason—luck, perhaps—Ioni and her followers had ignored the most important building of all, the one in which dried meats, grains, and vegetables were stored for a time of need.

Now was a time of need.

Once they had apprehended all the rogues from the Recovery team, Ezbai had summoned assistance. There was no point in not doing so. Obviously, the Culilann had seen too much already. Any hope of pretending that there was not Alilann intervention in their way of life had been shattered beyond repair.

Soliss and the Alilann doctor had worked together to treat the injured. Paris and Chakotay had refused assistance in deference to the more gravely wounded, and Paris was now regretting that. He felt weak as the proverbial kitten up a tree—or was that mixing metaphors? His head was so fuzzy he wasn't sure.

There had been anger, and fear, and sobbing and curses earlier. Now, everyone was spent. They were cold and wet and in shock from the events of the night before.

Trima sat with Paris as he leaned back against the charred trunk of an old tree.

"Things must change," she said.

"Yes," he agreed, looking over the black, soggy remains of what had once been a village. He couldn't believe no one had been killed other than Ioni, the ringleader. Trima's timely action had saved perhaps everyone in Sumar-ka, but the way the villagers looked at her, you wouldn't know it.

He knew that this was what was troubling Trima. "You did what you had to do," Paris told her. "If you hadn't contacted me, fired the phaser—"

"I know," she said, sharply. Her voice was tight. "But I still have lost everything. Look at them. They hate me. They think I brought this upon them."

From where she sat a few feet away from them, stubbornly refusing to be treated even by her own mate, Yurula stared at them. Her eyes looked like cold pebbles in her pale face. Even Tom felt the hatred in that gaze. This was a woman who had helped him when he was ill, had translated a ceremony for him so he wouldn't feel left out. And yet, with the cold loathing so plainly on her face, Tom felt as if he didn't know her at all.

"Everyone knows now." She hugged her knees into her chest like a little girl. "They know I've been lying to them, they know their gods aren't real, they know I've betrayed them."

"I know nothing of the sort," said Soliss, startling them both. He looked exhausted and was covered in blood and black soot. "I know that you have been responsible for seeing that our children have found loving homes rather than dying. Maybe the Crafters don't come right down to the mountain, but maybe they are working through you. I know that you've helped Strangers find their way home. And you can't have feigned your sincerity with the rituals, Trima. You can't."

Trima looked up at him. Tom felt hope rising inside him. Tears welled in Trima's eyes and spilled down her face, two clean streaks in the soot and sweat. "I hated lying to you," she whispered. "And I never wanted to be Culil. The rituals did mean something to me. Soliss, what do I do? I can't go back to the Alilann way of life, I can't! It's so cold, so sterile—there's no life to it. My life is here, and yet . . . ."

"No one wants you here," spat Yurula. "You don't belong. You've lied to us all along. We had privacy, but now we learn that you were telling everything we did to people who represent everything we hate. We had a way of life we loved, and you ruined it. We had gods, gods who walked among us and cherished our imperfect children, and now you've taken it all away from us!"

"Yurula," began Soliss, trying to placate his mate.

"And you!" Yurula whirled on him, her body tense with her anger. "You worked alongside the Alilann! The Alilann who burned our homes, stole our children!"

"These Alilann didn't burn your homes," said Chakotay, coming up behind Yurula. Ezbai walked beside him, the head injury inflicted by Yurula's hurled rock completely healed. "These Alilann helped save your lives. They are willing to work with you, to rebuild your village."

"Yes," said Ezbai. "We want to help."

Yurula spat on his face. Ezbai's eyes went wide, but he said nothing as he calmly wiped the spittle off his cheek.

"Oh, yes. We will rebuild our homes, but not with Alilann help. Not with your help, Trima, or yours, Soliss. You are no longer welcome here. No one who sympathizes with the Alilann is welcome here!"

Soliss stared at Yurula. "You are angry, and wounded, and exhausted," he began. "You do not mean—"

"Yes she does," said Resul the potter, stepping beside Yurula. "We will purge you from our memories, try to forget your lies."

Trima wiped at her wet face. "I never wanted to hurt you," she whispered.

"Trima, you can come back with us," said Ezbai gently. "I've seen a lot here tonight that has horrified me, and a lot that's touched me as well. There's got to be some middle ground, someplace where Culilann and Alilann can work together. I don't want to go back to that sterile place any more than you do."

"I cannot live in an Alilann dome," said Soliss. "But I cannot live here again, either. I want to learn your healing technology, but I don't want to give up my herbs. I know they heal, too."

Tom thought fast. "Maybe you can start a third way of living," he said. "I remember at the ceremony when the traders came, they gave the village a statue of a Way-Walker. You said the Way-Walkers were positive. Maybe you can be sort of Way-Walkers yourselves. Straddling two cultures, taking the best of both."

"Yes," said Chakotay. "Somewhere in between. A place for advanced healing technology and a cup of homemade soup as well. It has worked for us. Maybe it will work for you."

"We'll come with you." It was Winnif, carrying her

baby and holding the hand of her three-year-old. Her eldest walked close to her side. "Paris saved our lives last night. There is no hatred in him for our people. I know that. I had thought I was doing right, to leave my baby . . . I am so glad that he is all right. Do you think I could see him again? Do you think they would give him back?" She looked frightened and hopeful at the same time.

Ezbai smiled. "Perhaps." He turned to Chakotay. "There's still a lot of fear here, Chakotay. I don't know how the Implementer's going to react. But there may be more of us than he thinks."

"I believe you'll find your sister shares your views, Ezbai. On *Voyager,* she'll have been exposed to exactly that culture that you want to create here, one that takes the best of both worlds and makes a third culture," Chakotay said.

Ezbai sobered. "I hope she's all right. How will we get her back?"

"I don't know. But we have to hope—"

Ezbai suddenly looked fuzzy to Tom. For that matter, so did Chakotay, and Soliss, and Trima. He realized that he was being transported somehow, but it was nothing like *Voyager*'s transporter. He looked over at Trima, wanting to say something to her, to let her know that she was worthy, that she hadn't done anything wrong, that she was beautiful and that he would never forget her, but she was fading so quickly.

Then he saw her smile, and knew that it would be all right. She understood without a word spoken between them.

"Chakotay!"
"Tom!"

Many voices speaking at once. Chakotay blinked. They were back on the bridge of *Voyager*, seated in their proper places, as if they had never left. Kathryn was beaming, and reached to place a hand on his arm. He felt completely healed. Better, in fact, than he could ever recall feeling.

"Are you all right?" his captain asked.

"Just fine. We miss much?"

Janeway's smile melted into a full-fledged grin. "Not really. Just the near-end of everything."

"Oh, well, if that's all. . . ." He allowed himself a grin in return. It was good to be home.

Behind him, he heard Harry Kim utter a single, heartfelt word before he raced from the bridge.

"Khala . . . ."

"Hi, honey, I'm home." Paris's voice came through loud and clear. Torres's heart soared. Tom. He had come back.

"You missed all the fun," she said, hiding her pleasure.

"So I heard. Something about the end of everything."

"I'll catch you up tonight. In my quarters. Bring chocolate." Her grin faded as the door to Engineering hissed open and Kim bolted in. He looked around frantically. Torres knew whom he was seeking.

"Harry, I'm sorry," said Torres, sobering at once. "She's gone. Disappeared right before Tom and Chakotay returned. I'm guessing that Tialin somehow managed to take her back to her own universe."

Harry stared at her, brown eyes wide and filled with such pain that Torres had to look away.

"I didn't even get to say goodbye," he said. Without another word, he turned and strode out swiftly.

Torres looked after him, sorrow in her heart. Poor

Harry. They'd all thought this beautiful alien woman, with her sharp mind and warm heart, would be the one. Talk about being from the wrong neighborhood.

"This need to say goodbye," Seven said, interrupting Torres's thoughts. "It appears common to nearly every humanoid species. Curious."

Something about her tone of voice caused Torres to look around sharply. Seven's lip was trembling, ever so slightly.

"We missed our own goodbye to Telek R'Mor," Torres said, understanding.

"And now he is dead." Seven stated the fact coldly, almost as if forcing herself not to feel. "We did not thank him. That was an oversight."

"He has a daughter," blurted Torres. "Maybe one day we'll meet her."

Seven looked up. "Then we will tell her that her father was a noble man."

"Yes," said Torres, her own throat strangely tight. "We will."

Janeway sat on her bridge, smiling slightly. It was good to look down at the conn and see Paris sitting there, deft hands maneuvering the vessel with the most delicate of touches. It was good to sense the strong, quiet presence of Chakotay on her left. How she had missed him. She was sorry that he had not been privy to the amazing adventure her crew had undergone, but from the brief chat she'd had with him over a quick cup of coffee, she assumed he and Tom had had an adventure of their own.

She would miss Khala, but from what Tom and Chakotay had said, Khala and her brother were going to be key players in leading a revolution on their home planet. The best kind of revolution, too—one that involved changing minds and hearts, not firing weapons and taking lives. What was the term Chakotay had used? Way-Walkers? She liked the sound of that.

There was one who would miss Khala more than anyone else aboard the ship. Janeway had told Harry to take the rest of his shift off. He had thanked her quietly and gone to his quarters. She made a mental note to check on him later.

More of a loss to her was Telek R'Mor. He had become a friend, and a good one. It was unexpectedly painful to remember that he had died several years ago, when just a few hours ago she had pressed his hands between her own and lied about seeing him again.

"Captain?" Chakotay, perceptive as always. "Are you all right?"

She smiled. "Yes," she said. "And looking forward to that dinner you promised me. Southwestern cuisine, wasn't it?"

He nodded, and smiled, as if he had a secret. "Straight from Navajo country."

"Captain?" It was Tom Paris. It was good to hear his youthful voice on the bridge once more.

"Yes, Ensign?"

"I keep wondering—what's going to happen to us now?"

"Without the Shepherds, you mean?"

"Yeah. I mean, they've been doing this for eons. They have to know the equation. Yet Tialin said something about chaos. I would think they would know what's going to happen if they don't interfere, but maybe they don't."

Janeway frowned a little, thinking. "As I understand it, we're on our own. There's no more artificially perfect balance. A flat universe is almost impossible to conceive. I'd say the universe is either open or closed, now."

"So one way or another, it's going to end," said Paris.

"You're reckoning without the Q," Janeway reminded him. "Or the fact that perhaps other universes don't abide by the same laws that ours does. But whatever happens isn't going to occur for quite some time," Janeway said, chuckling. "I'd say there are many more-pressing things to worry about than the end of the universe, Mr. Paris." Her eyes lost focus, imagining the future. "And who knows, perhaps when that day finally comes, we'll have evolved to the point where we won't need a universe anymore."

"Anything's possible," said Chakotay.

She looked over at him, recalling Telek's words to her as he stood on the bridge. *Truly, anything is possible.* Their gazes locked, and she felt a slow, genuine smile spread over her face.

"Yes," said Janeway. "Anything *is* possible."

EPILOGUE

The Entity felt like a ghost. She couldn't bring herself to leave. She had to know if it would all work out, if her friends Chakotay and Tom, dear Tom, would return safely. Now that all was well, that the disaster had been averted, she found herself wishing she didn't have to leave. But she did.

Sadly, she withdrew, leaving this Voyager, *which was not her* Voyager, *behind. She would travel in the spaces between the stars once more, learning, growing, but alone. Suddenly a thought occurred to her, one which filled her with joy.*

This was not her Voyager. *But it was out there somewhere. A timeline in which the being named Kes had grown and evolved, had become the Entity, had done no hurt to those she had loved. She had a purpose now.*

The Entity would explore the universes, searching,

until she found her old friends. And then there would be laughter, and love, and belonging before a return to the spaces between the stars.

Her journey was just beginning.

The woman and the man walked hand in hand down the dirt road. Fields and orchards lay to each side, rich with color, heavy with fruits and grains. The small stone house waited up ahead, and its lights were on.

The pair did not hesitate. The woman strode forward and opened the door.

At least a dozen faces stared up at them. Recognition mingled with fear and suspicion. But the old woman who was the center of the circle of adults and young children alike merely met the interloper's gaze evenly.

"So, you have returned. To arrest us?"

"To join you, if you would have us." The woman knelt down in front of Dammik R'Kel, and gazed up into her lined, wise face.

"I had not expected to see Jekri Kaleh ever take such a position before me," said Dammik, mildly amused but also obviously pleased.

The woman shook her head. "That name is no longer mine. Name me. Teach me."

With great affection, the old woman placed a hand on the younger woman's sleek, dark head. "I shall," she whispered, and gave her a new name.

Harry Kim lay alone in his quarters. The lights were off. He liked it that way. He longed for the oblivion of sleep, but it would not come.

He lay now with eyes opened, seeing dark shapes in the dim lighting. Something bright red and flashing caught his eye. Someone had left him a message. He didn't want to hear Tom inviting him for a jaunt to Fair Haven, or a turn at Captain Proton. He didn't want to hear that Neelix had made his favorite dish, and wouldn't he like to come down to the mess hall and try it. He didn't want to hear anything. He just wanted to lie here and think about Khala, and all the tomorrows they would never share.

But finally, his innate sense of responsibility overcame him. It might be something important, after all, and Harry didn't want to shirk his duty.

He rose, feeling slightly ill in the pit of his stomach. "Heartache" was an accurate term. He thumbed the control and the small screen came to life.

His heart contracted. It was Khala.

"Hello, Harry." She smiled tremulously. How he longed to touch her. "I'm sorry about the informality of this message, but things are pretty hectic right now and I'm not sure how this will all end. I hope to be able to say goodbye to you in person, but . . . what am I saying?" She threw her arms up in exasperation. "I don't hope to say goodbye at all! Maybe there will be some way that I can stay. . . ."

Her voice trailed off. *Oh, Khala, if there had only been a way.*

She cleared her throat. "Well, in case I don't get to say goodbye in person, I'm recording this." She laughed a little. Harry loved that laugh. "We might even all be destroyed by Lhiau's dark matter before you get this. Who knows? I never realized just how important it is to fully live every day, every minute."

Her gaze locked with his. "Harry, there is so much we left undone, unsaid. Do you know I never got to hear you play your clarinet for me? I mean really play it, not just a few notes at that disastrous dinner. I so wish I had. I could hold on to that memory too. I want to thank you again for introducing me to this amazing world of art . . . and food!"

Again she laughed, brightly. "I love to eat now!" She sobered. "You've opened my eyes to so much. You've changed me forever. And I'm hoping that somehow I can find a way to live in my world with those changes, maybe even teach others about what I've discovered. You all kept talking about my world, my universe, as the Shadow universe. Well, to me, *you* are in the Shadow universe, and mine is the so-called real one. We could be mixing, even now, blending into one another without knowing it, thinking we're so far away when—"

Her voice caught. "I want to think of it that way. I want you to imagine that I'm right there, part of you, all the time."

Her image blurred. Kim blinked his eyes angrily.

"I am your shadow, Harry Kim." She was crying now. "I am your shadow, and you are mine. If we believe this, then we will never be without each other. Every time you stand in the light, you'll see me in your shadow, and know that I love you, and will remember you always. Be well, Harry."

She kissed her fingers and pressed them to the screen in front of her. Kim did likewise. Then the screen was dark. He sat for a long moment, then rose with purpose.

"Lights," he called. "Full brightness."

The room suddenly flooded with light. Before Harry lay the dark length of his shadow, its outline crisp and clean in the bright illumination.

Shadow universes, dark matter, unfathomable technologies, enemies who became friends, art, music, food, love. All rolled into one strange, precious ball called life. Despite all the pain and fear and losses and discouragement, he was glad he was living it.

I never realized just how important it is to fully live every day, every minute.

He gazed at his shadow, and remembered Khala.

CODA

Janeway was happily curled up in bed, a steaming mug of decaffeinated coffee at her side, with a book propped up on her knees. The door chimed.

"Come," she called, wondering who it could be at this late hour.

It was Seven. She had an expression on her face that Janeway couldn't quite interpret. "Please forgive the interruption," she said, "but I thought you might find this of interest. I found it in Dr. R'Mor's quarters."

Janeway felt a pang. Weeks had passed since they had said their farewell to the Romulan scientist and left him to his destiny. It had been fulfilled; Janeway had checked. Telek R'Mor had indeed died in the year 2367, as he was supposed to if the true timeline was to be preserved.

She rose and accepted the padd Seven handed her. Her eyes widened as she glanced at it. "Did you . . . ?"

"No. I did not read it, once I determined what it was." Again, the odd look. Janeway realized that Seven was struggling with grief, and compassion filled her.

"Thank you, Seven. Dismissed."

Seven nodded her blond head and left. Janeway sank back onto the bed, the coffee and book forgotten. Telek was not one to be caught off-guard. He had prepared for everything, even his eventual trial and Right of Statement.

Her eyes filled with tears as she read, sorrow warring with admiration for the keen brain as well as the bright soul.

FINAL STATEMENT OF DR. TELEK R'MOR
Presented as a Heartfelt Warning

I stand before you as a condemned prisoner. But prisoner or no, I am a Romulan, and to that end I have prepared this, my final statement. I do not question the decision reached by my peers, nor is this a plea for a different, more favorable verdict. Rather, I take this opportunity to warn you of a terrible danger that is encroaching upon us even as I speak.

It may seem peculiar that I use this last opportunity for my voice to be heard to speak of scientific matters. But hear me out, and perhaps this statement may serve some greater purpose. I speak of dark matter—and dark matters.

WHAT WE KNOW ABOUT DARK MATTER

A few hundred years ago, we knew very little about this matter which composes over ninety percent of our universe. We knew it was there only because we could see the effect it had on the galaxy. The outer regions of galaxies, for example, rotate faster than they should if visible matter was all there was in the galaxy. Like the hands of a puppeteer, whose gestures make the puppet dance, so dark matter exercises its gravitational power on visible matter.

There were two theories, both of which have proved to be correct, as to the identity of this mysterious matter. The first theory was that dark matter was composed of dark stars or large, planet-like bodies, or ECHOs— Enormous Compact Halo Objects, which for various reasons did not emit or reflect light or radiation. These would be composed of what we call "baryonic matter." Baryonic matter can also be called "ordinary matter," in that it is matter as we know it, made up of protons, neutrons, and electrons. This is the matter that makes up our bodies, our clothing, computers, and stars.

Observation nearly four hundred years ago showed that these ECHOs—which did indeed prove to be made up of ordinary matter—do exist. But this was only half the puzzle. Where, and what, was the rest of the matter of the universe? It could not be baryonic, or else we would have been able to identify it. It therefore stood to reason that the rest of the dark matter was made up of some kind of exotic matter with which we were entirely unfamiliar—and was nothing like ordinary matter.

It was only when we became capable of deep-space exploration that the second half of the puzzle fell into place. The rest of the dark matter is particles that interact weakly with other objects. We first encountered them a mere hundred years ago, when we became aware of the existence of something we call "dark-matter nebulas." These are collections of billions of dark-matter particles—which, in and of themselves, weigh an infinitesimal amount—into a visible nebula. I will refer to this later, in what I call the Colossal Mistake of dark matter *mis*-identification.

So—we were satisfied. All parties were correct. There were ECHOs and weakly interacting particles, all matter was present and accounted for—even if, to this very day, we still cannot say with any certainty precisely *what* the weakly interacting particles (which I refer to as "dark matter" from this point forward, as we do know what the ECHOs are) truly are composed of.

NEW REVELATIONS ABOUT DARK MATTER

We Romulans are concerned with things which are of value to us. We pursue paths that will help further the interests of the Empire. Scientific exploration of a venue for its own sake is not encouraged. As I stand facing my death, I speak up now, and condemn this policy. For thus it was that we made the Colossal Mistake.

We assumed that the reason we could not see dark matter was that it was too small to be viewed, unless it was gathered together in a dark-matter nebula with which we are familiar, or as a dark-matter galaxy—something which we have never yet encountered. We were wrong in this assumption.

Let me state this as plainly as I may, for this is vital to the comprehension of our present situation:

Dark matter is only visible when it interacts with subspace distortions, as in a dark-matter nebula.

We had made the Colossal Mistake of assuming that dark matter, apart from the known and understood baryonic-matter ECHOs, gathered together solely in clusters as dark-matter nebulas and galaxies. The truth is, dark matter is very nearly omnipresent. There are untold amounts of it in this room right now, perhaps hundreds of particles in a single strand of Romulan hair. We can't measure it—why? We can't see it—why? Why, when we can see and measure it in a dark-matter nebula?

The reason dark matter is detectable and even visible to the naked eye in a dark-matter nebula is that the interaction with subspace which renders dark matter visible *also pulls it completely into this universe.* The staggering secret behind dark matter is this—it exists simultaneously in *all* universes, never completely in one universe. This is why it is like the Earthers' "little man upon the stair." It is and isn't "there." It helps our universe exist in its present fashion—and who knows how many other universes it is helping to keep stable as well.

DARK MATTER, THE SHEPHERDS, AND US

We had no way of knowing the information I have just cited, but Lhiau did. He and the other Shepherds have spent eons manipulating dark matter, and they understand its nature very, very well. We know how the Shepherds' apparatus works. It gathers particles of dark matter directly to it, as a magnet attracts metal. We do not understand *why* the apparatus works, but our best minds are hard at work at deciphering this mystery. It is better to not be in debt to anyone. We Romulans know that.

Because dark matter is not completely of this universe, it therefore cloaks any object with a material that is not completely of this universe. What this does is effectively render the cloaked object utterly invisible, without moving it out of our universe. Any hints of its existence are wiped out. It is, as Lhiau promised us, a cloak without flaw.

The Shepherds' skill in manipulating dark matter has also enabled us to create wormholes of practically limitless size and of limitless stability. My years of effort at creating a stable wormhole of any useful size are well documented and I shall not waste precious time in summarizing them now. I will say that it has long been common knowledge that it is not finding the wormholes in space that is the problem, it is enlarging them and keeping them stable. Any kind of normal, baryonic matter tends to collapse under its own gravitational attraction unless something else stops it. We knew that the only way to keep a wormhole open would be to thread it with some sort of exotic material—something that has negative energy.

The same technology that summons dark matter to act as a cloak on our warbirds calls it to enter the artificial wormhole, providing that much-needed negative energy and resulting in stability and enlargement.

Now, such would seem to be a good thing, a powerful thing. But oh my colleagues, oh my leaders—we are blind children if we think these blessings all come without a terrible, terrible price.

THE TRUTH ABOUT DARK MATTER AND THE SHEPHERDS

Who were we, truly, to be the beneficiaries of such pure kindness? The Shepherds are no friends to the Romulans, to the Federation, to anyone or anything currently existing in this galaxy. Lhiau and his colleagues have an agenda, and it is one that calls for nothing less than the utter obliteration of every universe in existence.

And they are using us to bring this about.

Before I elaborate, let me digress briefly and refer to theories regarding the end of the universe. Many pages have been devoted to this eventuality. We know that the universe is expanding and has been since its creation. Some believe that the universe is "open," and it will continue to expand forever. Matter will be spread ever more sparsely, and the average temperature of the universe will fall steadily toward absolute zero. Pundits have dubbed this the "Freeze."

Others feel that there is enough matter present in the universe to stop this expansion. Everything will start collapsing back inward. The universe will become compressed, become a "closed" universe. This is called the "Squeeze."

Such playful terms are indicative of the cavalier attitude shown toward the eventual death of the universe and all things living within it. That is because, at its present rate, the universe should continue as it is for an unimaginably long time—1 followed by 100 zeroes. Our star system, in comparison, has a scant twenty billion years before it dies. We will be long gone before our universe is.

Or so we had thought.

Both theories on the universes hinge on the amount of matter present—too much, the Squeeze, too little, the Freeze. Therefore, obviously, dark matter, which comprises ninety percent of the matter in the universe, has a significant role to play in either scenario.

But there is a third option. It has long been dismissed by our scientists as completely unrealistic, and that is the concept that our universe is neither open nor closed, but flat. All theories involve the concept of a critical density, which is roughly equal to one hydrogen atom per cubic meter, or about one ounce for every 50 billion cubic miles. If the actual density of the universe were greater than this critical density by a factor as small as one part in a trillion, the universe is closed. If it were less by an equally tiny amount, the universe is open. A flat universe is one in which the density is exact. If our universe is indeed flat, it would keep expanding, but at a slower rate, never quite turning the corner. It would exist forever.

Of course, such a thing could never naturally occur. In that, I agree with our scientists.

But what about unnaturally? Suppose, for the last few billion years, the matter in our universe has been toyed with, a little taken here, a little put there, to keep it precisely at the critical density?

That, my colleagues, is what the Shepherds have been doing. They even took the name in acknowledgment of their actions; good shepherds, tending their sheep with care. For this, we ought to be grateful.

But there are other Shepherds who have long disagreed with this intervention, even though countless life-forms depend on this balance. Shepherds like Lhiau, who would destroy this universe and others as well, simply to see what else would happen, what new universes would crop up in our wake.

These rogue Shepherds have taken vows that forbid them to directly intervene, but there is nothing that prevents them from urging us, comparatively tiny, pathetic life-forms that we are, to unwittingly hasten our own destruction.

CLOAKS, DARK MATTER, AND THE SHADOW UNIVERSE

The gift of the dark-matter cloaks, the gift of the wormholes—these are but the weapons with which we will destroy ourselves and our very universe. We thought we understood dark matter, and to an extent, we do. In its natural state, it is utterly harmless. As I said before, it is likely passing through our bodies at this very moment.

But the dark matter that is summoned by the Shepherd technology, the dark matter that is brought into a wormhole, which is a different sort of space than any other—this dark matter has been mutated. We can detect it, much the same way we can detect it in a subspace rift, and for much the same reasons.

It has been changed.

There is a precedent for such mutations. We know that one type of neutrino can be changed into any one of another two types. An electron neutrino, the most common sort, can be changed into either a muon or a tauon neutrino. This is what has happened with the dark-matter particles.

No longer does it pass harmlessly through bodies, or machines. It is now fully of this universe, thanks to Shepherd tampering, and it lodges inside solid matter instead of passing through it. Once there, it acts like a foreign piece of matter—which indeed it is. It begins to replicate itself like a virus, ultimately destroying whatever is hosting it—the table, the star, flesh, mind, body. Our ships that have the dark-matter cloaks will eventually be useless, and the people aboard killed or driven insane.

Worse still, this tips the delicate balance so carefully tended by the Shepherds. There is more matter in the universe than there ought to be now, and this is disrupting the balance in other universes as well. Matter which exists in another universe is being pulled into ours at an exponential rate. Far sooner than anyone had dreamed— a few years, months, or perhaps days or even minutes—

our universe will have too much matter and undergo the Big Crunch. Other universes will suffer the same fate. Still others will have too little matter to continue, and suffer the Big Chill.

And all this, we have done ourselves. We, in our desire for conquest, have played directly into the hands of aliens who will not suffer for their crimes, for they exist in the rifts between universes. They will be fine. The board will be cleared, ready for a new "game."

The rogue Shepherd's diabolical plan must be stopped.

WHAT WE CAN DO

We are fortunate that in this battle for our very existence, we have allies—the true Shepherds, who are as appalled at Lhiau's renegade activities as we are. They have been busily trying to curb the damage themselves, by gathering up the mutated dark matter and rendering it harmless. To this end, they have enlisted the aid of the starship *Voyager,* as time is of the essence.

Yes, I admit it is true that the superior cloaks would give us a tactical advantage. The wormholes, aided by the mutated dark matter, enable us to open corridors virtually anywhere in this or other universes. But such advantages are not worth their price—the destruction of our universe at worst, the deaths of thousands of Romulans at best. We must no longer volunteer to aid our own destruction. We must cease using all Shepherd technology and lend our aid to the true, right task. And somehow, we must return the Shadow matter to its rightful universe.

In conclusion, there is only one enemy now—the rogue Shepherds, led by Lhiau. We have been gulled like foolish children, led to destroy ourselves. But now we know, and we shall not be misled any further.

We shall rally like the warriors we are, to save our universe and ourselves.

On a final, personal note, I hope that the above shows that I am no traitor. I am a true Romulan. I have lived like one, and now I am prepared to die like one, ever in service, mind and heart, to the Empire. I do not mourn death, for I shall merely be following my wife and my daughter—also true Romulans, who, I am certain, died well.

I thank you for this statement, and I hope you heed the warnings of one lone scientist. Long live the Empire!

"Long live the Empire," said Janeway softly, "when there are men such as you in it, Telek R'Mor."

He had never needed this statement. It served no useful purpose, and after their near-brush with the end of everything, Janeway realized that the less that was known about how close they had come, the better. Gently, she thumbed the controls and deleted the transcript.

She placed the empty padd down, and turned off the lights.

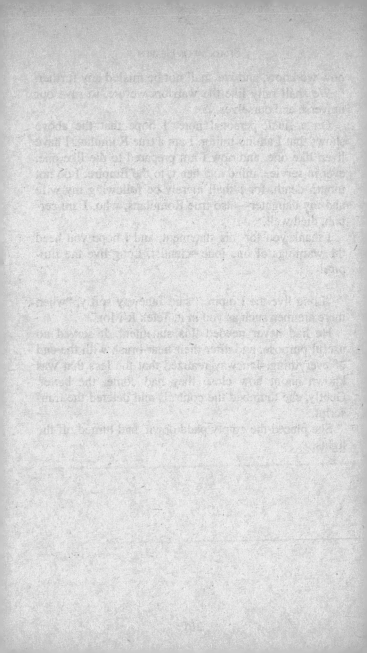

About the Author

Christie Golden is the author of thirteen novels and fourteen short stories. Among her credits are three other *Voyager* novels, *The Murdered Sun, Marooned,* and *Seven of Nine,* as well as a Tom Paris short story, "A Night at Sandrine's," for *Amazing Stories.* On the strength of *The Murdered Sun,* Golden now has an open invitation to pitch for *Voyager* the show.

In addition to *Star Trek* novels, Golden has also written three original fantasy novels, *Instrument of Fate, King's Man and Thief,* and, under the pen name Jadrien Bell, *A.D. 999,* which was the recipient of the Colorado Author's League Top Hand Award for Best Genre Novel in 1999.

Golden lives in Colorado with her husband, two cats, and a white German shepherd. Readers are encouraged to visit her Web site at www.sff.net/people/Christie.Golden.

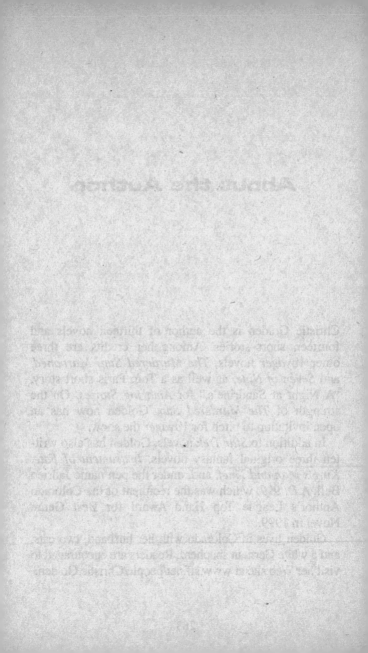

Look for STAR TREK fiction from Pocket Books

Star Trek®: The Original Series

Star Trek: Deep Space Nine®

Star Trek®: New Frontier

Star Trek®: Invasion!

Star Trek®: Day of Honor

#1 • *Ancient Blood* • Diane Carey
#2 • *Armageddon Sky* • L.A. Graf
#3 • *Her Klingon Soul* • Michael Jan Friedman
#4 • *Treaty's Law* • Dean Wesley Smith & Kristine Kathryn Rusch
The Television Episode • Michael Jan Friedman
Day of Honor Omnibus • various

Star Trek®: The Captain's Table

#1 • *War Dragons* • L.A. Graf
#2 • *Dujonian's Hoard* • Michael Jan Friedman
#3 • *The Mist* • Dean Wesley Smith & Kristine Kathryn Rusch
#4 • *Fire Ship* • Diane Carey
#5 • *Once Burned* • Peter David
#6 • *Where Sea Meets Sky* • Jerry Oltion
The Captain's Table Omnibus • various

Star Trek®: The Dominion War

#1 • *Behind Enemy Lines* • John Vornholt
#2 • *Call to Arms...* • Diane Carey
#3 • *Tunnel Through the Stars* • John Vornholt
#4 • *...Sacrifice of Angels* • Diane Carey

Star Trek®: The Badlands

#1 • Susan Wright
#2 • Susan Wright

Star Trek® Books available in Trade Paperback

Omnibus Editions
    Invasion! Omnibus • various
    Day of Honor Omnibus • various
    The Captain's Table Omnibus • various
    Star Trek: Odyssey • William Shatner with Judith and Garfield
        Reeves-Stevens

Other Books

Legends of the Ferengi • Ira Steven Behr & Robert Hewitt Wolfe
Strange New Worlds, vols. I, II, and III • Dean Wesley Smith, ed.
Adventures in Time and Space • Mary Taylor
Captain Proton! • Dean Wesley Smith
The Lives of Dax • Marco Palmieri, ed.
The Klingon Hamlet • Wil'yam Shex'pir
New Worlds, New Civilizations • Michael Jan Friedman
Enterprise Logs • Carol Greenburg, ed.

STAR TREK
THE EXPERIENCE
LAS VEGAS HILTON

Be a part of the most exciting deep space adventure in the galaxy as you beam aboard the U.S.S. Enterprise. Explore the evolution of Star Trek® from television to movies in the "History of the Future Museum," the planet's largest collection of authentic Star Trek memorabilia. Then, visit distant galaxies on the "Voyage Through Space." This 22-minute action packed adventure will capture your senses with the latest in motion simulator technology. After your mission, shop in the Deep Space Nine Promenade and enjoy 24th Century cuisine in Quark's Bar & Restaurant.

- -